a&b

The Dower House Mystery

A Case for Inspector Faro

ALANNA KNIGHT

Allison & Busby Limited
11 Wardour Mews
London W1F 8AN
allisonandbusby.com

First published in Great Britain by Allison & Busby in 2019.
This paperback edition published by Allison & Busby in 2019.

A CIP catalogue record for this book is available from the British Library.

10 9 8 7 6 5 4 3 2 1

ISBN 978-0-7490-2406-2

Typeset in 11/16 pt Sabon LT Pro by
Allison & Busby Ltd

The paper used for this Allison & Busby publication has been produced from trees that have been legally sourced from well-managed and credibly certified forests.

Printed and bound by
CPI Group (UK) Ltd, Croydon, CR0 4YY

For Barbara Wood,
with love and admiration

CHAPTER ONE

Had they been on the lookout for portents, the year 1907 did not begin auspiciously for newly wedded, recently retired Chief Inspector Faro and his bride Imogen Crowe.

After visiting York, they would live in Edinburgh. Their Dublin flat presented problems regarding Imogen's travels as a writer of historical biographies and the decision had been almost instant when a suitable Edinburgh house came up, with an accessible railway station to London and thence across to the Continent and beyond.

Aided and abetted in their search, they had been offered a permanent home with Rose, Jack and Meg Macmerry in Solomon's Tower at the base of Arthur's Seat. Large, ancient, romantic, its history lost in time, and almost ruinous in places, neither Faro nor Imogen were homemakers. Their thoughts did not linger on domesticity or the challenge offered by those vast empty rooms with their draughty stone walls, and they silently dreaded the possibility of a future living there, leaking pipes within, decaying stonework and foul weather without. They wanted a modern house, easy to maintain, where they could just settle down.

Even if Imogen's lifestyle had included leisure enough to yearn for pretty curtains totally inadequate on those massive stone windows, Faro had no wish to try his hand at building a flight of bookshelves. So, as both had succumbed to streaming winter colds, Imogen spent each day searching the newspapers for appropriate houses, while Faro remained crouched over the cheery fire in the massive kitchen, the Tower's only warm room despite the tapestries on the walls shuddering in the wind. He watched Imogen gallantly venturing outside, under shawls and umbrella, guiltily aware that his new role as husband sadly lacked the desirable and necessary ingredients of homemaking, such matters throughout his long working life having been the province and responsibility of Mrs Brook, his loyal and dependable housekeeper.

Grateful to Rose and Jack, who were relieved to see their marriage solemnised and made official at last after almost twenty years of living together, they were lured by the open aspects of the ever-expanding south side of Edinburgh, with sounds of the nearby railway line an added temptation.

The New Town constructed a century ago was solidly built with few open spaces and at a short distance from

Solomon's Tower. The one-time drove road down to the borders and thence to England now transported heavier traffic than horse-drawn carriages, and now renamed Dalkeith Road, sprouted a respectable vast terrace of six-storeyed houses.

The ever-expanding railway network had proved a great boon to the Faros, enabling them to visit places often difficult and almost inaccessible except by tortuous land and sea crossings taking several days. Until the turn of the century, Imogen Crowe had been classed as a non-desirable Irish woman with remote connections to the Irish Home Rule movement, before her free pardon from King Edward VII allowed her the right to settle in Britain and made living arrangements with Faro much easier.

While they were still hunting houses, by chance a suitable one came up. With Chief Inspector Jack Macmerry heavily involved in police work and Faro's daughter Rose McQuinn absent on one of her lady investigator cases, Imogen and Faro had taken their daughter, nine-year-old Meg, to visit a school friend whose grandmother had a rather pretty house near Sheridan Place, Faro's one-time home.

Imogen had been very impressed by the view from the house, with one large bay window looking across to Arthur's Seat and another gazing down towards East Lothian and the coast. Facing south and west, it had the advantage of sunny days and warm rooms, not to be despised in Edinburgh's somewhat chilly weather.

The owner, Mrs Mack, sighed. She was getting old, her legs bothered her and she didn't need all those now unoccupied rooms up two flights of stairs, while downstairs – once the dining room and housekeeper's domain of parlour and kitchen leading to the garden – was more than enough for her declining years.

She shook her head sadly, regarding Imogen with a gleam of hope. 'It is all too much for me, with Sandy gone now. I never needed a housekeeper, but I just hate living alone. I'm a bit nervous these days and I just wish I could rent the upstairs to some reliable folk. But I don't fancy having strangers living in the house.' She paused and looked again at her little granddaughter's escorts. The tall handsome man who, Janey whispered, was once a famous policeman. His wife, who seemed a lot younger, was lovely too, such a charming sympathetic manner. A nice, strong, respectable couple with good references.

She sighed and murmured, 'Someone I could trust and who might even keep an eye on things if I was taken poorly.' She patted her chest knowingly. 'Not as fit as I once was. Getting old.'

The Faros exchanged a glance. The first floor with its magnificent views would be perfect, and what had been the maid's room and the nursery on the top floor would provide extra space for the vast storage of all their books. It was an instant decision, the rent agreed and there was general jubilation from Mrs Mack, as well as the wee girls Janey and Meg, the latter in particular delighted at the prospect of her adored Imogen staying in Edinburgh. They had become great friends and the regard was mutual. Imogen had lots of time and hugs for Rose's wee stepdaughter, who was Jack's image.

A very excited Meg held both their hands skipping homeward along the one-time Coffin Lane. Once the end of the town and the last earthly sight of Edinburgh for condemned criminals, it had lost all sinister connotations and become just a pretty country road with hedgerows overflowing with colourful wildflowers.

Home up the hill to Samson's Ribs and Solomon's Tower, gasping to be first out with the news for Rose, Meg called: 'Isn't it wonderful, Ma? They'll be living so near. Fancy Imo and Grandpa living just as far away as the Crowe flies, eh?' she added, and they all laughed at the pun on Imogen's name. 'Isn't that great!'

And so matters were speedily arranged, and as the upstairs rooms of No. 2 Preston Drove were fairly empty, what furniture remained was purchased from Mrs Mack, with additions provided from the Tower and local auction rooms.

Preparing to move in, Imogen had no doubts. She had a feeling about houses and the moment she had stepped across the threshold had known this was a good place. 'My Celtic blood with its dash of Romany from my grandmother,' she told Faro.

Imogen had loved their tiny flat in Dublin, easily accessible from Glasgow, as long as one was a good sailor across the notorious Irish Sea to Rossclare. Before the decision to settle in Edinburgh, it had been convenient as long as their travels across Europe permitted, and as long as Imogen produced books that retained their popularity. This always surprised her, expecting that each new one would somehow not reach the mark. But, so far, the source had not dried up, the stories still came and as long as Faro accompanied her she would continue writing. Research intrigued her even more than the writing, she often said, and Faro laughed:

'You should have been a detective, like Rose, if that's what you enjoy so much. After all it's just searching for clues, isn't it?'

They were content together now that Faro had retired. During their first years, meeting intermittently when he was between cases, Imogen was always fearful. Fearful for his safety, that the bullet or the knife would bring their life together to a cruel end. She wished that their age difference was less than twenty years, aware always that in the scheme of mortality she would outlive Faro, and she thought with anguish of those years alone.

Faro was well aware of their shadow too. He constantly wanted to put the ring on her finger, have her respectably married so that he could provide for the rest of her lifetime. Until last year, she had continuously refused, saying she did not need a certificate or a wedding ring or to repeat after the priest, 'until death do us part', followed by a nuptial Mass to bind her to the love of her life.

Faro forgot sometimes that she was still a Roman

Catholic and occasionally when they were staying near a church she would take her rosary and disappear to Mass. In foreign cities, he was surprised. How did she understand it all?

She had laughed. 'It is in Latin, of course. The same for all Christians.'

Except for Presbyterian Scots, in the religion he had been born and bred in Orkney, although his appearances in St Giles in Edinburgh were limited to occasions such as official police visits, weddings and funerals.

Daughter Rose had married an Irish Catholic, Sergeant Danny McQuinn, brought up by the nuns in an Edinburgh orphanage, but neither Rose nor her second husband Inspector Jack Macmerry were keen churchgoers, although Jack's wee Meg was also being educated by the nuns in the convent at the Pleasance, chiefly because of its convenience as the nearest school to Solomon's Tower.

When Faro had tried over the years to persuade Imogen into marriage, she had laughed. 'You have a wife already, Faro. Sure now, it would be bigamy and you married to the Edinburgh City Police.'

And he realised then that she spoke the truth. The police, his dedication, had always been first in his life, even before his family. He had long ago known that he had neglected his first wife Lizzie, who had died in childbirth with their third child, a longed-for son. Rose and Emily had been shipped off to Orkney to live with his mother in Kirkwall and were rarely seen by their father, even on those dutiful summer holidays in Sheridan Place in Edinburgh – a father who was always too busy chasing criminals to spend an afternoon picnic with his two little daughters. He still carried guiltily the image of their upturned faces, their sad disappointed expressions, as Mrs Brook was allocated the task of deputising for this neglectful parent.

CHAPTER TWO

Faro had been both pleased and relieved by the prospect of remaining in Edinburgh. Much as he liked Dublin and the flat overlooking Phoenix Park, it could never become home. That was and could never be anywhere other than Edinburgh, although Yesnaby near Stromness in Orkney was close to his heart. This was home now to his mother, Mary Faro, who had moved in to look after his widowed daughter, Emily, and her little boy Magnus, although there was some question about who was doing the looking after. Neither Faro nor Imogen were sure, since Faro guessed that his mother – who had always kept her age a close secret – must be now well into her late eighties, although she showed few signs of slowing down.

But Orkney was too inaccessible for Imogen's travels and Edinburgh was where he had spent most of his life from seventeen years old until his retirement from the City Police last year.

He had to admit relief at Imo's delight in Preston Drove, slightly apprehensive that she might choose to return to Ireland and settle down back in Kerry at Carasheen, the family home of the vast clan of Crowes. He had been very wary in their pre-marriage days of their intense nosiness into his affairs and soon realised that although it was innocent enough and they meant no ill, the fact remained that privacy had not been invented for the Crowes: everyone who was allowed the privilege of stepping across their threshold brought with them their life as an open book to be scrutinised carefully, well read over and endlessly discussed in minute detail by all the family. Nothing was sacred, no secrets allowed, and what they didn't know for sure, they would patiently dig for until they found out.

Imogen never knew her parents. Her father, Padraig Crowe, a talented artist with paintings in the Dublin Art Gallery, was lost in a sailing accident off the Blasket Islands when she was expected, and her heartbroken mother died from childbirth complications when Imogen was three weeks old. Passed round the family, she was eventually adopted by her infamous Uncle Phelan, an Ireland freedom fighter who hanged himself in an English jail after an unsuccessful attempt to assassinate Queen Victoria.

He had brought Imo to England with him and as a fifteen-year-old she had been locked in a prison cell awaiting trial, accused of conspiracy. A year later, with no evidence against her she had been released but forbidden to set foot in England again. Determined to become a writer, born with a gift that she cultivated through years of hardship, she finally achieved publication and worldwide acclaim. And so the years had gone by until a meeting in Cork with Bertie, then Prince of Wales. He had been captivated by this lovely clever Irish woman and one of the first things he did on ascending the throne as King Edward was to grant her a free pardon.

Now that the stage was set, so to speak, with a home for the foreseeable future, Faro and Imogen could make plans. Her forthcoming talk in York had been cancelled due to the untimely death of the society's president and rescheduled for March 1907. As neither had ever been to York, they were looking forward to visiting the city built by the Romans and regarded as the most fascinating medieval city still intact in Britain, with its world-famous Minster.

Imogen had other plans too. The cold dead winter would soon be past, and they would be watching that annual reawakening of the world to another springtime. With Faro she had been consulting maps and had decided that, from York, with the now excellent railway, this presented a perfect chance of going over to the Continent from the port of Hull and in particular seeing Amsterdam.

She recalled being impressed on a brief visit, long before she met Jeremy Faro, by its new museum and always determined she would go back again.

She looked at their diary. Just weeks away, the wedding at Elrigg Castle on the Northumbria borders near Hadrian's Wall, where she and Faro had met twenty years ago and loathed each other. She was godmother to the Elriggs' only daughter, Mercia. It would be such a delight to go back with Faro as newly marrieds living, she hoped, happily ever after despite such a dire beginning. And a month later Amsterdam would be ablaze with tulips. Yes, she wrote dates in contentedly. Just another couple of weeks and February, never a good month, would be torn off the calendar for another year, with March and York in springtime to look forward to. Faro would love it, all that history and archaeology, museums and the rest.

But there was one more visit that must be included. Imogen produced her diary and pointed out that as the York event was still distant, either Faro or herself, but preferably both, must return to Dublin and release the flat. There were also several things happening that she was keen not to miss. Most important, a promise made to her friend Lady Gregory, whose new play *The Rising of the Moon* was to be premiered in Dublin's Abbey Theatre in early March and their presence would be expected at the opening night. Isabella Gregory and Imogen Crowe, the same age and friends for many years, were both dedicated, as were Isabella's plays, to the struggles for Irish freedom and a free state. A further bond was their passionate devotion to Women's Suffrage.

The visit went ahead as planned, aware that at their meeting the day after the premiere of the play the talk would not only be of the splendid reviews but also of the outrage regarding an older story that had hit the headlines beyond England: on 13th February dedicated and fearless suffragettes had stormed Parliament where sixty of them were arrested and thrown into jail. However, Isabella had shyly welcomed Faro, glad that Imogen's tall, handsome husband was not of dreaded English stock, but a Viking from Orkney (as Imogen always introduced him in Ireland). She tactfully refrained from adding to the introduction that he was or had been a chief inspector in the Edinburgh police.

The link with the Dublin flat severed, it remained to cross the Irish Sea to England and thence back to Edinburgh and their new home. Imogen was thankful on each crossing that both she and Faro were mercifully good sailors on often notoriously stormy voyages, while Faro, an avid reader of railway timetables, saw their decision to settle down and make Edinburgh their home with the widowed lady as an excellent choice. He was already looking forward to that cosy warm south- and west-facing house with the excellent views to coast, castle and Arthur's Seat, having taken into account and making particular note of the accessibility just two miles' distant of an excellent and frequent railway link with York.

However, the omens for their immediate travel were not good, in fact they were to be regarded with extreme caution. According to the philosophers of ancient Rome, mid-March, the date of the Faros intended first visit to York, was a significant and solemn threat not to be disregarded. Soothsayers of old would have warned him that since the murder of Emperor Julius Caesar in 44 BC, the ides of March was a cursed date and should be treated with caution by anyone setting foot in a city like York that owed its origins to and had been built by a Roman emperor.

For Faro and Imogen, the omens a soothsayer would have relished were all present, gathering patiently one by one on a horizon that, as twentieth-century persons basking in the wonders of a modern civilisation regarded as well beyond the dreams of ancient Rome, they were ready to ignore and amusedly dismiss as old superstitions . . .

At their peril.

CHAPTER THREE

Their sojourn in Edinburgh was a delight, but Imogen was doomed to go to York alone. Although the weeks were ticking away, the year, which had started badly, had some new hazards lying in wait in the form of a heavy snowstorm. On the eve of their departure for York, Faro was suffering from a lack of exercise and, regardless of the icy conditions, determined to climb that steep extinct volcano behind the Tower known to geographers and the world in general as Arthur's Seat. It was an ill-advised decision: he slipped, fell and limped home assisted by Rose's massive deerhound and family treasure, Thane. He had severely injured his right ankle. He had been shot in that leg during his service with the police, and it still troubled him. Now he was in great pain and could barely walk.

Rose decided a doctor's attention was needed and Imogen agreed that he was in no condition to travel anywhere and he must abandon any thought of accompanying her to York.

So Imogen, who loved trains, went alone. She had held her breath as York approached and the sunny day with its cloudless sky suddenly revealed the Minster dominating the horizon, before the train, amid dramatic clouds of smoke, steamed to rest alongside a platform in the handsome railway station.

She had taken barely a dozen steps into the city, towards the hotel where she would stay and be welcomed by warm breezes touching the River Ouse with shafts of pearl, when she looked over the bridge and knew this was a place that had been waiting for her. If one could fall in love with a city, then Imogen Crowe was head over heels with York.

That evening her talk on writing historical biographies of women who had shaped history was received by an enthusiastic audience who asked the right kind of questions and ones to which she knew the right kind of answers.

The chairman, Theo Hardy, was one of the team of local archaeologists. His wife Belle had organised a dinner party at Dean Court Hotel in Imogen's honour. The couple had been very impressed by Imogen's talk and Belle insisted that they did not want the evening to end. They wanted to know more about Imogen Crowe and her fascinating life.

Belle raised her eyebrows and sighed in envy at the courage of this talented brave woman whose travels took her to so many places in Europe, and further afield to North Africa, into dangerous and almost inaccessible places for research. It was beyond her understanding that this author could, undaunted, face the hazards that lay in wait for a beautiful woman travelling alone.

'Were you never afraid? I mean, of men?' Belle added in a whisper as Theo went in search of their transport.

'I soon knew how to deal with that situation, pick up enough of the language to make myself understood and so forth,' Imogen said firmly. 'A lesson I had to learn early on. And I also carried a gun.'

'A gun!' Belle shuddered. Travels among wild men always led to thoughts of rape. As for being armed with a gun, that was a very savage and unladylike addition to this picture of the lovely delicate-looking Imogen Crowe.

'Theo and I often go to Egypt and Greece, and the way the labouring men look at me, I would be terrified on my own,' said Belle.

At that moment, Theo returned. 'Our car is waiting. We will accompany you.' They insisted on driving her to the hotel, although she maintained that it was a short distance away and she would enjoy the evening air. York was so lovely.

They looked at each other. York had obviously enchanted Miss Crowe on her first visit. When was she leaving? Tomorrow? Oh, that was sad, she must come again very soon.

'Yes,' said Belle, clapping her hands and beaming at Imogen. 'And please do bring your famous husband next time. Such a pity he couldn't be with you tonight.' A swift glance exchanged with Theo who added:

'Of course, Inspector Faro. Everyone wants to meet him.' He smiled. 'I expect you know this already, but tales of his legendary career have spread far south of Scotland.'

That information always surprised Imogen as it did, in fact, Faro.

'We have lots of room at the Dower House,' said the eager ever-smiling Belle, 'and we would be delighted if you could spare the time to honour us with a visit, wouldn't we, Theo?'

Theo added enthusiastic agreement. Cards were exchanged. 'Let us know when you are arriving and we will meet you,' he said as the car stopped outside Imogen's hotel.

Leaving such a nice friendly couple, Imogen considered their card again, and thought that perhaps this had been a very fortunate encounter. The Dower House was an imposing address, and although she would take the precaution of booking hotel accommodation for their next visit, she decided to keep the Hardys' offer to herself until she had had a chance to inspect the premises and what might turn out to be a pleasant surprise for Faro, since he never enjoyed staying in a hotel, even a luxurious one, for an indefinite period. For anything more than a couple of nights necessitated by travelling, he missed the comfort and informality of home.

Before catching the Edinburgh train next day, with some difficulty and only by asking directions, she found the Irongate and had a look at the exterior of the Dower House. It was certainly large and imposing, even seen through the rain and a large umbrella that forbade a closer examination.

The weather was too depressing to explore York as she had hoped, and it remained to send 'thank you' flowers to Belle Hardy and scribble a special note for their kind offer.

The rain eased to a fine drizzle and on the lookout for a flower shop she walked down the Stonegate and there was one, the Four Seasons, with an attractive display outside.

The doorbell rang as she walked in and her entrance interrupted what sounded like a heated argument between a tall, fair-haired man she had seen somewhere before and the young woman behind the counter. Expecting to hear the local dialect, Imogen was surprised to recognise the familiar accent of home from the girl, and as the man made a hasty exit, Imogen saw that she was wearing the gold claddagh ring.

'Can I help you, madam?'

'Indeed you can, but you are a long way from home, are you not?'

The girl's eyes widened. 'I'm from Kerry. From Carasheen.'

Imogen leant over the counter and pointed to the claddagh. 'I recognised your ring. I'm Imogen Crowe.'

A shriek of pure delight. 'Dia dhuit, Imogen! We're related. I'm Kathleen Crowe.'

'Dia is Muire dhuit, Kathleen!' Imogen replied in the Irish and held out her hand to Kathleen who took it and, smiling, touched Imogen's third finger with the claddagh representing love, faith and loyalty. That was what Imogen had chosen in Dublin, rather than the normal plain gold wedding ring. The claddagh had been worn by all the Crowe family for generations past, as the traditional wedding band, and the two hands clasping a heart surmounted by a crown was said to have been worn since Roman times.

Anxiously, Imogen had told Faro of her choice and her reasons, afraid that he might object, but he wouldn't have minded had she chosen a curtain ring as long as she had decided at last to be his wife:

'You wear it with the crown pointing to the fingernail if you are married, and with the crown pointing downwards if you are unwed and on the lookout, so to speak. As it's for both men and women, would you like one?' But Faro declined; he had never worn rings and the claddagh, although looking so right on Imogen's hand, he considered would be a mite ostentatious for him.

The Four Seasons was a busy shop with customers considering what flowers to buy, so in the briefest of conversations Imogen was hearing that Kathleen was a widow, her young sailor husband from Yorkshire, whom she met on a visit to Kerry, having drowned shortly after their marriage.

Kathleen, aware of customers now waiting for attention, smiled at them apologetically and whispered to Imogen:

'I live just up the road there' – she gave a vague gesture towards the residential area beyond the Stonegate – 'but the shop closes at six,' she added hurriedly. 'There's a tea shop across the road, see!' She pointed through the window. 'We could meet there.'

Imogen agreed. She could get a later train to Edinburgh. Spend the whole day here. This was too good a chance fate had thrown her way, on her first visit; an astonishing coincidence, discovering by pure chance that here in York was one of the vast tribe of Carasheen cousins she had met only once as a child, now working behind the counter in the Four Seasons flower shop.

She knew vaguely from her uncle Father Seamus that Kathleen had married an English sailor and by all accounts had settled in England, but this totally unexpected coincidence had taken both of them by surprise.

Apart from the weather, the sudden rain showers, she would spend the day exploring. After walking the Shambles, she discovered the Minster in circumstances almost divine. Her visit coinciding with the choir practising for evensong, their voices echoing in angel-like chorus through the vast spaces, now seemed to turn her meeting with Kathleen in the Stonegate into a blessing.

Imogen was enchanted; she had fallen in love with York at first sight and was more determined than ever to bring Faro, certain that he would share her feelings; they always loved – or occasionally hated – the same places.

Before settling down in their new home in Edinburgh, they would get to know York, have it provide the holiday both sorely needed after a trying winter. After this first visit she resolved to return again in three weeks, give Faro's ankle a chance to mend properly, all the while bearing at the back of her mind the Hardys' offer. However, in case that did not work out, she would book a suitable hotel.

As well as getting to know this city that had captivated her with its brief glimpses, a longer visit would give her a chance to get to know more about Kathleen Crowe, this long-lost relative, more than had been possible in a few moments before customers who had entered the busy shop waited impatiently to be served.

As the hour approached, Imogen wondered what that her next meeting would be like with no childhood remembrance, aware only that four-year-old Kathleen had been tragically bereaved when her father hanged himself in a Stirling jail awaiting trial as an Irish terrorist. Kathleen had looked near to tears, telling Imogen about her brief marriage and how, after her husband's death, the wife of the boat's owner had given her a home in York.

As six was striking melodiously with chimes echoing from all across the city, Imogen folded her umbrella, and pleased with the day's activity of getting acquainted with York, but now footsore, was considerably heartened by the prospect of a cup of tea. Passing down the Stonegate, within sight of the Four Seasons, the 'Closed' sign on the door indicated that Kathleen would be waiting for her in the cafe across the way.

As she approached, she noticed through the window the empty tables, and trying the door, found it also closed.

She knocked timidly, and it was opened by a tall lady in smart black bombazine, her manner suggesting she might also be Mary who owned the cafe.

'We're closed, madam,' she said firmly. 'Sorry. Open again tomorrow morning at ten.'

As she made to shut the door again, Imogen said, 'Excuse me. I was supposed to be meeting someone here – my cousin, works at the flower shop, over there. Perhaps she left a message for me?'

Mary Boyd frowned as she peered across the road. She shook her head. There had been no message left for anyone. 'Are you sure this was the right cafe? We don't do evenings, just light meals during the day. And we close at five.'

Regarding Imogen thoughtfully and realising she was most likely one of the many daily visitors to York, she said: 'There are lots of nice cafes nearby, madam. Along the Stonegate, there's The Owl Barn and . . .'

But Imogen wasn't listening to the list. She shook her head stubbornly. 'My cousin definitely stated this was the cafe, pointed it out to me. Perhaps you know her? Mrs Roxwell?' she added hopefully.

Mary shook her head. 'Don't think we have ever met.' And aware of Imogen's bewildered expression she added: 'We don't get many shop girls in for coffee. It's difficult getting breaks during the day, when you have to be there for customers. And it's a bit expensive for the young girls, they usually bring their own food.' She paused. 'What does she look like?'

Having met Kathleen only once and so briefly, Imogen found her difficult to describe, just vaguely an ordinary young woman in her thirties, mid-height, brown hair.

Mary didn't think she had ever seen her, she had never served her in the cafe and this girl, whoever she was, certainly hadn't come in and left a note. She frowned. Surely working across the road she would be aware that the cafe closed at five, anyway.

It was useless to continue the discussion. There had been a mistake. Imogen apologised. Mary said again that she was sorry too. 'When you're a visitor,' she added by way of consolation, 'there's so many places in York, you can get lost.'

The door closed. Imogen crossed the road and lingered outside the Four Seasons until half past six, then realising that Kathleen was not likely to turn up, taking out one of her cards, she scribbled a message with their new address at Preston Drove, saying she planned to return.

Heading back to the railway station and boarding the next train for Edinburgh, she felt uneasy.

'Kathleen suggested the meeting, so why didn't she turn up? She had sounded sure about times and everything, so what had happened?' she said to Faro later, after recounting their extraordinary encounter and the events of her day in York, including her plan that they should have a holiday there. Although certain that Faro would love York, she did not mention the offer of accommodation at the Dower House, that was to be a surprise.

Faro agreed that York sounded quite perfect and had a list of consoling suggestions about Kathleen's non-arrival, none of them of a serious nature but it continued to bother Imogen. She was certain Kathleen had meant to meet her and each day she hoped the postman would deliver some message, some explanation.

It never came. Kathleen remained silent.

CHAPTER FOUR

There was much to keep the Faros occupied during the following three weeks, moving into the new home, and again Imogen discovered that she would be travelling to York alone.

Faro had to attend the funeral of one of his former colleagues from the Edinburgh City Police. The timing was unfortunate, the afternoon of the day before they were to leave for York, while Imogen had written to Kathleen suggesting that they meet at the shop when it closed, planning to take her to the hotel where they were staying for supper, she told Faro. And to meet him, of course.

He agreed. 'All things considered, I think you should go alone, and I will come on Wednesday. There will be people I haven't met for ages after Mason's funeral, as well as his family, and it would seem discourteous to rush away. Better if I take the York train next morning.'

Aware of her disappointed expression, he smiled. 'Besides, this will give the two of you time together.' In point of fact, this arrangement suited him well as he felt this meeting of the two cousins would be happier without his presence, since it would be overloaded with family news of Imogen's relatives known to him as little more than names in Carasheen.

Imogen accepted his decision and, more aware of the reason for his reasons than he guessed, she set off on a bright sunny day, elated at the prospect not only of seeing Faro but of being with Kathleen again. The city's history fascinated her; she felt all the excitement of opening a new project and determined to seize every opportunity, while Faro explored museums and art galleries, to research the conditions in women's prisons in York, particularly since the bodies of three females had been discovered during excavations in the 1850s.

'What is your man like?'

Gazing out of the window as the train sped past Durham heading for York, Imogen wondered how Faro would react to Kathleen, never able to conceal from her that he was always a little wary of her many relatives. She smiled at her own reflection as she remembered only one of Kathleen's eager questions at that first meeting.

'Uncle Seamus wrote that he's from Orkney, isn't he? I gather he's a policeman you married, and I bet he is tall and handsome.'

Imogen had laughed rather proudly. 'That describes him, more or less.' Although she carried a photo taken in Edinburgh last year, no likeness ever did him justice. How could she or anyone else who knew Jeremy Faro, retired Chief Inspector of the Edinburgh City Police, now her husband, answer that question. Glancing down at her hand with its wedding ring, she had firmly resisted a traditional occasion with many guests, family and friends. Such a ceremony was against all her principles, to be thus publicly linked even to the man she had loved for these many years. Marriage was for them a private business and thankfully Faro agreed.

She sighed. The upcoming wedding at Elrigg Castle would be a very different affair based on traditional pomp and splendour.

'He looks like a Viking,' was all she had said to Kathleen, her standard reply to anyone who asked. Good looks, yes, but there were lots of handsome men – Faro had much more than the requirements fitting the description. No camera existed that could capture his physical strength, the fine brain, his integrity and sense of purpose that had led the young lad from Kirkwall in Orkney, to seek his fortune in Edinburgh and rise from constable to chief detective inspector to become a legend in his own lifetime.

She smiled to herself. Even fifty years later, he had never lost it.

She gazed out of the window through the train's smoke, Durham with its magnificent castle briefly held the horizon. She made a mental note that was another place they must explore. An undulating landscape, flatter now, fields of sheep with young lambs whirling away from the smoking monster that thundered by.

More stations, platforms with anxious travellers, guarding luggage and small children.

'Your ticket, miss.' It was the train conductor.

Imogen frowned. This was his second time of asking. He had already seen the ticket when she boarded the train.

'Is there something wrong?' she asked as he handed it back. He shook his head, feeling guilty and a little ashamed. He gave her an appraising glance; didn't see many beautiful women on this daily journey between Newcastle and York, and this one was a stunner, the temptation for another look at her irresistible. He thought fleetingly of his wife working in a laundry in York, their life untouched by any kind of beauty or magic like the young woman who looked as if she had stepped out of a fairy tale with her mass of dark red curls and green eyes. A lovely voice too, an educated woman, one of the toffs, and he wondered why she was travelling alone. This second closer look revealed that she wasn't as young as he had first thought, a bit of a shock, she must be past forty and married. Lucky husband, he thought, closing the compartment door and sliding back into the swaying corridor of the train.

And now as the train steamed into York, Imogen gathered her luggage and stepped down on to the platform. Keen to have that promised look at the Dower House, she had sent the Hardys a telegram regarding the train's arrival at midday, which would give her plenty of time to spend with them before meeting Kathleen when the Four Seasons closed. However, she had her first misgivings as the platform emptied.

Then she saw a figure waving, Belle's smiling face.

She embraced Imogen and said: 'Theo is waiting.'

And there he was, smiling happily at the wheel of their handsome motor car, a new Ford tourer.

Imogen soon realised that the motor car had made its debut and settled in York. As in cities like London, Edinburgh and Dublin, it was fast replacing the horse-drawn carriage. She was seated comfortably beside the eager to be friendly Belle, who she was to learn was a local lass. Holding Imogen's hand and saying how wonderful it was to see her, Belle was asking where was her handsome husband.

'We were so looking forward to welcoming you both.'

Imogen gave a brief explanation about the funeral and told her that he would be arriving tomorrow.

Belle was saying Theo was dying to meet Inspector Faro, had heard so much about him. Then she giggled and confessed that her broad accent worried her husband who secretly thought it a mite common, moving as he did amongst mostly academics, but Belle merely laughed at him. She told Imogen that she was proud of having no edge, as she called it, a Yorkshire woman born and bred.

During the drive it emerged that Theo was a clerk in charge of records, keeping track of digs and artefacts rather than a working archaeologist. There was a surprise in store as they arrived at the Dower House. Glimpsed only briefly through rain on Imogen's first visit, it was not the kind of middle-class villa that might be expected as being within the means of an academic's salary.

As well as owning the motor car, the Hardys' residence was two centuries old, tucked away in the Irongate, a secluded cul-de-sac, a tiny oasis she had had such difficulty in finding on her first visit, hidden behind one of the Snickelways in the heart of the city. Like many ancient houses Imogen had encountered in her worldwide travels, it had an air of bewilderment, dwarfed by a city whose houses had sprung up alongside the old property, leaving it lost in time while the world around it moved on.

Now with leisure to regard her hosts more closely, she wondered again how the Hardys came to own and could afford the upkeep of such a mansion, which, as was pointed out to her, even possessed a private park.

The Hardys themselves were like many couples who had spent half of their lives together: blended by the passing years and approaching middle-age, few individual features remained to describe their personalities apart. Theo was tall, thin, balding and had never been a handsome man, but a distinguished scholarly manner hinted towards ambitions that at some time encompassed more than his present role as a mere clerk. Belle made up for his reserve with an air of faint but perpetual frivolity, the fading airs of a once pretty blonde with now thinning curls and abundant curves well controlled and corseted.

* * *

As Theo was handing Imogen out of the motor car, Belle was saying that the garden was older than the house. It was her pride and joy and they were looking forward to the pleasure of showing it to Imogen and her husband in some detail and at its best, in broad daylight, when Inspector Faro arrived.

Theo took up the story. 'There is clear evidence of an earlier building, fragments of stone,' he said excitedly. 'The remains of a mosaic floor were unearthed twenty years ago, that and some crumbling stone ruins over yonder indicate a Roman villa existed on this very spot. Emperor Severus was over sixty when he came to York in 208 AD with his wife Julia Domna and two sons. He had a huge retinue of servants and soldiers, including the Praetorian Guard. He was the only black man ever to be a Roman Emperor, and it is believed that he lived in the villa here. When he died in 211 AD, York gave him a lavish funeral.'

Theo went on to tell her that the Romans had occupied York in about 71 AD when Severus's predecessor, Vespasian, ordered General Quintus Petillius Cerialis, Governor of Britain, to march from Lincoln with the IX Legion of some five thousand men. Here they set up camp, where the rivers Ouse and Foss met, built a great fortress and called it Eboracum, their mission to conquer the Brigantes, a native tribe who occupied swathes of Britain from the Humber to the Scottish Lowlands.

'Digs of what had once been kitchen middens are the archaeologists' unfailing source of building up a picture of the past, and the Dower House has produced evidence of many buildings on this very spot over nearly two thousand years since the Romans left,' he added proudly.

'Absolutely fascinating, imagine living every day surrounded by such history,' Imogen was to tell Faro later. However, history had failed to supply an answer to the mystery of the IX Legion that had helped to found York. It was still a talking point among historians and academics as to why and where they vanished to after 117 AD, a mystery that has continued to intrigue, and for which all evidence has long been lost.

'No trace has ever been found of what happened after the IX marched north, and over the following centuries there have been many theories of how five thousand armed highly trained soldiers could disappear over the English border into Scotland,' said Theo. 'Had they been slaughtered or merely changed sides and decided to integrate with the Brits?

'As for the Dower House,' he continued, 'unfortunately, all the early documents were lost in a disastrous fire in the middle of the last century, so we know nothing of its owners and the part it and they might have played in the city's history.'

Imogen was intrigued and guessed that Faro would be too. Solving strange puzzles had been his life's work and here they were on the doorstep, one might say, of a house built over the remains of a villa once occupied by a Roman emperor who had died within its walls.

'Living here must have always been the answer to an archaeologist's dream,' she said to Theo, who laughed.

'It has failed to leave us any clues to its air of antiquity,' he said, to which Belle added sadly, 'Only those few remains of tiles of that faded mosaic floor.'

'Which covered most of the ground level of the villa in the Emperor Severus's day,' said Theo.

'And it is the most valuable part of the property,' Belle added proudly. 'Not something many householders can boast about.'

CHAPTER FIVE

Imogen followed Belle along the narrow twisting corridors inside the Dower House. The interior was like skinning an onion. There was a kind of magician's box of surprises about each of the small panelled rooms, where doors creakily opened to reveal windows often slightly out of alignment.

Imogen sniffed the air, overwhelmed by the feeling of a bygone age that recalled dallying in ancient churches and cathedrals across Europe. All had one thing in common, this unidentifiable yet familiar smell of past ages.

At her side, Faro in his practical way usually stripped away the romance and spoilt it all by murmuring that it was probably nothing more mysterious than dry rot.

From what Imogen had learnt, Faro would be intrigued about the IX Legion's role in the building of York, but would the Dower House also strike a chord, reminding him of Rose's ancient home they had just left at the base of Arthur's Seat?

Solomon's Tower's worn stone stairs, the creaking floorboards were all familiar here, so too the massive open fireplace in the large kitchen she suspected was also the warmest and most frequented room in the house.

The Hardys were cautious but welcoming and as they sat down at the table for lunch, from looks exchanged between the pair, Imogen guessed later that they had obviously talked over some proposition they were now about to present, once sure of her enthusiastic response to the Dower House.

Belle smiled, took a deep breath. 'How would you and your husband like to stay here? Theo is off on a dig.'

Theo looked at her and interrupted: 'My wife has decided to honour us with her presence in Egypt on this occasion.'

'I only go along,' Belle said with an apologetic shrug, 'if the place is guaranteed as sufficiently civilised nearby, like Cairo, to have the luxury of modern amenities where I can spend my time exploring shops, or failing that, traditional markets. I prefer to stay home,' she added, giving him a fond glance, 'when the dig is less appealing.'

She shuddered. 'I endured it when we were both young and such adventures had a hint of romance, but not now. Age and some chilly experiences of digs have changed that idea, although conditions have improved in the last few years. Once, Egypt meant those dreary pyramids, being in the desert with the sand blowing all day and sleeping in an uncomfortable tent at night.

Thanks to the success of the digs and their popularity, we now have decent hotel accommodation. Anyway,' she added watching the maid clearing away the dishes and exchanging a glance with Theo, 'we would be delighted to offer you and your famous husband—'

'I had the pleasure of meeting Inspector Faro in Edinburgh a few years ago, when we were on a dig at Cramond,' Theo interrupted, and to Belle, 'Sorry, my dear, you were saying . . .'

She was regarding Imogen anxiously. 'Well, Miss Crowe, what do you think of staying here, taking care of our little home while we are away, just for two or three weeks?'

Theo added encouragingly, 'It would be an excellent location, situated in the heart of the city for your research purposes.'

Belle nodded. 'You would be doing us a tremendous favour and hotel life is so dull, as I know to my cost, so please say yes, you will be much more comfortable here. Mrs Muir, our splendid housekeeper, is an excellent cook.'

Imogen had never envisaged such a generous offer as a certainty, a visit of a few days only in her mind, and accordingly she had booked rooms in the hotel where the limit of Faro's staying powers was a week. Longer and he would be looking for a self-catering house, exactly what she had in mind, ending with their visit to Elrigg and henceforth back to Edinburgh.

Now she was having second thoughts. The house was enchanting, and that sheltered garden would be an additional delight for Faro. He would enjoy a pipe in the evening sitting out there in peaceful seclusion, with birds flying home to their nests in its pretty huddle of trees, overlooked by the Minster's benign shadow.

Just as the house reminded her of Solomon's Tower, so there came another memory that would please Faro. Rose's sister Emily's house, Yesnaby in Orkney, where the family had gathered so sadly for her husband Erland's funeral last year. The Yesnabys' ancestral home also had a curious sunken garden with a strange magic, richly fertile in an arid treeless landscape.

'You will not be quite alone,' Theo said. 'Wilfred lives on the premises too. Belle is my second wife,' he explained giving her a fond glance. 'As we have not been blessed with children, Wilfred is a very welcome member of the family.'

'Wilfred is Theo's stepson,' said Belle, 'from the first Mrs Hardy. It's just as well we didn't have children, since the life of an archaeologist is somewhat hectic, and I know from experience over the years that would have meant I was trapped here with young children to bring up unaided.'

Later, alone with Imogen, still wrestling with this unexpected change of plans, Belle said: 'Wilfred's mother was a widow lady somewhat his senior, with a six-year-old when Theo married her.' She sighed. 'Theo has a kind heart, he was quite young, and I think it was more compassion than passionate real love. Wilfred and I have always got along well together, he's a clever lad, did a history degree at Oxford. Theo was hoping he'd be an archaeologist too, but no, not for him, that life. Very modern in his outlook on life, more interested in the present than past ages.' Again, she sighed. 'Not much taste for our society, he keeps to his own part of the house. Can be rather distant when you first meet, but if he takes to you, you will find him quite charming and very helpful.

'Wilfred isn't around at the moment and it's Mrs Muir's night off too, but they will take great care of you. Mrs Muir lives in, of course, but Molly, who served us, is our daily maid and there is John, a gardener-cum-handyman. He lives in the old-fashioned manner of a coachman above the stable to look after the horses.' She chuckled. 'These days, however, it is Theo's motor car he drives.'

And so, Imogen allowed herself to be persuaded. Belle was excited by her decision, quite rapturous and laughing happily, although Theo looked more solemn. He was a man of fewer words and less prone to expressing his emotions than his wife, Imogen decided, as she gave thought to the advantages of living in the Dower House.

The Hardys insisted she be driven back to her hotel when she had given a somewhat lengthy explanation for declining their invitation to begin her sojourn immediately at the Dower House by staying overnight. She said that a room had already been booked at the hotel rather than giving the true explanation that, always cautious, she had decided to examine the object of their offer first before committing herself and Faro.

It still sounds too good to be true, she would warn

him later, to which he would smile wryly and say that in his philosophy and long experience, things that sounded too good to be true usually were just that.

The motor car with Imogen installed purred into action, Belle issuing last-minute instructions for their next meeting, holding her hand anxiously and saying she was sure they would be happy here and that the inspector would love the Dower House, everyone did.

They waved her goodbye, driven by John as Theo had consumed a fair quantity of wine. Watching the motor disappear through the garden and into the Irongate, they went inside and leaning against the closed front door, Belle took her husband's arm and whispered: 'I think she'll be all right.'

Theo's thoughts were more regarding the absent Faro with his formidable reputation for crime-detecting. 'I only hope we've done the right thing.'

Belle gave him an anxious look. 'Of course we have. What could go wrong?'

He sighed. 'Plenty. But we will just hope for the best.'

Depositing her luggage which seemed hardly worth unpacking, as the city clocks far and near struck six, she was outside the Four Seasons where a young girl was already attaching a 'Closed' notice to the door. Imogen pressed firmly forward. 'Where is Kathleen?' She mouthed the words but the girl merely shrugged and pulled down the blinds obliterating Imogen's face from view. Hammering on the door, first politely and then intensely, made no difference. Telling herself that Kathleen had never received her letter, she retraced her steps back to the hotel where she determinedly pushed thoughts of her cousin aside, banished by the implications of a sojourn in the Dower House.

Following a pleasant, rather dull supper alone in the restaurant instead of the hospitality she had turned down with the Hardys, she found it difficult to fall asleep in the warm comfortable bed in the warm comfortable hotel, with niggling feelings about the failed meeting with Kathleen. She would be at that shop tomorrow morning when it opened, and after reasons had been sorted out regarding letters gone astray, she would give Kathleen a piece of her mind regarding shop assistants who closed the door in customers' faces at the stroke of six.

Having more or less dismissed that problem, the door remained open for yet another to slide in and she was now unable to keep out disquieting thoughts that she had been too impulsive about the Dower House. Faro's reactions might not be as she hoped, her changed plans no surprise for him but instead one of shock.

With a list of ready explanations composed, she closed her eyes at last and slept moderately well, apart from some very odd anxiety dreams confusing Carasheen and Edinburgh, with a dash of Dublin, in which she was always searching, waiting.

Opening her eyes next morning to brilliant sunshine

flooding the bedroom, delicate clouds floating like silk, drifting in a gentle haze across to the Minster, she stretched her arms above her head. Birds were singing, and this was spring, the world around her awakening again from its long sleep. She bathed, went down to a substantial breakfast and gazed at her smiling reflection in the window, pleased to have taken the initiative about the Dower House, reassured to have cancelled the hotel booking.

Very soon she would be meeting Faro off the morning train from Edinburgh. At the railway station, they would take one of the new taxi cabs through the city's twisting streets and down into the Irongate. To the Dower House.

She clasped her hands delightedly, excited now at the lovely surprise she had prepared for him, now certain she had done the right thing, glad she had resisted the temptation to mention the Hardys' offer.

Walking down the hotel steps, she took reassurance, made confident by the sunshine, that this day promised to be the beginning of a delightful holiday for them both. Her misgivings in the dark hours of an unsettled night were banished by a surge of excitement with so many advantages to consider, certain that the Dower House's history would gladden Faro's heart, staying on the very site of the original Roman villa with its faded remains of that mosaic floor once walked on daily by the Emperor Severus, his family and retinue of servants.

First of all, her day would begin with the pleasant task of seeing Kathleen again. Making her way towards the Stonegate, she told herself she would soon realise that she had been worrying unduly. There were many reasons why she had not heard from Kathleen, and Faro had assured her that letters frequently were delayed when forwarded to people moving to new addresses.

Perhaps it would have been better to have given her Solomon's Tower as her address, he added, which too late was not much in the way of consolation. By the time she met him off the train and took him to meet Kathleen, and introduced him to the Dower House, she would have all the answers to that one imponderable thought at the back of her mind that refused to be banished.

How on earth Theo, a clerk and record keeper with the archaeologists, unlikely to earn much more than a working man's wage, could, along with his wife and a stepson who had no fixed employment, afford to live in the Dower House and employ a housekeeper, servants and run a motor car that even a professor's income would find it difficult to maintain?

Meanwhile, as she approached the Four Seasons, Jeremy Faro, who loved train travel, was sitting back comfortably, enjoying the morning sunshine streaming through the carriage window, his nostalgic thoughts wandered over the happiness Imogen had brought into his life in their years together.

CHAPTER SIX

Faro laid aside the guidebook he had intended reading on the train journey in favour of the fascination of an ever-changing landscape. He sighed, thinking happily of Imogen and another new experience they were to share. Indeed, each time they were separated by even a few days, he found himself counting the hours until they would be together again.

He had never grown used to spending long periods apart, never got used to the demands of her life as a writer of some repute traipsing across Europe, her biographies of historical figures in high demand and always the need for research taking her to yet another country. He had been glad before his retirement to accompany her but relieved that the turbulence of Irish history had brought her nearer to home.

Home for her was in Kerry, where they had been married by her uncle, Father Seamus Crowe in St

Katherine's Church in Ventry. An almost secret marriage, more like an elopement rather than the family wedding expected to be enjoyed with an overabundance of food and drink by the Crowe family in Carasheen, an occasion both of them were keen to avoid.

As the train swept past Durham, the sight of its splendid cathedral reminded him that they must visit that city, especially knowing that the university had asked Imogen for a lecture on her biographical series on the female Irish saints.

Far below the railway line a car was speeding along the road, aiming to keep pace with the train, and he wondered if a day would come when the motor car would replace the railway for speedy travel. While staying with Rose in Edinburgh, he had learnt to drive Jack's motor car. It pleased him that Jack, like Rose's first husband Danny McQuinn, who had disappeared while working for Pinkerton's Agency in America, was also a policeman. There were no shopkeepers or bankers, no doctors or priests in the Scarth or Faro families, and like his own father, PC Magnus Faro, who had died on the job, it seemed that Jeremy Faro could never entirely escape from the world of violence and crime.

As the train reached Darlington, drawing Imogen ever nearer, Faro was in a nostalgic mood. They would be going to Elrigg Castle for a wedding shortly, and as the train steamed through Berwick Station, it had reminded him of their first meeting in Northumberland – a disastrous occasion. Possibly because his male ego was insulted when she refused to share the only carriage waiting outside the station, he had taken an instant dislike to this young woman, an impossible creature, only to discover they were staying at the same hotel.

There had been other incidents: judging from the literature she carried, she was one of the dreaded suffragettes, as was revealed when meeting her among the standing stones at Elrigg. She had rushed off at his approach, run down the hill, tripped and sprained her ankle.

He could not leave her there and had to carry her down to the road. Not that she was grateful for his assistance, protesting all the while, but he could remember the warmth of her, the delicate perfume, and when they met later socially, as guests at the same dinner table, he had to grudgingly admit that she was quite a beauty, clever and witty too – but with a heart of stone, he did not doubt.

However, by the time they said goodbye at Berwick Station he had learnt a lot about her and that she was an authoress doing research. As the train steamed out of the station, he was left wishing he had kissed her goodbye instead of that mere garbled politeness in which he had talked vaguely about the possibility of their paths crossing – some day – in Edinburgh.

Indeed, their paths did cross in Edinburgh and Faro was to discover that one should be careful what one wishes for, since the suppliant has no advance knowledge of the means by which it could be granted. This time it was near disaster: the case involved a royal scandal and Imogen's cousin, another Crowe, hanged himself awaiting trial as an Irish terrorist in a Stirling prison. Rose Faro had been seized as hostage by the Fenians and Imogen – a member of the organisation – put her own life in danger to save Inspector Faro's daughter, aware that by so doing she had a price on her head if she entered Britain again.

Thus, exiled forever it seemed, in recent years she had unexpectedly received a royal pardon.

Despite it all and the dour face of destiny, Faro never forgot Imogen Crowe or the fact that she was the enemy and he was a policeman, his life dedicated to defending the Queen's Empire, destroying criminals and all they stood for, with Irish terrorists high in that category. Her face haunted his dreams, and occasionally he would wake up feeling as if she too remembered and he had held her willingly in his arms. But what was there to remember really, merely a kiss blown across from a departing ship to Ireland and the possibility that they would never meet again.

He read about her sometimes, saw reviews of her books, once or twice picking up a copy and buying it, not to read, its content of little interest to him, but because it had her photograph on the book jacket, which never did justice to her beauty.

One or two books was all he ever had, all that he could expect. Except that fate had one more card to play. The years passed, and Faro was invited to a police conference in Dublin, where desperate measures had been taken by the patriot Daniel O'Connell in the last century to seal centuries of wounds inflicted by the British.

Chief Inspector Faro was already well known for his integrity, his sense of justice and admiration for men like O'Connell and Henry Parnell, regarded as traitors by the English. He was pleased and indeed flattered to be asked; also taking part in the meeting that evening was Arthur Griffith, editor of an Irish newspaper who went on to found Sinn Fein in 1905.

As Faro went to the lectern to give his talk, lecture notes in hand, he found himself face-to-face with a smiling woman: Imogen Crowe was seated in the front row of the waiting audience. He was never sure how he got through the rest of the evening, what he said, only that it went well.

Arthur Griffith and the officials were ushered from the stage amid tumultuous applause. With the flimsiest of excuses, Faro politely declined to join the platform party for a drink afterwards. He rushed downstairs in time to see the hall emptying. He panicked, realising Imogen was gone, would have left after the applause died down. He stood there, feeling a cold chill that he had lost her once again, without even a word or a smile of greeting.

But this time he was wrong. As he left the hall, outside she was waiting by the carriage that was to carry him to his hotel. She smiled, and he took her hand, held it a moment too long and smiled back. 'May I drop you off somewhere?'

'Where are you staying?' she asked. He told her, and she nodded. 'Sure now, me too.'

They sat side by side in the carriage, silent in the short distance, and at the hotel took their keys from reception and climbed the stairs. Reaching her door, she held it open. Following her, Faro closed the door, and without a word being spoken, both aware that destiny had held this moment in wait for a very long time, they fell into each other's arms, the massive four-poster bed an invitation not to be denied. There fulfilment awaited, a bridge across the years. Tonight they belonged to each other and they would never be parted again.

Through those missing years before they found each other, Imogen had known many brief loves and each time she stayed at a hotel, when her door opened she had hoped that it would be Faro who would appear, the imagined magic of a kiss repeated on each occasion. She had fled from Scotland, forever an exile, but always aware that tonight it would be his face, his mouth she kissed, his body that fitted so well into her own, rather than the man she had invited, a passing love, an attractive man, a fleeting acquaintance soon to be forgotten.

Faro had not been so fortunate, although he had met women who attracted him too. But the real loves of his life had been few. His first love at seventeen in Orkney had been Inga St Ola. They had met over the years when he returned home, and the flame had rekindled but Inga had steadfastly refused to follow him to Edinburgh. In many ways she was Imogen's only predecessor. They would have got on well together these two women, he often thought, for the qualities of Inga were also recognisable in Imogen. Both were independent, both demanded more of life than the conventional image society provided of women's role as being little more than a breeding machine and a slave to man's bodily requirements. With scant regard paid to any spiritual qualities they may possess, women were generally viewed by society – and even by the Church – as being lower than man, whom God had created in his own image.

As well as Inga there had been Amelie, Grand Duchess of Luxoria, goddaughter of Queen Victoria. That sad, brief passion and her love for Faro ended with her returning to a cruel tyrannical husband and a childless marriage; then came a short cryptic message: WE have a son. The boy prince George had ruled over Luxoria since his mother's early death, the son Faro could never acknowledge.

Then there was his wife, Lizzie, to whom he was grateful for his two daughters, Rose and Emily. By extension, his family now included Emily's son, Magnus, and Meg Macmerry, Jack's daughter from his brief unhappy marriage on the rebound from Rose's rejection Finally, there was Faro's stepson, Dr Vincent Beaumarcher Laurie, who was now Dr Vincent Beaumarcher Laurie, now junior physician to the royal household. Vince had been of assistance in solving some of his early cases and Faro felt fortunate indeed to have been loved at all with a life so dedicated to the demands of being a chief detective inspector.

The train was approaching York. Imogen would be waiting.

Faro closed his guidebook that provided all the necessary information for someone visiting a city for the first time. Before leaving Edinburgh, he had purchased this important part of any journey, for it was essential that he knew in advance exactly where he was going and what to expect. In their new flat he had already a stack of similar guides to every city he had visited with Imogen during their years together.

Already he had a rough plan of York's city centre so that he would not get lost and embarrassingly have to ask for directions. He also had a pretty good idea of the main places of attraction. Most importantly he had to know where and why each city began from a bleak wilderness that existed through the centuries before man had discovered that this was a place to build, a place to expand. In York's case, man had been signified by the Romans who had set down Eboracum, and when they moved on it became Christian when Constantine the Great was proclaimed emperor in 306 AD. It had been a garrison town ever since, captured and burnt by the Danes in 867 AD, becoming their capital of England for one hundred years.

Renamed Jorvik, York's original name, the use of 'gate' a reminder that they had settled here. When the

Normans invaded in 1069 they found a thriving little trading centre, burnt it and proceeded to rebuild the walls and two castles that saw the founding of most institutions that flourished during the Middle Ages, although little had survived apart from the ruin of a partial Norman house.

Seizing his luggage and thrusting his guidebook inside, he was satisfied to have absorbed the details and information that would mean not always being seen as a stranger.

Imogen would be well ahead of him regarding places to visit and he needed to keep up with her, realising that he probably would not have come at all if this return visit was intended mainly to see again another Crowe relative from Carasheen. As always, he would be surplus to this family reunion, and he was thankful that the two stranger cousins would have met by now and the funeral in Edinburgh had provided a solemn if useful excuse to let her come alone.

As the train slid to a standstill at the platform and the steam cleared, he looked round eagerly. Expecting to see Imogen, she wasn't there.

The platform emptied of departing passengers and he made his way to the entrance. A line of taxicabs waited, the sun shone, but Imogen was nowhere to be seen. He had only the name of the hotel where they were staying.

With a weary sigh he boarded a cab, fighting off vague feelings of anxiety new to him. In the weeks since Imogen's first visit, apart from worries about not hearing from Kathleen, she had been deliberately vague about York, hiding something else, some other concern.

And that was not like her, nor was this failure to meet the train; Imogen was meticulous about such things, checking arrangements had always been part of her way of life.

As the cab rattled across the bridge and made its way past the Minster, the bells were ringing. Bells of another kind – of warning – were ringing for him. He had a gnawing sense of fear that something had happened to Imogen.

He was right.

CHAPTER SEVEN

Faro's anticipation of a pleasant holiday with Imogen were to be rudely shattered when they met and instead of the glories of York, he heard how on the previous day, as six o'clock was striking and the shops closing, she had left the Dower House, hurrying down the Stonegate full of apologies for Kathleen who would still be waiting in the flower shop, only to find a 'Closed' notice was already on the door.

There had been no sign of Kathleen. Had she mentioned in her letter from Edinburgh or in that previous brief conversation where she was staying, given the hotel a name? Yes, she was sure she had done so and said they would go there for supper. Hope renewed, she decided that might be the answer and that Kathleen was there already waiting for her as she hurried to the hotel. At the restaurant, tables already filling up with diners. No sign of Kathleen. At the desk she asked if any message had been left for her. Giving both names as Mrs Faro and Imogen Crowe, she watched anxiously as the receptionist inspected the boxes where the room keys were kept.

'No, madam, there are no messages or letters for you.' She gave Imogen a strange look as she added in response to her question: 'No, madam, your husband has not yet arrived. We are not expecting Mr Faro until tomorrow.'

Did that slightly knowing look indicate that the girl thought she was having an illicit meeting, Imogen wondered, as wearily she took her key and climbed the stairs to their room. What to do next? Go to the restaurant? But she had guessed wrongly hoping that Kathleen might have assumed there had been travel complications and worked out that Imogen would be waiting here at the hotel.

She looked round the empty unwelcoming room. Realising she was hungry and hadn't eaten since lunch at the Hardys', she went back down to the restaurant and ordered a light meal. As she ate, always keeping an eye on the door of the hotel, she tried to reason out what had happened.

Kathleen had waited for her and, disappointed, had gone home. Or, the letter she had written from Edinburgh had never reached her. She wished Faro had not had to change his plans for that funeral and had travelled with her. She needed more than ever his practical logical mind in this crisis, his consoling presence and soothing words.

By eight o'clock she knew waiting any longer for

Kathleen to appear was useless, and back in her room she read for a while and went to bed, telling herself that all was not lost. There was one sure solution to seeing Kathleen again. She would be at the flower shop when it opened next morning.

After a quick breakfast, she went once more to the Stonegate where her enthusiasm was greater than their opening hours. The 'Closed' notice told her that she was perhaps too early, although a group of men in overalls were unloading a van of containers that looked like flower boxes. A tall, well-dressed man, obviously the boss, was giving them directions in what she realised was a foreign language, probably Dutch.

Seeing her standing outside the shop, the man stared across at her. Pointing at the shop, she smiled and asked him when it would open. He was watching her with the intent look she was used to from strange men. It told of admiration and more that she didn't want to know about. In answer he shrugged, gesticulating, obviously not understanding her question.

For a moment she continued to look at him, wondering where she had seen him before and remembering that it was on her first visit to the Four Seasons, when she had interrupted an argument with Kathleen. A tall, fair-haired man who had looked angry, bowed slightly and walked away.

And Imogen realised that it was his image she had seen in a gallery long ago in Amsterdam, and she recalled how she had returned again and again after that visit because it had so fascinated her. Perhaps all Dutchmen looked alike but she had fallen in love with 'Andres', the sixteenth-century portrait of a young man by Vermeer, the same fair colouring and neatly pointed beard, in his outstretched hand a goblet of wine, a gentle, slightly mocking expression as if inviting the viewer to participate.

How extraordinary, she thought, as she looked in the Stonegate for a shop selling newspapers to take one back to Faro. Then she walked back once more towards the Four Seasons and, seeing the 'Closed' notice was still there, the containers inside and the unloaders vanished, she continued down the street to the cafe where she had intended to meet Kathleen on that first visit. She walked across and glanced in the windows at some smartly dressed ladies who were obviously enjoying morning refreshments in what was a very respectable coffee house that lived up to its reputation for excellence. Taking advantage of the pretty young waitress's friendly manner, as she paid for the delicious cream scone she mentioned the flower shop. Did they open later than the usual shops in the area?

Mary Boyd, the owner and manager, overheard the question and came forward. She vaguely remembered this very elegant and lovely woman. Hadn't she arranged to meet someone who hadn't turned up?

She didn't want to appear nosey, it was none of her business, after all. She merely shook her head. She had no idea, but if it was flowers madam wanted there were other shops and she thought there would be plenty of spring flowers and tulips about at this time of year. That wasn't very encouraging, and paying her bill, Imogen said casually the Four Seasons had been particularly recommended.

Oh yes, this was definitely the same lady. Mary again shook her head and smiled apologetically. She hardly ever went into a flower shop. No need, really. They were too expensive when she had lovely flowers in her garden at home.

As Imogen was leaving the Ladies' room, hovering indecisively, wondering what to do next, four tough-looking men, grim-faced despite their smart suits, walked rapidly to the table she had just left. Her umbrella was still there. They looked up sharply as she approached and apologised. One of them was Andres come to life from the Dutch portrait, who she had noticed superintending those flower boxes outside the Four Seasons.

When she said: 'My umbrella, if you please', without a word or a glance he pushed it towards her irritably, hardly interrupting his conversation.

What manners and a disappointment, she thought, not much like the portrait of that gallant sixteenth-century young man, and looking across she saw the expression on Mary's face. Imogen could almost feel her annoyance and fears for what the presence of such men would do for the coffee shop's business and reputation.

It was clear what Mary thought as she glanced anxiously in the direction of her tables full of smartly dressed York matrons, regular customers enjoying their morning coffee, as a male hand raised and fingers snapped sharply and impatiently for her attention from the newly entered quartet of men who seemed like strangers in this area.

It wasn't Mary's first encounter with these unpopular customers and anxiously considering her ladies she hoped these common individuals weren't going to make a habit of coming into her cafe. She did not like the look of them. She had an instinct about people. Something in their appearance said trouble and seeing them sitting there would undoubtedly spell disaster for her business.

She remembered that first time, last week. The four men had gathered around a corner table. Four well-dressed but unprepossessing men whose gloomy appearance and muttered conversations hinted to Mary that they were conspirators. Her ladies already looked scandalised, whispering among themselves. Not good news for the clientele since it was only in very recent years that middle-class ladies had gone out unattended by their maids. The intruding males belonged to a definitely lower echelon of the social system and from her vast experience she would have hazarded a guess that at least one of them had a criminal record and carried a firearm in the jacket of that smart suit. She enjoyed reading short stories in the *Strand Magazine* about a detective called Sherlock Holmes and she was momentarily intrigued.

'Up to no good, mark my words,' she said to her pretty young waitress Amy, preparing their coffee.

Amy gasped, 'How do you know that? Just look like ordinary men from the offices to me.'

'Foreigners,' Mary sniffed, 'not a nice local lad among them.'

Amy darted a look at the table as she heaped rolls onto a plate. She did not share her boss's misgivings. One of them looked young, not bad-looking, and Amy was on the lookout for a new young man – not one of the rough kind she met at the Saturday night dance hall who worked on the railways. She had her sights on some fellow with a good steady job and a bit of money as a matrimonial prospect.

She giggled and shook her blonde curls. 'Not all foreigners. I think I heard one Irish accent. I recognised it because the matron at the home was from Wexford. She was awful nice to me.'

'Irish,' Mary repeated, unimpressed by this observation. 'Well, that's bad enough but the others sounded like those sailors we get in sometimes from Hull, even if they are better dressed. Some too dark to be Dutchmen,' she added.

She knew that the Dutch accent might be mistaken for German. Two of them looked like Arabs. She sighed. What was York coming to? No longer good-humoured, tough but kindly solid Yorkshire lads working on the railway, always good for a laugh or even a wee flirtation, but always plenty of compliments and a good tip. But these foreigners didn't even have the manners to say thank you miss. Took their coffee and rolls all straight-faced or scowling and left no tip either.

CHAPTER EIGHT

As Imogen retraced her steps towards Kathleen's shop, the Minster chimed ten. Ah, the shop was open and the doorbell rang as she entered. It wasn't Kathleen as she expected but the young girl she had seen putting up the 'Closed' notice who stepped forward from behind the counter.

'What can I do for you, madam?'

'I'm looking for Kathleen – Mrs Roxwell?'

The girl looked round nervously and shook her head. 'I am sorry, madam. You must be in the wrong shop.'

'I most certainly am not,' Imogen said. 'Mrs Roxwell is a relative of mine and I visited her in this shop just recently.'

'You must be mistaken, madam, there is no one of that name here.' The girl's voice held a note of panic.

'I think it is you who are mistaken, miss. Mrs Roxwell has managed this shop for some time.'

The girl gave a nervous laugh. 'I have never heard of this person and I am in charge here.'

Imogen regarded her sternly. She was very young to be in charge of anything, not more than seventeen or eighteen. She looked like a schoolgirl with her long fair hair, straggly and thin. Shivering slightly, she reminded Imogen of a lost puppy and her appearance was no great advert for the flower shop.

Imogen's annoyance was overtaken by pity. She leant forward and asked: 'Is there something wrong?'

'What do you mean, something wrong? Nothing is wrong.' The note of panic was almost hysteria.

'Are you sure, miss? You look rather poorly.'

The girl made an effort to straighten her shoulders. 'I am quite well.'

And Imogen, who was good with voices, had detected a foreign accent in the girl's quavering replies. Her curiosity aroused, she said: 'How long have you worked here?'

The girl frowned, thought for a moment. 'A long time.'

'Mrs Roxwell was here three weeks ago.'

The girl was gaining confidence. 'I have no idea, madam, who was in this shop before me.'

The doorbell pinged. Here was a customer. Obviously relieved at this interruption, the girl moved Imogen aside: 'If you will excuse me, madam, I must attend this gentleman. There are many other flower shops – you made a mistake here.'

'Very well, but may I know your name, miss?'

The girl bit her lip, gave Imogen a doubtful glance and seemed about to refuse. Then she shrugged. 'It . . . it is Sofia.'

Although the man had his back to them, studying various bunches of flowers, Imogen recognised Andres again. She wanted to say to him, *You were here that last time I came in, talking to Kathleen.* But she was too confused at that moment and left the shop, not only frustrated but also anxious and for the first time afraid.

What had become of Kathleen? Where was she? Where did she live? She should have asked that young man. He might have known. All she remembered was Kathleen pointing vaguely towards the residential district, her apologetic manner indicating that it was near the flower shop.

She heard the city clocks strike again. Heavens above, Faro's early train would have arrived. She should have been at the station meeting him half an hour ago. She looked round frantically but there were no cabs in sight, so she had better go straight to the hotel where he would be wondering what had become of her.

As she quickened her steps along the Stonegate, her anxiety and fears for Kathleen increased. The fact that the foreign girl in the flower shop was lying was assuming sinister proportions and awakened a feeling in her stomach that one of her intuitions of disaster might be moving rapidly in her direction, and was not merely due to that rich cream scone, the sort of indulgence she was very strict about before ten in the morning.

Reaching the hotel, she hurried up the steps into reception to be told to her great relief yes, Mr Faro had arrived. He had been served coffee in his room.

She ran upstairs and threw open the door.

He unwound his tall frame from the sofa and stood up to greet her.

'Imogen, where the devil have you been? I thought you were meeting me at the station.'

'So did I,' she groaned as he kissed her. 'That was my intention,' she said throwing down her cloak, 'but something dreadful has happened.'

He regarded her calmly. 'I rather gathered that from reception, since you had cancelled our reservation.' He frowned. 'What is going on? Why this change of plan?'

Of course, he didn't know about the Dower House. She sat down. 'Well, you see, I have been offered a better place to stay here in York for a couple of weeks. It's a lovely house—' Her voice broke, she couldn't go on.

She was obviously very shaken, and Faro was troubled by this reaction. This wasn't at all like his Imogen, usually so calm and collected, able to deal with any situation. Bewildered he sat down beside her and held her close, stroking her hair. 'This lovely house?' he asked gently.

She stood up sharply. 'No, no – tell you later.' She gulped, and the tears threatened as she whispered, 'Faro, oh, Faro! Something really awful has happened. Kathleen has disappeared.'

CHAPTER NINE

It took Faro a moment to identify who this Kathleen was and he put an arm around Imogen. 'Now, keep calm and tell me what has happened.' Reaching over to the table, he poured out a brandy as an instant cure for all ills.

'Thank you, but I don't need that,' she said.

'Drink it. There now, try to be calm.'

That seemed to have the right effect. She put down the glass, took his hand and told him how she had gone on a quick visit to Kathleen before his train arrived, only to find that the flower shop denied all knowledge of her. She was to go over the incident many times, without mentioning the customer she called Andres, too embarrassed to admit to Faro how many years ago she had fallen in love with a sixteenth-century portrait, and even if she did tell him, there was no way of tracking down this man who happened to be in the shop when she first met Kathleen.

She said: 'The girl this morning claimed that she had been the only one working there for some time, that she had never heard of Kathleen. She insisted there were a lot of flower shops in York and I had come to the wrong one, made a mistake.'

'And could that have been possible, do you think?' asked Faro gently. He had been listening very carefully and hoping this story was not as sinister as Imogen implied.

She laughed scornfully. 'Come now, Faro, you know me better than that. It's the girl who is foreign and might have got her facts wrong, not me.'

'Very well,' he said. 'Let's go back to the beginning, surely we can track her down. But before we start, do you mind telling me where we go next, and why you have cancelled our reservation here.'

'Oh, the Dower House.' She told him about her meeting with the Hardys and their offer, and briefly about its history and connection with the Roman occupation. 'I hope you will approve. I'm sure you will love it.'

She stopped and sighed, tightened her hold on his hand. 'I never mentioned it in Edinburgh, you see. Knowing how you hate hotels, I wanted it to be a pleasant surprise.'

'It certainly is a surprise,' he said wryly, thinking such an offer from a stranger was more than generous, and was definitely to be regarded with caution. 'Do go on.'

'I just know you'll love it. But at this moment, I am more concerned about Kathleen. We must find her.'

'Of course we will. Where did she live?'

Imogen regarded him blankly. 'I didn't have her exact address, she told me in a house near the shop, no distance for her to walk each day.'

'No street number, nothing?'

Imogen shook her head.

And Faro realised guiltily how he had dismissed as of little importance Imogen's plan regarding Kathleen in this opportunity to spend a few days exploring York together, something he had always wanted, before going on to the wedding at Elrigg Castle. All he vaguely knew of Kathleen was that she was one of Imogen's innumerable Crowe family. In truth, he hadn't been particularly interested in meeting her, glad Imogen would have that visit behind her before he arrived. He had learnt to dread and keep to an absolute minimum visits to Carasheen, where Imogen's family were very direct and had been in the past, not to put too fine a point on it, vulgar in their queries about his intentions.

And when are you putting the claddagh ring on her finger? was the main one. Then the scornful sniff and reminder that of course he wasn't Irish, making that sound like an incurable disease and that such behaviour was only to be expected of the English. The kindlier, more diplomatic Father Seamus, Imogen's uncle and also the parish priest, explained tactfully that Imogen's man wasn't the hated English but from Scotland. No, Imogen pleaded, not Scottish, from Orkney. That made matters worse. Shrieks of dismay. And where in the name of God was that? Suspicious looks followed, as if he was a Hottentot.

Faro had looked around him and despaired; among the vast army of females, he wondered how they had managed to produce Imogen. Small wonder that he limited himself to no more than token visits, avoiding the relatives one had never met and would hope never to do so. He found it particularly wearisome when there were no faces to put to the vast chronicles of who had died, got married, or been born since the last visit. The only person Faro felt comfortable with was bright, clever Father Seamus.

In her anxiety over Kathleen's disappearance, Imogen had only briefly mentioned the change of their plans for York. Now calmed by Faro's reassurance that they would conduct an immediate search and having utmost confidence in his remarkable abilities, she was content to be persuaded to wait until tomorrow morning. Certain that they would find out where Kathleen was and contact her, she returned to the subject of the cancelled hotel booking and that they were to stay at the Dower House.

'I hope you approve, Faro, darlin',' she sighed. 'It really is lovely.'

Faro nodded vaguely; his reaction was a disappointment too. Yes, she had said something of the sort, but affected by her distress, his main concern was now for the business of this missing girl to be settled, and having asked her for more details, Imogen continued:

'Kathleen told me she managed the shop and was in every day, and quite honestly, at that time, I had no idea we would have the chance of meeting again and an opportunity to get to know each other. I hadn't seen her since she was a wee girl. It was only through a chance encounter that I discovered Kathleen was here.'

Imogen paused and sighed. 'She's had a hard life, Faro, in her thirties now and I would never have recognised her. It was all very garbled, that first meeting, interrupted with customers in the shop all the time. When I thought about it afterwards and knew we were coming back in three weeks, I scribbled our new address on one of our cards and pushed it under the shop door. I'd hoped we could spend some time together, get to know her, that sort of thing.'

'You were the one to be surprised, my darling,' Faro said and thought how, in a few weeks, whole patterns of life could be completely altered.

'Did she have your address?'

She nodded. 'Yes, I put Preston Drove on the card. I had told her that I was married to a policeman, a retired detective inspector, and that we had been staying with your daughter Rose in Edinburgh. That piece of news was unlikely to reach her from Carasheen.'

'Let's hope a telegram to Uncle Seamus will provide her address.'

It was all very vague, not much to go on for a missing person investigation, Faro thought, the unsatisfactory product of a few minutes' conversation in a crowded shop.

He regarded Imogen sympathetically; he thought he knew her so well, but he was now aware of seeing a new version of her usually efficient manner of dealing with important issues in her busy life.

He realised she was particularly upset due to her seeing again and reliving in Kathleen's misfortunes her own bitter experience as a fifteen-year-old from Carasheen. That, thought Faro, was the reason behind Imogen's acute distress, her anxiety that something dire had happened to the girl and that she had not just walked out of the flower shop one day. Imogen was determined to find out exactly what had happened; any hope of a satisfying answer he realised was going to be up to him.

He said: 'The most likely answer is that she has gone home again to Carasheen.'

Imogen shook her head. 'That hasn't been home for years, since she got married. After that business with her father I only saw her the once. She was just a child, but it was somehow a slur on the family honour that he had taken the coward's way out and not awaited trial and died with a curse on his lips for the hated English.'

And the inevitable verdict and sentence of hanging, Faro thought grimly as she continued:

'I felt so sorry for Kathleen's unhappy childhood, but there was worse to come. Desperate to escape from a claustrophobic dull Carasheen, where a private life was impossible and everyone knew not only what you were doing but what you were thinking and privacy was unknown, she married an English sailor from Yorkshire, met when he was visiting Kerry. He was ill-received by the Crowes, as you can well imagine; there was a quarrel and he was shown the door.'

'So that was how she came to be living here.'

'Yes, Henry was in the merchant marine, on a cargo ship that had a regular route between Hull and Rotterdam, and after the ship was lost with all hands, the owner's wife took pity on her being so young and suggested she stay in York.'

'What was her married name?'

'Roxwell. Kathleen Roxwell.'

Faro smiled encouragingly and put down his pen. 'That is fairly unusual, we should be able to track it down.'

'You'll help me, Faro?' she said.

He hugged her. 'Of course, that's what husbands are for, my darling. First, you send a telegram to Carasheen asking if they have had any word, such as a forwarding address. There is always the possibility that she has returned there.'

Imogen looked doubtful indeed, so he added: 'Surely the whole of Carasheen can't have blacklisted her. Had she no sympathetic family friend?'

'Only Uncle Seamus.'

'Then address the telegram to him and hope for the best.'

Imogen had little hope for the best as Faro continued: 'While we are waiting for a reply, we go to the council offices and look at the census list for this particular area and see if there are any Roxwells – that will give us an address.'

Faro was always very thorough, Imogen decided with relief. If anyone could find out what had happened to Kathleen, she had great faith in him. Maybe those dark clouds of despair were shifting a little, and drawing a deep breath, she smiled at him hopefully.

'I'm sure we will find her.'

He didn't like to spoil it by saying the census was taken every few years and success depended on where they lodged the year they were married. Imogen calculated that it was the summer of 1886, more than twenty years ago.

She shook her head. 'They were only married a few weeks. It was all very tragic, Faro.'

As she spoke Faro was busy scribbling down relevant details.

With so many mysteries during his working life, the habit of carrying a notebook, which Imogen found rather endearing, was one that he had not yet learnt to discard.

Faro sighed. Poor Kathleen, married at eighteen and widowed in the same year.

'I don't suppose she told you the name of the ship?'

'No. We only talked for a few minutes at that first meeting.'

The ship's name would have helped, he sighed, making another note. 'We can try the shipping authority at the docks, their files will have records of merchant vessels trading between Hull and Rotterdam. They will certainly know of any accidents, lost at sea, in past years.'

He put his arm around Imogen. 'Now, you are to get rid of that worried frown, Imo – what we need is some fresh air. How about a walk on the city walls while it is still daylight, and first thing tomorrow morning we'll have a look for that street Kathleen pointed out to you?'

It was all very encouraging, and they got as far as the first set of steps up on to the wall when the rain had them hurrying for shelter in a pleasant cafe, where they enjoyed an excellent meal before returning to their hotel. As they settled down for the night, Faro's thought turned again to the missing woman.

'I expect it is too much to hope for that your uncle or anyone over there has a photograph of her?'

'That is rather doubtful since she left years ago.'

'What did she look like?' Faro asked.

Imogen frowned and thought. 'Now that you ask me, I would find it very hard to describe her. Medium height, thinnish, thirties with brown hair pulled back tightly.' She sighed. 'Very unprepossessing, really. The kind of person you would pass by in the street without giving a second glance.'

Unlike you, Faro thought fondly. Imogen's striking looks were memorable indeed. Perhaps she had inherited all the good looks being handed out in the Crowe family.

CHAPTER TEN

Faro felt guilty, having slept better than Imogen, to awake and find her up first, which was unusual, ready to go down to breakfast and dressed for the outdoors. The Dower House was their destination once they had found out what had happened to Kathleen.

Imogen seemed to have forgotten all about Elrigg. At this time of crisis, family was more important than a goddaughter's society wedding. As they walked briskly in the direction north of the Four Seasons that Kathleen had vaguely indicated, Faro realised they both knew this was not going to help since the horizon was held by a long line of identical terrace houses.

The houses were shabby and had been built closely packed together, probably for railway workers in the mid 1840s. The windows were dirty, the doors looked poor, lacked paint and their atmosphere was distinctly unwelcoming.

And Faro's reasoning rebelled at the prospect of knocking on doors. With painful recollections of his early days as a beat policeman walking the streets of the poorer districts of Edinburgh regarding some criminal activity, he was well aware of the reception they could expect in the vague hope that some neighbour would remember Mrs Roxwell.

Imogen had been overcome by a new wave of optimism at what she considered a splendid idea. In dismay, he realised she was even hopeful that Kathleen might come to the door herself and tell them exactly what had happened, why she had left so suddenly – disappeared – and why the new girl in the flower shop had never heard of her.

Faro's stern expression, his hand on her arm said that this was indeed a wild goose chase. But Imogen wasn't to be put off by the formidable prospect before them.

'Oh, now that we're here, let's cross our fingers and try one or two,' she said eagerly. 'We might be lucky.'

Luck was not with them. Suspicious faces looked out of grimy windows, there was a slight delay, even a hesitation, before doors opened reluctantly. Only a few inches, and soon Imogen realised why. They were scared.

Faro still looked like a policeman, he had never lost that, and perhaps the wariness of one in plain clothes asking questions with that air of authority was a message of caution for even the most innocent. The inevitable sharp response. No, not here, never heard of her.

But there was a corner shop at the end of the

long shabby street, a general store that many such working-class areas possessed and where Faro knew from long past experience that such shopkeepers, for their own protection in the matter of paying for goods, made it their business to know all there was to know regarding the street's inhabitants.

Once again, however, Faro's tall striking appearance, his non-local accent, threw up a wall of hostility. A policeman – oh aye, there's danger here.

He couldn't hide it. Imogen decided a woman's wiles might work. She gave the man her most charming smile and said: 'I am looking for my cousin, but I've lost her address. She is in her mid-thirties . . .'

Listening to that very inadequate description, both she and Faro were certain that the man behind the counter was speaking the truth when he said rather sharply he had never heard of Mrs Roxwell. The shopkeeper regarded Imogen again, detected her accent.

'She's from Ireland, this lass you're looking for?'

Imogen beamed at him. 'Yes, from County Kerry.'

The man did not respond to her smile. The newspapers told them that the Irish were big trouble, not to be trusted.

A firm shake of the head. 'No Irish folk in this street or hereabouts that I know of.'

'It's hopeless, isn't it?' said Imogen over a refreshing pot of tea that Faro hoped would banish her glum expression as they made their way back to the hotel. As the Minster far above their heads cheerfully struck out the hour he said: 'You might try one of your prayers as a last resort. How about one of your saints, the one who deals with lost causes?'

Beyond the windows the benign sunlight had faded, and Imogen frowned. She didn't like being teased about 'a saint for everything'. Helping himself to a second scone, Faro pretended not to notice the slight pursing of her lips.

'I take it you mean St Jude,' she said. Irish families with generations of sea captains believed in his powers. 'Indeed, he might help us.'

Faro already had an uneasy feeling they were going to need all the help available to find the present whereabouts of Imogen's missing relative. A woman in her thirties, now unrecognisable as the orphaned girl Imogen had met briefly once in Carasheen umpteen years ago. Their only link was a few minutes' conversation in a flower shop in York, in which Imogen had learnt nothing more than the bare details of what seemed to have been a rather tragic life.

Their search had already established all the elements of failure and with it Faro's pleasant anticipation of a few days in York. A city about which he knew little, still steeped in medieval England, he had been ready to enjoy its ancient history, walk its walls, explore its old buildings and museums as well as their anticipated stay in the Dower House that Imogen had considered such a lucky break. Now all such happy options were vanishing as fast as had Kathleen Roxwell.

When they retired to their room after supper that evening, neither felt disposed to take a walk in the city, for the rain had increased and fell in heavy sheets down the handsome window overlooking the city walls.

'The flower beds are lovely at this time of year and so well kept,' Imogen had remarked. 'The tulips are lovely; the soil must be very good.'

Faro said, 'I'm sure of it. I don't suppose the manager makes it known, perhaps even tries to conceal the fact that his hotel was built over the old plague pits.'

'How do you know that?' Imogen gasped.

'Because victims of the Black Death – and there were many later plagues – were always buried outside the city walls and the phosphate in all those bones makes good soil and grows pretty flowers.'

Imogen was impressed, where some hotel guests might have been horrified. She could imagine sensitive women screaming in horror and demanding that they leave immediately as she said, 'Sure now, isn't it great to know that good can spring from evil.'

Faro might not have put it so eloquently himself as he drew out his notebook and, pointing across at the other armchair, said, 'Now, my dear, back to our missing Kathleen. I want you to tell me right from the beginning everything you know about her, every detail of that brief conversation.'

Imogen sighed. 'Very well, but you have heard it all before,' she added reproachfully.

'I know, I know, but it was all rather garbled, you

weren't thinking as sharply as you normally do. You were tired and worried. Now that you are calm you will, as I know you always are able to, give me a clear and precise account of your second visit to the flower shop. Every detail. Yes, every one. There may be a link, some clue that we have missed.'

When Imogen somewhat wearily reached the meeting with the new girl, and the foreign accent, she paused again. 'I've travelled a lot and I can recognise most of the obvious European ones, but further afield, I'm not sure.'

She thought for a moment, and then said: 'Oddly enough, I now seem to remember that it was the same as the men in the cafe across from the flower shop.'

'What men?' he demanded eagerly.

This was where she should have introduced Andres, but no, instead she said: 'Just some rather shady-looking characters whose presence had shocked and alarmed some very respectable local ladies having their coffee,' and as the carriage headed towards the Dower House, she held his hand with all the excitement of a child offered a sudden treat. She was not disappointed, the ancient house meeting all Faro's requirements for charm and beauty as well as possessing a beautiful garden. In every possible way, it far exceeded his intended stay or any hotel in York.

Much to Imogen's surprise, the Hardys had already left. Wilfred, warned of the Faros' arrival, was at home to welcome them and extend his stepfather's apologies. The archaeology team had had an unexpected change of plans, something to do with ships to Egypt, he had ended vaguely. They were to make themselves at home.

Belle's description had been accurate. He was rather untidy, as if he did not care for appearances, with a general air of self-sufficiency that Faro often encountered in the young who were rebelling against society. There was nothing striking or even memorable about his appearance, in fact he seemed to blend chameleon-like into his surroundings, Faro thought. Polite enough, but Imogen guessed that he was glad to escape back to his own rooms when he declined to have supper with them.

The maid Molly served them an excellent supper, hovering anxiously. No, she didn't live in, she was only a day-girl – went home each night after supper was served and the dishes washed. Well, Mrs Muir had excelled herself, Imogen decided, if this was what they were to get used to.

The housekeeper put in a brief appearance to show them up the twisting stone stairs to where their rooms were situated. She was a bespectacled, middle-aged woman whose shapeless uncorseted figure and rather untidy grey curls were not disciplined in the usual tightly pulled-back hairstyle favoured by housekeepers and upper servants.

Mrs Muir encountered difficulties transporting their luggage up the stairs, which was immediately taken over by Faro, thinking this task was one Wilfred might have spared her. Faro was rewarded by a whispered *Thank you, sir*, as she ushered them into the room with a brief curtsey. As Imogen turned to add her thanks, the housekeeper nodded sharply, murmured breakfast was at eight-thirty and was already hurrying back towards the stairs.

Closing the door, they took in their surroundings. A beautiful room, doubtless one of the best in the house, with a bay window gazing down across the tranquil garden with green, well-kept lawns extending towards parkland behind an ancient stone wall overlooked by the now distant Minster.

Faro sighed pleasurably as he hung their outdoor clothes inside the substantial wardrobe. 'What a lovely place, Imo. Well done, and so kind of your new friends.'

'Listen,' said Imogen. 'We can hear the trains.'

'It must have good acoustics too,' was the reply. 'I hope we can get a glimpse of them.'

The ancient house at least had modern amenities, and they were glad to see across the corridor a room with bath and toilet facilities.

Having tacitly agreed to relish the present moment, with thoughts unspoken that there would be no more discussing Kathleen with nothing to be done until tomorrow, they settled in to the handsome room, tastefully furnished and carpeted, with a pleasing lack of the bric-a-brac, the samplers and heavily embroidered cushions that had characterised rooms of the last reign, its good fire adding a warm welcome towards the postered bed and a good night's rest.

Next morning, Faro awoke early. He looked down on his wife's sleeping face, his thoughts still quoting (with apologies to Shakespeare) the description of Cleopatra, for age had not wearied Imogen either nor custom dimmed her abundant red hair and green eyes. He sighed happily, for this was still the beautiful woman he had met twenty years ago, his longing to make her his wife legally at last fulfilled. He got out of bed carefully so as not to disturb her and scribbled a note saying he was off to explore York and would see her in the lounge of the hotel they had just vacated, situated conveniently in the centre of the city for morning coffee.

With a definite plan in mind, he would visit the Four Seasons. A gentleman buying his lady flowers the perfect reason, a good excuse to perhaps find some clue that Imogen had overlooked to account for Kathleen Crowe's disappearance. The mysterious and somehow sinister fact that the flower shop denied her existence was certainly worth investigation. Last night, as they prepared for bed Imogen had decided that they were wasting precious time and should go immediately to the police and register Kathleen as a missing person.

Faro had doubts about that, well aware from his early days in that particular department of the Edinburgh City Police that extreme caution was involved. He had vivid memories of hysterical women, so often wives with their missing person being the husband who had just walked out to escape an unhappy marriage, or the mother whose son or daughter had too much to bear at home and had decided to leave.

He did not fancy Imogen's hopes of police cooperation or sympathy. She knew so little about this woman, having had a minutes'-only encounter in the flower shop, and he strongly advised awaiting a return of information from Carasheen.

Imogen had sent a telegram to her Uncle Seamus, head of the Crowe family. As the parish priest, Faro speculated that if he didn't know Kathleen's whereabouts he might provide valuable information from the confessional.

That shocked Imogen. Such things were never discussed, the secrets of the confessional were sacred.

Faro thought this extremely tiresome and inconvenient, especially in his own experience as a policeman, where such information would have been valuable and, most importantly, time-saving in apprehending a criminal.

He had a solitary breakfast served silently by the housekeeper at the table in front of a good fire. The kitchen seemed to be accepted as the most comfortable living room rather than the formal-looking dining room glimpsed on their arrival, with its twelve chairs at a long, well-ornamented table.

Indicating the two set places he informed the housekeeper that although Mrs Faro preferred to take breakfast in her room, he was well pleased to tackle bacon, eggs and sausages each morning. Imogen ate little. He sympathised, for she was never at her best in the morning and by her own account was an owl not a lark and liked to take her time. Let the streets get aired first was the Irish description.

His attempts at polite conversation were foiled by Mrs Muir. He glanced at her as she poured the tea. Grey-haired, with a slight stoop, chronically short-sighted, he suspected, behind those thick spectacles. Never good at guessing women's ages, she could have been anywhere between forty and sixty. Her answers were almost monosyllabic, and he concluded she was either deaf, painfully shy or even disapproving of these new strangers taking over the house.

CHAPTER ELEVEN

Leaving the house after his substantial breakfast, Faro crossed the garden, pausing to consider the faded colours and indecipherable pattern of a once bright mosaic-tiled floor, all that remained of the Roman villa where the Dower House now rested. Impressed that any hint of that original building had survived wind and weather almost two thousand years later, he headed towards his destination.

The Four Seasons in common with the rest of the city's shops had its window shutters closed and they would remain so until nine o'clock. With time on his hands, he would take the opportunity to acquaint himself with York, especially as the early morning was pleasantly warm and sunny, the streets still almost empty.

His footsteps took him towards the Minster, which never closed and was already teeming with a flurry of black-cassocked clerics engaged in the routine sacramental daily offices of a great church.

He would not need his guidebook and thrust it aside to join an early morning group of tourists under the guidance of a very learned lady. She had paused to explain that the walls of the fourteenth-century chapter house with those seven lovely windows had no support, just the great buttresses on its eight sides, and that this was the greatest concentration of thirteenth- and fourteenth-century stained glass in Britain. Pausing before the most famous, the magnificent fifteenth-century east window, the group looked in wonderment at its two thousand square feet of glass as she explained further that in a time where few people could read or write, stained-glass windows were the nearest equivalent to learning the story of the Bible.

As the group moved on, he remained to gaze in awe at the splendour surrounding him, in particular the magnificent windows depicting the end of the world, and although not what anyone might call a good churchgoer, the sanctity, the benign atmosphere of a church – which he preferred empty – always held him. On such occasions he envied Imogen her unwavering faith as she paused to reverently light a candle and offer a silent prayer.

Far above his head the clock boomed out nine hours, and as he was leaving there was a shout: 'Inspector Faro, sir!'

He turned quickly. 'Good heavens. Joseph Ingles, is it not!'

'I thought it was you, sir. What are you doing here?'

'I might well ask the same question,' and as they

shook hands Faro considered the young man he had last encountered in policeman's uniform in the Central Office shortly before his retirement. Tall, exceedingly good-looking and well set up with great promise of a future in the Edinburgh City Police, this man with a warm attractive personality that included an eye for the ladies was now in the clerical attire of a priest.

He repeated his question and Joseph's smile had not lost its charm. 'A change of mind and a change of heart,' he added soberly. 'Which way are you going, sir?'

Faro vaguely indicated the Stonegate and Joseph said: 'Then I'll accompany you, if I may, Inspector.' He smiled again. 'I can't let you disappear so soon after meeting you. Is this just a fleeting visit, or are you staying long?'

As explanations were made they left the Minster. Heading eastward with this unexpected knowledgeable guide, Faro's attention was brought to St William's College, home of fifteenth-century chantry priests.

Joseph smiled. 'They did not live such a holy or celibate life as one would have imagined. Fortunately, it was only a step back over to the Minster where they infrequently appeared for matins, much the worse for earthly wear. In the Civil War it housed the forbidden Royalist press. There was also an abundance of guildhalls, three of the original still remain.' Pausing for breath, he added: 'Do see the Merchant Adventurers' Hall in the Fossgate. It still gives the clearest picture of the powerful institutions that once ruled York.'

He stopped and grinned apologetically. 'Sorry,

Inspector. I do go on a bit. Get carried away by the grandeur around me. Your turn now. Tell me, how have you been since your retirement?'

As they continued walking together, two men of equal height, two individuals, the young and the elderly both of striking appearance, Faro said: 'Travelling, mostly. I'm married now,' he added shyly.

Joseph's eyebrows raised in surprise. In his Edinburgh days, Chief Inspector Faro's apparently non-existent love life had long been a matter of speculation among the junior ranks. So long an attractive widower, past sixty and now married. Well, well.

'My wife is an author. She had an event here, was quite carried away by York and persuaded me to come join her for a short break.' Faro looked at him quizzically. 'But what about you, Joseph, what brought you here?' He paused 'A very different sort of life to the Edinburgh police.'

The young man smiled. 'Where are you staying, sir?'

When Faro said the Dower House, the young priest's eyebrows raised as he continued, 'You had such promise as a policeman, a great career ahead. I had seen so many young fellows in my time, but you were quite exceptional. I expected you'd have passed detective sergeant and be well up the ladder to inspector by now. That was where your talents lay – you showed remarkable dexterity in the homicide section.'

Joe shook his head and said wryly. 'That was exactly the career I intended.' He pointed to a bench nearby. 'Have you a minute to spare, Inspector?'

Faro nodded and taking a seat in the parkland crossed by distant figures hurrying to begin their day's work in shop, school and factory, Joe said, 'I had always loved solving mystery puzzles and being a detective in the police, that was what I had hoped for.' He paused, shrugged. 'But then everything changed, almost overnight, you might say. I was twenty-two, had a steady young lady and hopes for a future together.' Pausing, again, he sighed in search of the right words. 'It was not to be. We were planning to marry, she took diphtheria and died within days. I was heartbroken. But that wasn't all. My mother took seriously ill. She was rushed to hospital and unlikely to recover. She had always been a good Christian, went to church regularly and now she was dying. She begged me to pray for her. The doctors had shaken their heads: cancer, they said, she had not long, and my father was an invalid, still suffering the effects of his war injuries. He was desperate, I was their only son. Pray for her, son, pray to God for a miracle, he said. And so I did, I went across the road from the Central Office every day to St Giles and I made a promise to God and to myself. For a long while, although I was doing well in the police, the inevitable end of seeing men and women sentenced and hanged had been giving me sleepless nights.'

He shook his head. 'You see, Inspector, I didn't believe they were all evil, I believed in redemption. So I made a promise. If God listened to my prayer and answered it, which seemed very unlikely, I would give up the police and become a priest; instead of hunting down criminals I would try saving souls.'

He looked at Faro. 'Against all the odds, my mother recovered, the cancer disappeared. The doctors were astonished, one said to me. It was like a miracle.' Pausing, he laughed. 'And she lives now, happy and healthy. Does that seem odd to you, Inspector?'

Faro shook his head, silent for a moment. 'No, not odd, I think we are called to what we become, that it is a kind of destiny. Maybe already decided, if I believed as you do, even before we come into this world.'

Joe regarded him intently and nodded. 'Yes, sir. I think that is why I always felt that, although I was just a young policeman and you were a great man, a great detective, yet we shared a common bond.'

And Faro had felt it too, remembering how just sometimes in his profession he encountered a stranger, as PC Joseph Ingles had been, with whom he felt an instant rapport. Imogen was the exception to the rule. They had both disliked each other intensely at their first meeting, travellers off a Borders train to Elrigg.

Joe stood up. 'This is where I leave you, Inspector.' As they shook hands, Faro said: 'Thank you for telling me all this, Joseph.'

The priest shook his head. 'It's Joe. Everyone calls me Father Joe.'

Faro laughed. 'Then you are not to call me "Inspector". That belongs to the past. I am just plain Faro now.'

Joe regarded him gravely. 'As you will, sir. But

you could never be plain anybody. Great men who are legends in their own time can never shake that off.' He held out his hand and smiled. 'We may meet again in the Minster. It was a lucky chance seeing you there. I just looked in to see someone.' He straightened up. 'There was one thing I should add. I'm a Roman Catholic priest, my church St Columba's is very small, tucked away in one of the Snickelways just across from the place where you are staying. From the eleventh century onwards there were forty parish churches in York, many survive and mine is one of them. However, the most interesting is the fifteenth-century All Saints in North Street, it has unique windows and medieval woodwork.' He paused and smiled again. 'I hope you enjoy your day exploring York. If you get lost, they'll tell you the way to the Dower House.'

Faro shook his head. 'First of all, I'm heading for a flower shop in the Stonegate.'

'Flowers for the missus, sir.' The young priest smiled as they shook hands again. 'It has been great meeting you again, sir. So unexpected.'

'My wife is doing some historical research here. She is very interested in the Minster and the early churches.'

Joe's face lit up. 'Then I would love to meet her. I'm very interested in York's history. Reading about the Romans' and the Vikings' occupation is my favourite hobby. I have lots of books, so do tell her to come across to St Columba's and see me. What is Mrs Faro's name?'

When Faro told him, he repeated. 'Imogen Crowe. I have heard of her, she's famous and I think I have one of her books. Now, isn't that amazing.'

Faro smiled. 'She's Irish and Roman Catholic, like you, but believes one shouldn't be bigoted and that all churches are the houses of God.'

Joe laughed. 'Quite right too! And I'll hope we shall have the pleasure of meeting her – and indeed you both – again.'

'I certainly hope so,' said Faro, and as Joe walked briskly away he continued his walk towards the Stonegate, and going over the strange story that the young priest had told him knew that Imogen would be very interested. Hurrying towards the Four Seasons he found the shop already a scene of busy activity, an early delivery from a van outside, with men briskly unloading boxes of flowers.

As he approached they stood up, regarded him stolidly and he thought just a little warily as he entered the shop.

And so did the girl behind the counter, she was the one Imogen had described. Very young and looking rather scared, as she watched the boxes carried in, perhaps anxious about the fate of those fragile flowers after their long journey. Tulips from the bulb fields of Holland at this time of year, he guessed, although there was no sign denoting place of origin on the van outside.

The tall, fair young man who was the driver was talking to the girl urgently, presumably about the delivery, and she was replying, talking rapidly. Here was some kind of an argument and he remembered Imogen thought she was foreign. There was no doubt about that. Faro was familiar with French, and although it was almost a whispered conversation, he was near enough to the pair in that small area to know that this was a Teutonic language but not German – no, he guessed, this was Dutch.

Faro coughed gently to make his presence known.

The girl turned sharply, said: 'I will be with you in a moment, sir.' And instead rushed to the door after the young man. A lot of head shaking and gesticulation suggested a further urgent exchange of words between them. When she returned, Faro could tell that whatever had been said had upset her.

He examined a possible purchase for Imogen, although this was hardly necessary – from the extensive gardens of the Dower House, there were vases of flowers everywhere provided by Mrs Muir.

However, needing an excuse to justify his visit to the shop he was sure Imogen would love a small posy of violets. The young girl, he noticed, had long straight hair pulled back and held in place with a particularly pretty hair clasp, very like one Imogen wore in the same manner to hold back her abundant tresses.

The girl, who did not seem inclined for conversation, handed him the posy. As he paid for it, he indicated the pile of flower boxes. 'You will have a busy time unpacking all of those. Tulips, are they?'

She stared at them apprehensively, then nodded vaguely.

As Faro had intended this visit to yield some information about Kathleen, smiling pleasantly, he said: 'May I ask where you come from?'

Again, she stared at him blankly, shook her head as if not understanding. 'You are not from these parts, I take it. Not English?' he said slowly.

She understood, shook her head. No, not English.

Faro gave her a gentle smile. 'May I ask, what is your name?'

She frowned before replying: 'Sofia.'

'Have you worked here long?'

A vague nod this time, but there was to be no more pleasant conversation hopefully revealing some hints about Kathleen Crowe. At that moment a tall, fair young man entered. Better dressed than the driver who had argued with the girl, he had an air of authority that suggested he was the boss.

Faro saw the girl's hands clench suddenly, her knuckles whiten. She was afraid, perhaps her job was in danger. All was not well, certainly something was amiss.

Brushing Faro aside abruptly, she said: 'Good day, sir. I have another customer to attend,' moving swiftly to open the door, a clear indication that he was to leave.

It was very frustrating but there was no way he could stay, and making his way back to the Dower House, his mind was also very busy going over all he had seen and heard in the hour since he had left. Imogen was waiting and he had a lot to tell her.

CHAPTER TWELVE

Imogen listened carefully, less interested in his meeting with the young ex-policeman priest than the latest developments at the Four Seasons. Although he did not wish to alarm her, he realised his account of the visit to the shop was achieving what he least wanted at that moment: merely convincing her that something dreadful had happened to Kathleen. There was a sinister element about the conversation with the flower delivery man and he felt concern for the girl Sofia, a lot younger than Kathleen, with the responsibility of running a shop.

When he said so, Imogen shook her head. 'Not much to do more than arranging flower bouquets and wreaths, sweeping out the shop, counting the cash and being polite to customers.'

Faro thought about that. 'She just seemed very young and insecure—no, scared.'

'Did you think she was pretty, this Sofia?'

Faro frowned, he had never excelled at describing young lasses and had to confess that they all looked rather alike to him and looking nervous hadn't done much for this particular one's appearance or attraction.

He said, 'She wears her hair long, like you.' And that triggered a thought. 'In fact, she was wearing it pulled back with a jewelled clasp very like the one I bought you when we were in Venice.'

Imogen nodded vaguely. She had never been fond of that clasp, but Faro liked to see her wearing it. He knew little of women's fashion and she was overwhelmed by elaborate costume jewellery, de rigueur in London, and felt that the clasp belonged to evening dress occasions only. She remembered having it with her on her first visit to York. On an impulse and with nothing to give Kathleen – a Crowe family tradition when meeting a relative for the first time – and because she had long, pretty hair, Imogen had handed her the clasp.

'I'd like you to have this, it will look good on you.'

Ignoring Kathleen's apologies about not having anything to give her, she decided not to mention this to Faro, embarrassed at having to tell a lie, that she was often careless about losing personal possessions, umbrellas were a speciality, and gloves left in carriages. However, she now resolved to personally investigate this incident and the clasp that Faro had seemed to recognise the girl wearing, as well as earnestly hoping that it was not the same one she had given Kathleen.

'What shall we do now?' Faro asked.

'Are you sure we shouldn't go to the police?' she said anxiously.

'Please, Imo, do try to be calm. There's nothing we can do until we get confirmation from your uncle that she isn't at Carasheen.'

Imogen frowned. 'It is taking him a long time to answer.'

'We only sent it yesterday,' Faro said consolingly. 'We need to give it a day or two. If there is still no reply and Kathleen has not turned up, then we consider our next move.'

Ignoring his advice, Imogen insisted: 'The police station and missing persons, Faro, that is what we must do.'

Faro nodded in agreement, and then said firmly, 'Meanwhile, my dear, while we await developments, we don't waste time. We explore York, try to enjoy this new experience. There is so much to see.' He held up a booklet. 'Such a history, the Roman occupation, the Vikings – there is an excellent museum.'

'I know, I know.'

Faro thought she might also be using this as valuable research time, their reason for being in York, instead of agonising over this second cousin she had met only once as a child.

He also suspected that he knew a lot more about human nature from years of experience than Imogen and guessed that Kathleen had accepted their first meeting as a pleasant surprise but had no reason for keeping in touch with this older relative. Essentially, he considered that all they had in common was membership of the Crowe clan, were both orphaned at an early age and had unhappy experiences of relatives who were Irish terrorists and died in British jails.

Imogen came out of the bedroom fastening on her jacket. 'You are quite right, Faro. Sure now, there is nothing to be gained sitting around here worrying myself sick. I am off to do a bit of shopping. No, no,' she added hastily, 'this is lady's business, I won't inflict milliners and costume shops on you.'

Faro grinned with a sigh of relief. 'Thank you for sparing me. I shall tackle the museum and see you back here for lunch.'

They kissed, and Imogen watched him striding away through the garden with his usual purposeful air. She smiled fondly. Vikings, indeed. He would have fitted so well into that page of York's history. All he needed was a horned helmet and a dragon-headed boat to drag along the river to complete the image.

As she prepared to leave, she thought guiltily that she hadn't told him the complete truth. Before any shopping, she intended paying a visit to the Four Seasons and having another chat to this Sofia. The incident of the hair clasp had to be investigated.

The day was at its best, the bright sunshine spread across her shoulders like a warm and welcoming cloak. There was no wind, a benign sort of day with the Minster towering above all, the stones of the ancient wall enclosing the city; holding it close and protective in less happy centuries, it now gleamed golden. She felt mankind hadn't progressed very much sometimes, women were still disregarded, their place in society ignored. She thought of the suffragette march imminent in London, hoping that would change women's status and put a foot over the threshold of a different future.

Walking in the direction of the Four Seasons, the windows of the Shambles' ancient houses leaning towards each other threw a shadow over the sunlit day. She paused, looking around. There were already many people stopping to gaze into shop windows, many were visitors unaware of the darker issues of this great city where history books could never fully appreciate the tragic history of the Jews who had been massacred, the place of Roman and Viking invaders readily taken by another race of men whose lives were corrupted by religious intolerance and the lust for vengeance.

At last she was in the Stonegate, the flower shop with its tubs of tulips outside an attractive sight. The bell rang as she opened the door where the girl Sofia was serving one customer while another examined flowers on display, their pleasing perfume spreading through the shop.

Sofia hadn't seen her yet, or perhaps recognised her, and it was not until she turned her back to put money into the till that Imogen saw the hair clasp. She gave a gasp of astonishment. The jewelled clasp was undoubtedly hers, the one Faro had bought in Venice, that she had so gladly but guiltily passed on to Kathleen.

The shop emptied of its customers. Sofia turned

to her. 'Can I help you, madam. What is your wish, a bouquet, perhaps?'

'My first wish is to enquire where you got the hair clasp you are wearing.'

The girl looked alarmed, a trembling hand went to her hair.

'A present, madam.' A nervous smile.

'Indeed. It is most attractive. Where can I get one in York?'

The girl shook her head. 'I-I do not know, madam.' Her face was flushed, she paled.

'Is that so?' Imogen paused for a moment, then said sternly: 'My reason for asking you, miss, is because I believe it belongs to me. I was wearing it on my first visit to your shop.'

The girl looked flustered now, clenching her hands.

'It wasn't a present now, was it?'

'No, no – madam. I found it lying under the counter.' As she spoke, she unfastened it hastily and held it out to Imogen. 'If it is yours, please take it back.'

Imogen's heart was racing. 'Thank you. When did you find it?'

'I do not remember. A while ago.' An attempt at a thin smile. 'It is very pretty, and no customer claimed it. If you lost it, then I am glad to return it to you.'

Fastening it on to her hair, Imogen said, 'Let me tell you when I lost it.'

The girl's eyes widened. 'You remember? When was that?'

'On my first and only visit to your shop. I didn't lose

it, I gave it to the young lady who was serving here, Mrs Roxwell – she is a relative of mine. She was in charge of this shop a few weeks ago, at the beginning of this month, but you denied all knowledge of her. You insisted that you had never heard of her. But here you are and wearing the very hair clasp I gave her.'

'I do not understand,' the girl stammered. 'I found it, just as I told you—'

There was a throat clearing behind them. The door had been left open after the last customer so no bell rang. Sofia's eyes opened wide, her face paled and Imogen swung round to find herself face-to-face with one of the four men she had first met in the elegant coffee shop.

It was Andres. He stared at her and she thought he recognised her as he said in perfect English this time, 'Are you buying flowers, lady? I am in a hurry.'

This was her perfect opportunity and ignoring the question she said: 'You were in the shop here talking to Mrs Roxwell who was serving customers a few weeks ago. You must remember her.'

A moment's hesitation, a blank stare, a shrug. 'I do not remember the occasion.'

'But you must,' Imogen insisted. 'You seemed to know each other well from the way you were talking together.'

'We were talking together, were we?' he repeated slowly, frowning. 'I talk to many people.' He shook his head, spread his hands wide. 'I do not understand. I do not remember this woman, it has always been this young lady serving in the shop.' And turning his back on

Imogen, he spoke to Sofia in his own language, pointing to a tub of flowers.

They had lied about Kathleen, but there was nothing Imogen could do but leave the shop and, looking back through the window, she beheld the terrified girl. Although she could hear no words, she saw him grab her arm, leaning forward in a threatening manner. While she was making up her mind to intervene, it was too late, as behind her another customer was entering the shop, a woman with a child in her arms.

In despair and with a new set of terrors concerning Kathleen that she was sure were linked to the Four Seasons, she made her way back to meet Faro and this time tell him all. However, before doing so, feeling shattered by this unpleasant experience she decided to sit down, have a coffee in the very agreeable nearby restaurant.

From a window table, surveying the other customers revealed the same clientele as on her first visit, quartets of middle-aged affluent-looking York ladies, fashionably dressed.

Heading towards her armed with the menu, Mary was pleased to see this new customer again. Although no longer in the first flush of youth, and about the same age as herself, this elegant lady had not lost her looks, the beautiful red hair and green eyes of youth still remained. Such a lovely combination, quite outstanding, Mary thought enviously, and remembered Amy saying her accent was Irish.

Suddenly she was curious and wanted to know more.

A friendly greeting, the coffee and scone ordered, she was wondering if it would be rude to ask what she was doing in York, was she on holiday, and she remembered her enquiry on that other first visit.

'Did you meet up with your friend from the flower shop, madam? Maybe she didn't know when we closed if she came to leave a message for you.' Seeing the lady frown, she said: 'Perhaps it was another flower shop. There are lots in York.'

Imogen was startled by the question, especially after her recent encounter with the girl Sofia. There was a little confusion, but this friendly waitress might help, perhaps she had known Kathleen. Some explanations were necessary.

'I was on a visit to York and sending thank you flowers to a lady I had met when I discovered one of my relatives from Ireland working in the Four Seasons.' She shook her head. 'Perhaps you remember, I had called on her – it was a few weeks ago, but now there's this new girl who says she's never heard of my cousin Kathleen.'

Mary frowned. 'Foreign, was she?'

'Yes, maybe she didn't understand.'

Mary continued with the place setting and said nothing.

Imogen asked: 'Do the flower shop girls come for coffee?'

'Very rarely, madam. We close about the same time each day. They only come in very occasionally if it is a special occasion.' She paused apologetically and repeated again that the girls who worked in shops usually had something to eat on the premises. 'They bring in their own sandwiches. It's cheaper on their wages.'

The lady looked a bit distressed, and wanting to be helpful Mary said: 'What was your relative like, madam?'

Imogen was once again faced with the difficulty of describing Kathleen in any way to make her memorable. There was nothing striking about her appearance, just an ordinary girl you would pass in a crowd and never give a second glance. She said: 'She's about thirty-five, straight brown hair, my height, and she has an Irish accent.'

Mary shook her head.

They regarded one another helplessly, nothing more to be said, really. Imogen was sorry, but not surprised, and as she asked for the bill, Mary, realising she couldn't delay her, asked weakly: 'Staying long, madam?'

When Imogen responded and handed over the coins, Mary thanked her and said: 'I hope you'll enjoy York.'

Imogen summoned a smile. 'My husband and I both think it will be a great experience. We are staying at the Dower House,' she added.

Mary's eyebrows raised at that. The Dower House, indeed. They must be important people.

Watching her leave, Mary was more intrigued than ever and said to Amy, 'That lady I was serving is staying at the Dower House.'

However, Amy, who was attending a man who had

just come across from the flower shop, was less impressed than she had hoped, her thoughts entirely preoccupied with this tall, fair young man, and Mary observed that she had a glow of excitement.

When he left she said, 'Guess what, Mary. He said he'll be coming in again.' She giggled. 'I think he likes me.'

Men frequently liked the pretty young Amy and most of them said they would come to the cafe again, but rarely did, and the young man she was always wistfully hoping for failed to materialise.

Mary considered this one to be very unsuitable. He was smart-looking and well behaved without his comrades, who she suspected were gangsters.

'He's from Amsterdam.' Amy clasped her hands excitedly.

She ignored Mary's warning glance. 'Well, don't count your chickens, Amy. These foreigners are all after the same thing,' she said sternly. 'Remember that.'

'Just like our local lads,' Amy flashed back at her. 'Don't you worry about me, I can look after myself.'

When the restaurant closed that day, Mary was regarding the flower shop thoughtfully. That Irish lady staying at the Dower House was very troubled about that foreign girl saying her relative had never worked there. At home, she picked up her newspaper. The sensational headline was a domestic murder in Tadcaster. A railwayman had murdered his wife.

Mary sighed. If she had a secret wish stretching well beyond the confines of the cafe, it was that she had been a man and could be a detective. She loved a mystery story and suddenly she began to wonder if there was something sinister going on much nearer home, and hoped Amy wasn't going to get herself involved with this smart young Dutchman.

She decided to keep a watchful eye on happenings at the flower shop across the road there, and she would have been very surprised that her Irish lady was having much the same conversation with her husband in the elegant surroundings of the Dower House.

CHAPTER THIRTEEN

On hearing the details of Imogen's visit to Sofia, Faro reluctantly considered this as a new and sinister development regarding the missing Kathleen. He could well understand Imogen's alarm and it certainly gave the lie to the denial that Kathleen had ever worked at the flower shop, especially when she told him that she recognised the male customer as the one who had been talking with Kathleen on that first visit, but when she tackled him on this occasion, he denied it entirely.

Faro was not surprised by that, however, as although Imogen was very observant, in her subsequent anxiety over Kathleen, she might well have made a mistake and had embarrassed an innocent man who was merely in the shop buying flowers.

There had been no response from Uncle Seamus and Imogen said, 'Don't you think that we have wasted enough time? I am going to the police right now and registering Kathleen as a missing person.'

Faro frowned and held up his hand, as she prepared to leave. 'Wait. Sit down, Imo, and let's go over the facts carefully before we go any further. First of all, you really must give your uncle more time to reply. I doubt that matters move as swiftly in Carasheen as they do here in York, and he will also need time to make enquiries among members of the family. Perhaps one of them—'

'A complete waste of time,' Imogen interrupted with an impatient shrug as he continued: 'We know that Kathleen had worked at the shop, the proof – if needed – the fact that the new girl Sofia was wearing the hair clasp you recognised as the one you gave to Kathleen on your first visit.'

'She didn't deny that it wasn't hers and she had found it in the shop,' said Imogen triumphantly. 'That was guilt enough that she was telling a lie.'

Faro gave her a wry glance. 'You should have told me that the hair clasp wasn't quite to your taste or style, you know. I would have understood that you were happy to part with it.'

Imogen felt guilty, but she wasn't prepared to go over all that again as she demanded: 'So how did Kathleen lose it in the first place? Surely that strikes you as having alarming possibilities?'

Faro thought for a moment. 'I think Sofia was telling the truth and she did find it.'

'Sure, but how and when? Had Kathleen dropped it, or had it been pulled from her hair in a struggle?'

Faro looked at her. 'You think now that she has been kidnapped?'

Imogen shrugged. 'I think that is a possibility, don't you?'

Faro put his hands together and frowned. 'There has to be a reason for kidnapping, Imo. A very dangerous business indeed, and usually a ransom is involved.'

He did not care to suggest that getting rid of her in a more permanent manner would have been much more credible.

Imogen shook her head and he realised he could no longer try to salve her misgivings. He had to tell her his own conclusions.

'Tell me, how well did you know Kathleen? I gather you had only met her once in Carasheen and that was more than twenty years ago.'

Imogen nodded, and Faro went on: 'Just a small girl, and you knew nothing of her adult years at all, only what she told you of her brief marriage and widowhood.'

Leaning back in his chair he regarded her thoughtfully. 'Think about it, Imo. You are basing the theory that something dreadful has happened to a girl who, although kin to you, was also a complete stranger. You have no idea of her character development in those missing years – you are merely presuming that she grew up to be a nice good girl.'

Imogen sighed. Faro was right. She did not want to think ill of Kathleen but that was merely because she was blood kin. There was so little to go on, she knew Faro was right as he continued:

'You have all along the line been jumping to conclusions, my dear, just because the flower shop have denied all knowledge of her.' He paused. 'There might have been many reasons of their own that you are presuming as not only suspicious but sinister, but might not be so at all, merely business reasons that they did not wish made public.'

'What about my hair clasp? How do you explain that?'

Faro shrugged. 'That she spoke the truth and merely found it without any sinister explanation. All we know for certain is that Kathleen left the flower shop or was dismissed for reasons unknown to us. She did not get in touch with you – was it likely that she would have done so, even if she had your address?' He paused. 'As far as she was concerned, you were a visitor to York, who surprisingly claimed to be related, one of your numerous family, met only as a child.' He shook his head. 'Probably forgot all about you five minutes after you left the shop . . .'

'That is not so,' Imogen exclaimed. 'We were to meet again at the coffee shop across the road when the shop closed.'

Faro sighed wearily. 'Let's face facts, Imo. It slipped her mind and she never, ever gave an instant's thought to this odd customer and that brief conversation about Carasheen, your only link.'

Imogen looked doubtful and he patted her hand, saying gently, 'Think about it from her point of view. She never expected to see you again, perhaps she had other plans for that evening already and there was no reason for a lasting connection, not even her home address. So why on earth would she get in touch with you to apologise for not turning up at the coffee shop?'

He paused. Imogen had said nothing, listening, biting her lip. 'You must have had many such occasions in your own life, Imo, travelling as you have done. People you have met, and on brief acquaintance, although you might have given them your card, you would have been very surprised if you had ever heard from them again.'

There was a moment's silence as Imogen considered his words. She knew he was right, and she allowed her emotions to get the upper hand merely because Kathleen was one of her family. Nevertheless, that did not account for her gut feeling that there was something amiss at the Four Seasons.

When she added: 'I wouldn't have been worried – would have just accepted the fact that she had left, and I couldn't see her again – if only Sofia hadn't said she'd never heard of her, while brazenly wearing the hair clasp I'd given Kathleen.'

Faro shrugged. 'As I've said before, Imo, business is business. There's nothing sinister about the flower shop being wary and not wanting a complete stranger, a mere visitor to York, to know their affairs.'

He stood up. 'Now I think we should try to dismiss Kathleen and her affairs, whatever they were—'

'I just wish word from Uncle Seamus would set our minds at rest,' Imogen interrupted.

Faro smiled. 'And aren't we going to feel complete idiots if she is there at home, while you have been worrying yourself sick about her.'

Imogen squeezed his hand. 'Please God, I do hope you're right, darlin'.'

'Well, if that is settled, let us take this opportunity of enjoying York. You can do your research while I do the museums, and if the weather holds, we can enjoy sitting in this lovely garden and the privilege of having a delightful historic house at our disposal. As for Kathleen,' he added, 'don't be surprised if we walk into her in the Shambles or somewhere around and she looks very surprised to see you, or even finds it difficult to recognise you again or where you met.'

Imogen added a silent prayer that would be so, resolving that tomorrow she would begin her research in the library and newspaper archives and leave Faro to his own devices – he was good at that.

Two pleasant days followed enjoying Mrs Muir's splendid cooking; although invisible, she provided breakfast and supper, served by the maid Molly, but the meals were of such proportion that a midday break to ease tired feet and have a scone in one of the many coffee shops was all the sustenance required.

Away from each other for long intervals, Faro and Imogen's thoughts were their own. Behind the pile of material accumulating while she made copious notes in the library, Imogen firmly banished Kathleen from her thoughts, except when her research notes led her into the Stonegate.

She was close to the Four Seasons and curiosity led her to stop and look at the bowls of flowers outside, which also allowed a glimpse through the window, and there was Sofia behind the counter serving a customer. Looking up, she gazed directly across at Imogen who hurried past, too embarrassed after the hair clasp incident to risk another encounter.

As for Faro, filling in time while accompanying Imogen giving talks and attending conferences abroad was a usual occupation. Now, two days of rain and high winds cast a blight on their York sojourn, the garden drenched, and indoors, the panelled rooms of the Dower House chilly and unwelcoming, the seldom-used fire smoking in the drawing room no longer a place to linger in those once comfortable armchairs.

Suddenly the splendid surroundings of the Dower House had been transformed into a setting for a sinister tale by Edgar Allan Poe, so apart from meeting Imogen for a brief lunch, Faro soon grew restless and when more time had passed without any reply from Carasheen, because his entire working life had been based on solving mysteries, the disappearance of Kathleen hinted at an interesting interlude. A possible innocent mystery to be solved, which would please Imogen and put her mind at rest, dismissing the more sinister version of Sofia, the flower shop's denial and the hair clasp incident.

Matters might well have stayed that way until, leaving the museum between showers and heading across to St Mary's, he encountered a well-kenned face from the past.

CHAPTER FOURTEEN

'Faro! Thought I recognised you! What on earth are you doing so far from Edinburgh?'

Faro looked away from his contemplation of the ancient stones to see at his side Inspector Dave Stokes, retired from Edinburgh City Police six years ago.

'Faro, man. The years have been good to you,' Dave said with a touch of envy for his one-time colleague's still youthful figure, his thick hair now tinged with silver. For himself, time had taken its inevitable toll, for he was now corpulent and almost bald.

As they shook hands, he stepped back and said: 'You still look exactly the same. And what brings you to York?'

'My wife is a writer, she has been here on a business trip.'

'Wife, eh?' Dave's eyebrows raised in astonishment. 'You're married – at last. Well, that's a turn up for the books.' His reaction was similar to that of Joe Ingles and

Faro smiled and said: 'I was about to ask, what are you doing here? On holiday?'

Dave grinned. 'No such luck. Same answer as yours – my wife. If you remember, she hailed from York and when I retired, the family were grown up and she decided she had always wanted to come home.' He sighed. 'So commanded, I had to obey. But it was a good decision,' he added hastily. 'My father-in-law is an inspector, so I managed to get into something to keep my mind busy with a desk job in the police here.' He stopped. 'Time for a dram?'

In the nearby pub as they raised their glasses to old times, Faro's mind had also been busy. If matters were the same in York, then a desk job with the police often meant being in charge of records.

With a sudden vision of Imogen's still anxious face, her worried frown each morning at the absence of word from Carasheen, ordering a second round he leant over the table and told Dave as briefly as possible that his Irish wife had expected to see this young relative who worked here but had left her job and apparently vanished.

He ended: 'I realise there is probably a perfectly good reason, of course, but Mrs Faro is very upset.'

Dave smiled. 'Don't tell me. My wife gets agitated over the smallest detail, and heaven help me if I keep her waiting: her mind immediately turns to a traffic accident or a heart attack. She has substituted these as an alternative to when I was in the police and she was sure I had fallen victim to a murderous attack.'

Faro nodded sympathetically. 'My wife is all for going into your office and registering this young woman as a missing person.'

'Have you checked her home, she could be back there? Where is she from?'

'A place called Carasheen in County Kerry,' Faro continued. 'We got in touch, my wife's uncle is also the parish priest, but there has been no reply.'

Dave shook his head. 'These small places in the back of nowhere, they are hardly reliable for urgent communications.' He sighed. 'The trouble we have with information about this Irish Republican movement, you have no idea the time it takes to getting answers and being kept up to date on what they're doing. And it's getting worse.'

Faro realised that there were fewer problems in Scotland, regarded by the Irish as fellow sufferers from the hated English and their tyranny over the centuries.

Dave was saying: 'As for the young ones these days, they are all a bit cavalier about keeping in touch with their aged family, that we know to our cost. Our two sons . . .' He went on while Faro was remembering the police procedure at the Central Office for missing persons. First check the list for name, age and description, then the hospitals, then that last resort, the mortuary.

Nodding sympathetically over Dave's family problems with those two sons, the conversation turned to other matters bridging the years, and when they were about to part, Dave said: 'If it would help your domestic harmony with Mrs Faro, I could do a wee check of our records.'

Faro sighed with relief at this unexpected piece of mind-reading. He had been wondering how to tactfully put the question to him.

'Would you? That is so good of you. My wife will be so grateful.'

'Not at all.' Dave smiled. 'Glad to be of any help.'

Faro had not much to offer beyond scribbling down Kathleen's married name, but could provide no helpful physical description apart from age and that Imogen believed she had lived near the Four Seasons.

'The flower shop.' Dave looked at him, seemed about to say something and changed his mind. 'Where are you staying?'

'The Dower House.'

Dave looked even more interested. 'That old house could tell many a tale if walls could speak.'

'My wife met the owners when she was giving a talk here a few weeks ago. I had agreed to join her and the Hardys, who own the house, said if we were to stay in York for a while, would we consider making the Dower House our base for a couple of weeks. I gather they are away with the archaeologists on a dig in Egypt.'

Dave frowned. 'Interesting. I often wonder how on earth they can afford to live in that historic place.' He paused, looking at Faro as if expecting some comment. 'An archaeologist working with the local team can't be earning much. All the ones I've met complain about low salaries for hard work, and it is really hard. One chap I meet in the pub says that unless you are a qualified man with a degree and all that sort of thing and some capital behind you, you aren't much better off than the chaps working on the railway.' He gave Faro a quizzical glance. 'Must have come into a fortune, rich uncle or something, for a fortune is what it must cost, especially as they have servants and a motor car too,' he added with a touch of envy.

Dave's reactions were identical to those of Imogen and Faro, but they had decided that it was none of their business. When he had no comment beyond that to hint at, Dave sighed.

'About Mrs Faro's missing relative. I'll do what I can, Faro.' And as they parted he added: 'I'll be in touch. Give my regards to the missus.'

'I'll do more than that. I'm sure Imogen would love to meet you and Mrs Stokes.' Sure of Imogen's reaction and gratitude for this unexpected offer of help, he said, 'Please come along this evening and have supper with us.'

Dave's eyes gleamed. 'Babs will be delighted, she has always wanted to have a look inside that house.'

Taking a chance that the efficient Mrs Muir would have no trouble dealing with the extra food situation, Faro now wished he had suggested two days ahead. That, he decided, making his way to tell Imogen the good news, would have given Dave, if he was true to his word, ample time to instigate some enquiries.

Imogen would be so relieved.

After a successful morning in the library armed with a pile of notes, she had almost, but not quite, succeeded in dismissing Kathleen lingering like a dark shadow at the back of her mind. While still hoping to hear from Uncle Seamus, of course Faro was right – he usually was, she told herself – and she had been making too much of the missing girl, turning it into a sinister mystery for which he was now almost convinced there would be a perfectly logical explanation.

As for Faro, he was going over again the possibilities of that chance meeting with Dave and how his access to the police's missing persons records might put Imogen's mind at rest and persuade her to believe that Kathleen was still alive and well – somewhere.

Crossing the garden to the Dower House, Faro thought this was the oddest house he had ever encountered, even odder than Solomon's Tower, which had stood for centuries past at the base of Arthur's Seat in Edinburgh.

He was not a fanciful man but Imogen could have told him that beyond mere bricks and mortar she was aware of a personality – almost human – as if its walls, its ancient panelling still breathed with the life of its creators; where doors waited to be opened, and dark corners with shelved cupboards, long boarded up and untouched by the passing centuries, waited to be opened and explored. This house held close its secrets, ivy-covered walls almost hiding window-like eyes watching all newcomers like themselves.

Even crossing the garden suggested a degree of reverence for the past, although that might well be only the fragment of the mosaic floor dating back to the very origins of York itself and its associations with the Emperor Severus. One thing for sure, as she daily set foot in the garden she longed to thrust aside that wilderness of creeper to reveal what the original building of the Dower House had looked like two centuries ago before adopting the mantle of ivy to disguise it from mortal view.

Imogen had just disappeared into the house as Faro entered the garden, pausing a moment at the pleasing sight of ornamental flower beds, besides which delicate trees and velvety stretches of lawn, occasionally disrupted by fragments of stone, marked earlier long-lost and unchronicled ancient dwellings. In a more practical manner, there was a flourishing kitchen plot where a woman was gathering vegetables into a basket.

The normally invisible housekeeper.

'Ah, Mrs Muir. Good day to you.'

She straightened up somewhat startled, and returned his greeting, hands clasped neatly, eyes modestly downcast, the very model of a Victorian housekeeper meeting the master of the house or an honoured guest.

Faro felt that he was neither, but here was someone who, with encouragement aided with determination on his part, might provide interesting information about the area, the house and even the owners. First of all, he congratulated her on the excellent food she was providing and mentioned that there would be two further guests for supper. He hoped this would not inconvenience her and this was obviously the right move as, within seconds, she was extolling the merits of various ingredients from the vegetable plot that were included on her menu.

Asked if she had long been in the employ of the Hardys, she looked towards the house, shrugged and replied: 'A while now.'

'You are not from these parts, are you?' He was good at accents and no trace of the unmistakable Yorkshire one was evident.

She shook her head. 'From further north.'

'Hello!'

She was interrupted as Imogen had appeared heading towards them. With almost a curtsey, Mrs Muir picked up her basket and departed briskly towards the kitchen. Imogen smiled. 'So she can speak.'

'Indeed, she can,' Faro said. 'We were having an interesting conversation.'

'Not shy any longer, that's a relief.' She gave him a fond glance and thought: or it could be she is only with ladies – nothing like a charming gentleman for drawing a shy lady out of her shell. And taking his arm, she asked:

'Sure now, and what have you been doing while I have slaved away in the library?'

When he told her about meeting Dave Stokes, a

retired colleague who was now a clerk in police records, with access to missing persons, she sighed.

'Now isn't that just wonderful?' At last, hope loomed on the horizon and even negative answers would indicate that Kathleen was still alive – somewhere.

CHAPTER FIFTEEN

'Now you can stop worrying,' Faro said.

'I suppose you are right, as usual.' She laughed. 'It will just have to remain like one of your past unsolved police mysteries, but at least one without a crime or a corpse this time.'

Not even that. Despite that Crowe connection as far as Kathleen had been concerned, Imogen was just an Irish visitor to York, who happened to be from Carasheen buying flowers at the Four Seasons.

Imogen's thoughts were rather different. With only the weird question of the hair clasp still unanswered, she resolved that it must remain so. She had no intention of spoiling for Faro what could be a memorable time, a very pleasant break in a lovely city.

As for Faro, he was considering why he had now involved Dave Stokes in the search for Kathleen Crowe. An unsolved puzzle was always for him an itch that needed scratching. A problem to deal with himself and let Imogen do her research and enjoy everything that York and this strange house had to offer.

The maid Molly knocked at the door while they were having tea.

'Someone . . . for you, sir.'

Perhaps it was the sight of a uniformed young police constable standing on the step that had made her look so anxious. Her hand was trembling as she handed over a brief note from Dave asking what time they were expected for supper.

'I'll deal with this, Molly. If you will ask the constable to remain a moment, please.'

As Faro went across to the kitchen table to write a reply, his noiseless footsteps had not disturbed the three faces peering out of the window at the policeman – Wilfred and Mrs Muir, now joined by Molly.

'Obviously the Dower House doesn't get many visits from the law,' he told Imogen after the three rather guiltily dispersed.

When Molly reappeared, he passed on the message regarding the changed arrangement to Mrs Muir.

After a whole day of exploring York, the medieval city walls, rebuilt in the thirteenth century on the foundations of the Roman and Norman footpath, provided him with an interesting circular walk passing the remaining 'bars' or exits at Mickelgate, Bootham, Monk and Walmgate.

He walked the gates down into the city descending at Mickelgate and Bootham where the Georgians had built their handsome town houses that provided an excellent social centre for county families, with a racecourse at Knavesmire as well as a Theatre Royal.

Victorian York saw the beginning of a flourishing confectionary industry as well as the City Art Gallery in Exhibition Square, opened in 1879. Besides an imposing array of old masters, it also boasted the presence of a son of York: William Etty, famous for his scandalous portrayal of nudes, he had shocked society in the last century.

Faro did not always walk the walls alone and on one occasion, after promising to take Imogen out on the River Ouse, as they were returning to the Dower House, Imogen decided to look in at the Minster once again. It fascinated her, as did its history, and as they were leaving who should they see walking towards them but Father Joe Ingles, who was delighted to meet Imogen. While having learnt in his previous encounter with Faro that he was now married, Joe was still surprised that the retired chief inspector had won such a beautiful woman who, he suspected, was very much his junior in years. Joe was soon to discover Imogen's secret: she had not only outstanding beauty but also brains to match Inspector Faro's own.

As a writer of some import and experience, she shared Joe's love of history and Faro was amused to note that, as so often happened with those meeting Imogen for the first time, he was suddenly of no interest as the pair were quickly absorbed in York's historic past.

Joe offered to show them both the remains of the original Eboracum the Romans had built, upon which the Minster had taken shape. As they descended the steps, Joe took the opportunity to tell Imogen about his church near the Dower House.

'I'm a Roman Catholic but I have many friends among the clergy here.' He smiled. 'We say the same prayers and we're all brothers in God's sight.'

An emotion that would not be shared by many Presbyterians, Faro thought, noting Imogen's delight in meeting this charming young priest.

The Roman remains were an impressive sight and as they returned and walked down the nave, Faro, now tired and hungry, had an idea. Would Joe like to come and have supper with them. Imogen was pleased when Joe eagerly accepted the prospect of this unexpected invitation to the Dower House. And so it was arranged. All that was needed was to inform Mrs Muir of the extra guest.

Refreshed after a brief rest that afternoon, Faro and Imogen took a short walk to the Shambles and Imogen said she was glad he had invited Joe. She expected him to provide a fountain of information and knowledge for her research, as well as being an amiable attractive young man, and she was particularly keen to see his little church just around the corner. As a good Catholic who had never escaped the roots of her early upbringing, Imogen told Faro she would get up early one morning and go to Mass. Although Faro was merely a nominal Christian, as he put it, he rather envied her absolute conviction.

Promptly at seven o'clock that evening the doorbell rang and Dave Stokes arrived apologising for being alone. His wife sent her apologies, very disappointed to miss such an occasion, having developed a shocking head cold, which she would nurse behind her own closed doors. She had no intention of passing it on to anyone. 'However, she hopes that she will sufficiently recover so that we can have a meeting together before you leave.'

He smiled at Imogen. If anyone could have read his mind at that moment they would have seen that he had, as almost every man including the young Catholic priest, an identical reaction to meeting Faro's lovely wife. The thought was almost visible: how had he managed to land such a stunner?

'I have put in some enquiries on your behalf, Mrs Faro,' he said.

'Thank you, and please call me Imogen.' She smiled.

He bowed and continued: 'There is no immediate trace of your relative, Mrs Roxwell, or indeed of any young woman of her description in our missing persons records.' Tactfully, he did not mention specifically the hospitals or the mortuary, although they were both aware that these would have been included.

Molly was attending to the fire as the doorbell rang again. They heard Mrs Muir's footsteps as she attended to the new guest's arrival, and a few moments later Joe entered, looking solemn, with apologies for being late. Introductions made, hands were shaken, Joe murmured something about a sick parishioner but was soon absorbed into the conversation and very pleased to recognise Mr Stokes, whose wife was a local worthy. Although one of the Minster's regular congregation who played a leading role in their many good works, she had taken the young priest under her maternal wing and helped him when he first came to St Columba's.

Imogen sighed and exchanged a relieved look with Faro. It said they had found themselves in an ecumenical society, vastly different from their own bigoted religious backgrounds in Catholic Ireland and Presbyterian Scotland.

As Molly served the meal, which lived up to Mrs Muir's trademark of excellence, the talk turned to Edinburgh and the nostalgic reminiscence of the years spent there by the two retired detectives. Faro suspected that Dave's disappointment in leaving it was evident. He would have loved to spend his retirement, the rest of his days, where he had been born, but loyalty to his wife decided otherwise.

The wine was running low and as there was no bell visible to summon Molly, Faro decided to go through to the kitchen in search of a replacement. Opening the door, he almost tripped over Wilfred, who jumped up, ostensibly from tying his bootlace.

His ear had been suspiciously near the keyhole. He had been listening to their conversation and Faro demanded rather sharply, holding up the bottle, 'Is there another one of these?' The young man looked considerably embarrassed, snatched it from Faro and mumbled: 'I am sure there is. Molly will fetch it.'

'Not at all, I will wait,' Faro replied, following him to the kitchen where Molly and Mrs Muir sat at the table, both looking up sharply in the expectant manner of those awaiting news, and none of it good.

They jumped to their feet and Faro suspected that behind his back they intercepted a warning glance from Wilfred.

'Another bottle, Mrs Muir, if you please. As it is red, it will not require chilling.'

But with it in his hand, heading back to the dining room, Faro's thoughts *were* somewhat chilling, remembering the policeman's visit, how they had stared out of the window unaware of his presence, and now this eavesdropping.

Were they merely curious or was his naturally suspicious nature seeking a more sinister interpretation?

As the visitors were about to leave, Molly handing the visitors their outdoor garments, Joe, halfway into his overcoat, pointed down the corridor.

'Is that the kitchen?' Molly nodded, and heading to it, he said over his shoulder: 'Won't be a moment. Must thank Mrs Muir for that supper.' He smiled. 'Best I have had in a long time.'

When he appeared again a short while later, having heard indistinct murmurs of Joe's voice, which was well adapted to large churches, Imogen whispered to Faro: 'Well, there is someone else she isn't shy with. Or is it just women she doesn't like?'

Faro grinned. 'Maybe she's one of his congregation –

anyway, there is a tradition that all curates are popular with women – of all ages. Perhaps even more when they become good-looking reverends.'

Preparing for bed, Imogen decided it had been a very successful supper party with all the right ingredients, including Mrs Muir's excellent menu and splendid wine.

Faro agreed and when he told her how going for another bottle he had caught Wilfred listening at the keyhole, she frowned. 'Perhaps we should have invited him. By all accounts he is a solitary sort of chap. It would have been a nice polite gesture, Faro.'

'Rather than the impolite one of having his ear to the keyhole.'

Imogen laughed. 'Just being curious, I expect, or maybe he had been told or had a righteous feeling that it was his duty to keep an eye on strangers in his stepfather's house.' Aware of her husband's doubtful expression, she added: 'You are no longer a policeman, Faro.'

'And policemen aren't welcome. You should have seen them, all heads together, staring out of the window when a policeman appeared to deliver Dave's note.'

Imogen shook her head. 'A quite normal reaction, I should think, in any house in York. Only a policeman would think it suspicious and that they had something to hide. Remember the way the doors closed when we were going door to door looking for Kathleen's address? And they were just ordinary folk, not a criminal among them, I'm sure.'

Mention of Kathleen brought them back to the fact that

with no dire information from the police records supplied by Dave, unless they heard from Carasheen there was little they could do. Leaning against his shoulder as he looked out of the window where a new moon slid sleepily between fleecy clouds, Imogen yawned and said, 'If the weather holds tomorrow, might we take a boat out on the river?'

That was to be delayed, however. As they were preparing to leave after breakfast they had another visitor. Announced by Molly, she looked a little shaken to usher in Dave Stokes and a uniformed police officer.

Faro was wondering what bad tidings this portended, heartily glad that Imogen was upstairs, having availed herself of the luxury of a morning bath. He ushered them into the small dark study, apologising for the fire not yet lit. Dave declined the offer of refreshment, saying this was a short visit. He nodded towards the man with him. 'This is Inspector Eastlake, Inspector Faro – someone I think you should meet.'

As they shook hands, the inspector apologised for this early morning intrusion. 'The name of Chief Inspector Faro and his reputation gets around, and as I had business in the area, Mr Stokes' – he paused and considered Dave critically – 'who is also my son-in-law, suggested I might call upon you for a few moments, if this is convenient.' Faro remembered that in the course of conversation Dave had mentioned that his father-in-law was in the York Police.

Dave smiled. 'I have an appointment, so I will leave you gentlemen.'

With a bow, he was gone and Faro indicated a chair and said: 'Please, take a seat, Inspector.'

Eastlake sat down and said, 'I have also heard of your wife, Imogen Crowe. A lady with a reputation almost as great in the literary circles as yours is in the police.' He sighed. 'And she is the reason I am here.'

Faro stood up. 'Then I shall call her.'

Eastlake held up his hand. 'No, no, if you please, I think you should hear this first.' He looked uncomfortable, cleared his throat. 'It was the name Crowe that interested me.'

'She has a young relative here in York.' Could this be news of Kathleen at last?

The inspector looked up. 'So I understand. The reason that I came was I learnt that Dave was conducting a search among our records for her present whereabouts.'

He paused, and Faro said: 'My wife is most concerned for this young woman from her family in Ireland who has unaccountably disappeared. She worked in a flower shop and Mrs Faro, expecting to see her, was informed that no one there had ever heard of her. What my wife desperately needs to know, sir, is what has happened to her, and we will be most obliged for any information, such as her address—'

He got no further as the inspector interrupted with the question Faro had been dreading. 'How well does Mrs Faro know this young woman?'

'Not well at all. Merely a meeting over twenty years ago in Carasheen where they both lived. The girl was orphaned—'

'I am aware of that and I believe closely related to a terrorist who hanged himself in a Scottish jail.'

Faro's eyes opened in amazement as Eastlake continued. 'I realised that your wife is under a misapprehension about this young woman. We are aware from sources in Ireland that Kathleen Crowe may well have had a troubled childhood – being passed from cousin to cousin indicates to everyone an abused unhappy upbringing of a young child.' He shook his head. 'That may well be so and could account for the person we encountered as an adult.'

'Encountered?' Faro demanded. 'In what way?' he added, thinking surely not a police record.

'Kathleen Crowe grew up to become a trusted member of the Irish Nationalist organisation, following in the footsteps of her family. We now have Sinn Fein newly created two years ago, which I fear will give us even more grief to deal with.'

Pausing, he regarded Faro thoughtfully and sighed. 'This is confidential information, but I am trusting you as a former police officer. I think it is only right that you should be told, and your wife should be warned, that she is treading in dangerous territory.'

Faro's heart sank with the realisation that Imogen herself once belonged in that dangerous territory and approved heartily of Sinn Fein. With a glimpse of a hopeful sign that the inspector might know Kathleen's whereabouts, he asked eagerly:

'Do you know where she is since leaving the flower shop, Inspector? What was her last address?'

The inspector shook his head. 'I am not at liberty to

divulge that information as there are others involved who we are also keeping an eye on. All we know is that she is no longer living at that address. She has disappeared. We have always maintained a watch over her, as one who has a criminal record.'

He smiled wryly. 'She is also a thief, involved in stealing a large sum of money from a local bank – I will spare you the details since there is no absolute proof, only circumstantial evidence, but we are anxious to apprehend and question her. However, our last sighting was two weeks ago, when a constable saw her heading towards York Station. He followed her, but she gave him the slip and he did not see her board the train that was leaving for London. The various railway and police stations en route were alerted with her description, but there has been no information thus far.'

'Do you think she might be heading back to Kerry?'

'There is always that possibility, however there are Irish terrorist nests the length and breadth of Britain.' The inspector stood up and smiled. 'I must take my leave of you, sir, I thought your wife ought to know all this and spare you both the anxiety of a continuing search for a missing relative.' He bowed. 'It would have been a greater pleasure to meet you, sir, in other circumstances than with such disquieting news.'

CHAPTER SIXTEEN

Faro was in a quandary. What and whether to tell Imogen, whose footsteps he could hear on the landing upstairs. He was not a good actor; this, added to the fact that Imogen had an invariable habit of reading his thoughts, he could conceal little from her, so opening the door he went out into the garden for time to think up some plausible story.

He must at least emphasise the reason for the inspector's visit and Imogen would be relieved to learn that her young relative was not dead, or kidnapped. The fact, if it was only that, of her early upbringing with criminal tendencies would be distressing, but Imogen could deal with that – after all, how could anyone possibly know from a solitary meeting with a young girl, how she was to evolve or what destiny held for her?

That she was suspected of having affiliations to the Irish Nationalist movement would not dismay Imogen, it might make her proud of a girl whose secret dealings with that organisation she had shared in the past. However, that the girl she had regarded as innocent and ill-used had a police record and was being hunted down as a thief was another matter entirely.

Footsteps as Imogen hurried across the path towards him.

'Who were your visitors, Faro? I heard talking and recognised Dave's voice.' She paused, frowning. 'Who was the other fellow I saw leaving from our window? Did they bring news of Kathleen?' she added anxiously.

He shook his head.

She was regarding him intently and he was sure she knew something was wrong as she said reproachfully: 'You should have called me.'

He ignored that. 'Dave had brought his father-in-law, Inspector Eastlake, who wanted to meet me.'

She smiled. 'Was that all? Sure now, that reputation of yours. Follows you everywhere.' Looking up at the sky, she sniffed the air. 'Well, a lovely day, is it not? Mrs Muir has prepared a picnic basket for us, so let's make the most of it.' And taking his arm she smiled up into his face. 'We are going to enjoy every bit of York, there is so much to see,' she continued excitedly, pointing to the table. 'Read these when you have a moment.'

Faro listened patiently, well aware that Imogen had been enchanted by her first visit and had eagerly absorbed the history of York lying at the junctures of the three Yorkshire Ridings but with its own administration, acting as a regional capital more often than a county one.

'Did you realise it was bypassed almost entirely by the Industrial Revolution and even today in the 1900s, York has retained its ancient character and remains more medieval than most English towns?' She thrust the leaflets into his hands. 'We are so lucky, Faro. This great city and we have this historic house to come back to each night.' She laughed. 'And I promise, no more fretting and worrying about Kathleen, though I expect we will hear – sometime – from Uncle Seamus.'

He told himself that Imogen had made his decision for him. There was nothing he could do; the police had the matter in hand. What was the point in upsetting her with the inspector's revelations? Let the disappearance of Kathleen remain a mystery, as Imogen had been convinced there was no real cause for alarm beyond her own wild imaginings. Kathleen had left York, there was no reason for her to expect ever to see Imogen again, no reason for a forwarding address. Doubtless the girl had friends the length and breadth of Yorkshire. And was waiting an opportunity to travel back to Ireland.

As for Faro, although relieved to see Imogen happy and sharing the enjoyment of this totally unexpected treat that the owners of the Dower House had generously offered, he was guiltily aware that, although the new information from Inspector Eastlake had solved the disappearance of Kathleen Crowe, it hung like an inescapable cloud between himself and Imogen. He wasn't used to keeping secrets from her, but this was one – should he pass it on

– he was certain would distress her more than ever. And had the inspector revealed her address, he could well imagine Imogen rushing to it and ringing the doorbell – with the awful consequence of falling foul of a web of conspirators. He shuddered; that was one can of worms he refused to allow either of them to open, thankful that they were only here for a few days.

The wedding at Elrigg first, then once back in Edinburgh and settled in their new home, Imogen's search for Kathleen would hopefully become part of the past. Meanwhile, the inspector's information lay heavily on his conscience, another mystery, a sinister secret not to be shared.

But in that he was wrong. There were others who knew the truth about Kathleen and one was Seamus Crowe. After an exhausting day of exploring York in and out of the quiet closes called Snickelways, looking in modern shops and examining ruins of ancient buildings with their handbook, they retired footsore to sleep very well, and leaving Imogen still asleep, Faro went downstairs to breakfast. There on the hall table was the long-awaited letter from Ireland. Faro seized it eagerly, prepared to carry it upstairs to Imogen, when he noticed that it was addressed not to her, nor to them both, but marked personal to Mr Faro.

Dear Faro,

I hope this finds you and Imogen both well. My reason for writing to you is that what I have to tell you is up to you to share with my niece or not, regarding her anxiety over Kathleen. I have to tell you there is no news of her in Carasheen and I would not have expected any. The family have disowned her long ago, not because of her marriage to an English fellow but because long before that she disgraced herself in their eyes by her moral character. In more recent years when we have met, to my amazement she wanted to stay in touch with me. However, I have grave news to share. I have to tell you that Kathleen from her earliest days was not to be trusted. She stole money and jewellery from members of the family. It was a disgrace that no one could forgive her. As for her present whereabouts, perhaps she will be in contact with Sinn Fein—

Faro read no more: footsteps warned him of Imogen's approach and he thrust the letter into his pocket. It was too late, she was smiling, excited.

'Molly said there was a letter from Ireland. So Uncle Seamus has written at last – news about Kathleen. Is it good? Is she there?' And looking at his solemn expression, she held out her hand.

'Come on, now, Faro. Where's the letter?'

Damn Molly, he thought, taking it out of his pocket aware that there was no possible way of shielding her from the truth. As she sat down and began to read, he thought that out of this bad news some good might come. At least this would herald the end of her concern about Kathleen.

Silently she read and finally, with a sigh, threw the letter down on the table. 'Sure now, I see it was addressed to you, Faro. It would seem that my own uncle did not know me or trust me as well as I thought. A family matter to be avoided,' she added bitterly.

'I am so sorry, Imo. I realise this must be quite a blow for you.'

She shrugged. 'Not as long as she is alive. As for her early days, the Crowes were always ready to see the worst in her. Many children steal things, just being naughty, and perhaps poor little Kathleen had more reason than most, maybe driven by neglect and desperation to steal money for food from their purses or a piece of jewellery, perhaps even a childish desire to run away, but I believe they were all biased. They clung to this past against her and it all blew up when she married an Englishman, this Henry Roxwell' – she paused and sighed – 'the last straw, the final disgrace; I can just see them mulling it over, making it worse than it was in reality to justify their feelings.'

She stopped again for breath and Faro who had listened in silence could think of no words. He was sure Imogen was the one biased in Kathleen's favour, although he was aware how readily the female members of the Carasheen family eagerly seized upon every scrap of gossip. They would talk endlessly on the subject matter, adding fantastic theories to blow up even the smallest happening into a family incident of mammoth proportions.

He looked at Imogen. 'Well, this changes things, does it not?'

She said sharply. 'In what way?'

'In view of what we have learnt,' he said slowly, 'I don't think Kathleen is any more your vital concern, my dear.'

'Do you now? Well, that is where we differ. I still want to know why the Four Seasons are pretending that she was never with their shop.'

Faro sighed deeply. Back to square one again. 'I agree,' he said wearily. 'That is strange, but your uncle's letter suggests that she is very able to look after herself, and as for being missing, doubtless she has her own reasons.'

While considering telling her that Inspector Eastlake's revelations about her stealing money was perhaps an excellent reason for the flower shop denying any association with Kathleen, he was aware of Imogen's expression, regarding him tight-lipped and angry.

'Tell the truth, now, all you want to do is forget about this unexpected news since it got in the way of the pleasant holiday we planned in York. Such a relief to be rid of one of my tiresome relations.'

'That is not fair, Imo. You know me better than that. If I felt she was in the slightest danger, relative or not, I would be the first to do something about it. But as I have tried to stress to you a hundred times, this girl maybe blood kin but she is also a stranger. As we know of her sympathies, perhaps she has a contact with Sinn Fein and is with them now.'

And that decided him. With a sigh, he began cautiously: 'The inspector said the police were looking for her, that she would go to prison for having stolen money. He hinted that there will be bad times ahead for Britain with Sinn Fein.'

Imogen laughed scornfully. 'And that was no doubt why she stole money – to help them. We can't blame her for that. A good cause and good luck to them. It is only what Britain deserves,' she responded sharply. 'If I was still at home, I would be joining them too.'

Faro regarded her narrowly. 'Is that so? Like you went to Dublin two years ago in 1905. You persuaded me not to accompany you to hear Arthur Griffith and meet Maud Gonne MacBride and Mary Ellen Butler, saying it was a women's suffragette thing and that I would be bored.'

'And so you would have been,' Imogen replied sullenly, embarrassed but defiant as he went on.

'Look, Imo, your politics and your religion are and always have been your own business. We have agreed to differ. You are Irish, you must go as your heart and your conscience move you—'

'But you would rather I didn't,' she interrupted. 'You don't approve of Sinn Fein – like the rest of your countrymen, you are scared of the truth.'

'My countrymen are Orcadians,' he reminded her stiffly.

'They are indeed. I am in no danger of forgetting that. But you still spent your entire working life and earned your living with the Brits in the Edinburgh City Police.'

Imogen's face was flushed, her temper rising, and he realised with a growing sense of horror that this was the nearest they had ever come to quarrelling in their life together.

He stood up, drew her to her feet in one swift gesture and into his arms. She remained there, her head against his shoulder. Then she sighed, put her arms around his neck, drew his face down to hers and kissed him.

The dangerous moment was over and stroking her hair back tenderly, he said: 'Imo, my darling one, I won't be brought into any argument. All that matters in the world to me now is being with you, loving you, making you happy.'

She looked up at him. There were tears in her eyes. 'Oh, Faro darlin', and I love you. Forgive me, you are all the world to me. No more worries over Kathleen, I promise, that is finished. Let Sinn Fein and the Brits go hang.'

They kissed again, but Faro had a fleeting sense that danger had only been averted, an instinct to be aware that there were more dangers imminent that neither of them could foresee nor avert.

CHAPTER SEVENTEEN

Later that day news came in the form of a telegram from the Hardys. Theo had had an accident to his leg at the Egypt dig, and was unable to walk. Could they possibly extend their visit for another week?

Imogen sighed. 'This is a bit inconvenient,' she said. 'What about our important engagement at Elrigg Castle?'

They would have left for the wedding in two days' time before heading back to Edinburgh, nicely timed to coincide with the end of what was originally intended as their stay in York.

Standing by Faro as he penned a telegram in the affirmative to the Hardys, Imogen sensed that they were now under an obligation to return to the Dower House once more and remain until the owners returned.

Faro had certainly not forgotten Elrigg. One of Imogen's goddaughters was getting married and she had promised long ago, so she said, to dance at her wedding. To make up for being childless herself, Imogen had accumulated as many godchildren as she had cousins in Carasheen.

How did she manage to keep in touch with them all, Faro wondered, when he had difficulty with birthdays or special occasions in his own small family? He was prone to forgetting his mother's and two daughters' birthdays and yet Imogen now reminded him gently, adding them to her vast horde as she went spinning about Europe through the years, now taking Faro with her.

Mark, Lord Elrigg, had married the daughter of the local vicar, Rev. Cairncross, much to his family's displeasure. They had wanted him to marry a wealthy heiress, but he and Harriet had been childhood friends and in love. Their quick marriage had a further shock in store when the Elriggs observed that Harriet was pregnant with their first child, son and heir Nicholas. Mercia their daughter came two years later.

Imogen smiled at him. 'Sure now, I'm hoping you will enjoy Elrigg Castle. One of your old hunting grounds,' she added tenderly.

Faro would never forget it: an investigation commanded by Her Majesty, the king's mother, to prove that her wayward son, Prince of Wales and now King Edward the Seventh, was not a coward who had left his equerry Sir Archie Elrigg to be gored to death by a wild bull.

Faro had proved his innocence in regard to that matter and narrowly escaped death himself. It was not a happy time, a Gypsy woman's prediction had been almost right and he recalled his scorn hearing that abominable woman

Imogen Crowe addressing her in her own language and how she had turned on him and said proudly that her grandmother was a Romany, one of them.

He shuddered, and Imogen's eyebrows raised. 'Our second encounter, Faro, and not a great deal to be said for it.'

'And I'm not sentimental about that, either,' but his smile was gentle.

She took his hands and whispered: 'Sure now, and we both knew, even then I think, there was no escape. We were trapped, although wild horses wouldn't have dragged the truth from us.'

'You're right there! We damned well detested one another.'

'I thought you were the handsomest as well as the rudest man I had ever met. You looked like a Viking and scowled when I said put on a horned helmet and you'd have every girl within miles run screaming.' Pausing she gave him an impish smile. 'I didn't say in which direction.'

'What cheek!' he said, hugging her. 'Of course I want to come to Elrigg. Wouldn't miss it,' Faro said.

'No savage white cattle this time, only nice wedding guests from miles around, all very civilised.'

'After Elrigg, Edinburgh soon, thank God. And when is your next engagement?'

Imogen said, 'I have the summer free. Thought it would be so nice to have time to explore Britain for a change. I've never really had the chance since my pardon.'

She was saying: 'We'll come back as promised to the Hardys until Theo is able to travel. We owe them that much.'

She paused. 'However, when we are in Northumberland, it would suit me fine for my next book if we could have a look at Hadrian's Wall.'

'I don't imagine there are trains in that area, so how do we travel?'

Imogen had already been busy with timetables in the city library. 'There are trains between Newcastle and Hexham, and Mark will send a carriage for us and take us to the wall. Archaeology is his hobby: there has been a team led by his cousin Hector, digging in the castle grounds, since Harriet's father found a Roman coin. He has always been intrigued by the Roman occupation.'

She went on: 'My main concern with York has been finding out more about the female prison but I have always been intrigued by how women on both sides of the border lived during the Roman occupation and the building of the wall, either as respectable legionnaires' wives or as the local prostitutes. There is still plenty of material to be explored and I want to know more about how the Romans and Britons treated their womenfolk after Constantine became the first Christian emperor. Did you know, York is still a garrison town?'

Faro smiled. At that time women had a very insignificant role to play and there were few who stood out like Boadicea, the warrior queen of the Brigantes who had fought against the Romans. Women's suffrage was a new movement, a rebellion that had taken centuries to take shape. Beyond some minor scuffles among women considered mad idiots, and under the watchful gaze of the Edinburgh police in case occasional incidents became a movement that boiled over, he had not expected to hear of suffrage on a personal level, until he learnt of his daughter Rose's obsession as chairwoman of the Edinburgh branch, a passion she shared with Imogen.

He had to agree with the growing knowledge among writers like Robert Louis Stevenson who were appalled that women in nineteenth-century Britain – even aristocratic ones – had never heard of contraception, willing to endure a child a year, treated as little more than mindless breeding machines.

After sending off the message to the Hardys and deciding that it was perhaps fortunate that they had the extra time, Faro had to admit he would be sorry to leave the luxury of Dower House; he had developed a great fondness for York, never weary of exploring its historic artefacts.

Waking early in the morning, shortly after dawn, an old habit from his Edinburgh days that he had been unable to shed with marriage, he crept out leaving Imogen still soundly asleep. He was particularly addicted to the daily routine as an Edinburgh detective of walking on Arthur's Seat. It had often helped him clear his mind of other thoughts and work out problems and even conclusions to a crime. In retirement he now enjoyed a pipe exploring the still quiet cities they visited, and here in York, walking the wall surrounding the city, taking a seat to enjoy the view at the 'bars' as the four exits were called.

It also gave him time and opportunity to think of

marriage, and in particular his own and how it had changed his life – how very different since they became lovers who travelled the world together. He recognised that as a husband he had taken on a new persona, as had Imogen as his wife.

He realised where once she was her own woman, she now leant upon him and he had a responsibility towards her needs and indeed her whims. It was a new role, he had never had any one dependent upon him – even his two daughters after Lizzie's death, taken over by his mother, Mary Faro, to live in Orkney, had removed that commitment from him.

He sighed. He loved Imogen, that had not changed, he loved her more as wife than lover, but there were odd jolting moments – perhaps the worse in the 'better or for worse' warned in the marriage vows.

Back in the Dower House Imogen had been busy consulting railway timetables. Fortunately, York was well served by trains up and down the east coast, and trains from Newcastle to Hexham on the Carlisle line were also frequent. She decided that they should arrive the day before the wedding and afterwards, on the next day perhaps, Mark would take them to Hadrian's Wall.

'We should not be absent for more than four days,' she informed Wilfred, who said Mrs Muir was shopping. She had Molly with her, who would be doing most of the carrying, according to Wilfred, in sole possession of the kitchen and lifting his head from rapidly demolishing a plate of freshly baked scones.

It was with a sense of relief and pleasant anticipation that Faro and Imogen prepared to set off for Elrigg, with Faro already in his very best suit and cravat. Imogen, however, was still completely undecided within hours of departure on what she would wear. She was particularly concerned about the Northumbrian weather, known to be unreliable, as well as the cool, not to say bitterly cold, interior of Elrigg Castle's bedrooms.

Faro en route from the barber shop, Imogen having insisted he must look his immaculate best, encountered Inspector Eastlake in the Stonegate and was persuaded that a light refreshment be taken, not in the form of a glass of ale at the inn near the police station, but as a coffee across the way.

Mary was interested in these new customers. She had seen the tall, handsome man walking past with the Irish lady and guessed that the way they looked around they were tourists in the area. However, the man with him today as they sat at a table was a different matter.

Even out of uniform she recognised a policeman. There was something unmistakable about the breed. At least these two were respectable gentlemen who would not frighten off her lady regulars, not like those foreigners who sometimes lingered in the vicinity of the flower shop and who, despite their smart suits, she was certain were up to no good.

She was worried about Amy, who seemed to have got off with one of them and was behaving very secretively, not saying much about it but smiling to herself a lot. Mary didn't like it: Amy was young and pretty and with not much sense in her head where lads were concerned – believed every word they said. She was off work today, had a bad cold she said. Mary shook her head and, menu in hand, went over to the two men who were in amiable conversation.

The policeman had a Yorkshire accent, he was all right, but the other taller man, very handsome he was, sounded Scottish.

While they waited for the coffee, Eastlake said there was still no news of the missing Kathleen and stressed that knowing what the police did of that young woman's reputation he assured Faro that he and his wife should not be alarmed. 'Mrs Faro must accept that she has narrowly escaped the consequences of a criminal offence and is well able to look after herself. She is probably back in Ireland with her fellow conspirators enjoying the money she stole,' he added gloomily.

Faro acknowledged this without revealing the information they had received from Carasheen, and said it was fortunate Imogen had now also accepted that Kathleen was not a missing person but was alive and well. The flower shop had doubtless its own reasons for not acknowledging that she had ever worked there. He added that they were going up to Northumberland for a wedding but would be returning to York again immediately, explaining about Hardy's accident and that they had been asked to remain at the Dower House until he was fit to travel home.

The inspector looked grave. 'It's as well that you can be there, Faro, a man with your reliable experience.' He sighed, considering Faro thoughtfully for a moment before continuing: 'This is also for your information only. We have been keeping the Dower House under surveillance for some time now.'

'Is there some problem?'

The inspector sighed. 'Perhaps you are unaware of this, but there is a thriving trade in smuggling Roman artefacts and stolen goods across to the Continent via Hull and Amsterdam. There are keen buyers on the European market, well-known connoisseurs, millionaires willing to pay high prices.' He frowned. 'The Dower House is particularly vulnerable. As you know, it was the site of the Emperor Severus's villa during the Roman occupation. The mosaic floor would be worth a fortune.'

'Surely that would be difficult to take up?'

'Indeed, it would, but the removal of a few tiles would be possible, and its very existence hints at what further excavations on the site might reveal. There have always been substantial rumours of other valuable artefacts, especially some discoveries during repairs after the fire during the last century. The usual fragments of pottery, coins and some Roman jewellery.'

'Treasure trove, you mean?'

'Indeed, yes, and that is the reason we believe that

Hardy refuses to allow the archaeologists any access to the grounds.'

'Rich pickings and understandable that he wishes to keep any treasure under wraps as his own,' said Faro. 'What's the rule up in Scotland?'

'We call it bona vacantia – owners' goods. Treasure trove in any form – coin or plate, gold and silver vessels or utensils or bullion – hidden and rediscovered, which no person could prove ownership of, is claimed by the Crown.'

'Yes, it's much the same here in York if we find hoards buried with the intention of retrieval. It is most often personal loot where people running for their lives hastily buried jewellery and money with every intention of coming back for it when peace was restored. But that never happened – in the case of soldiers they had undoubtedly been killed. As for the Romans and the Brits of that time, there were more peaceful items such as votive offerings or grave goods.'

'You are very knowledgeable,' Faro laughed.

The inspector shrugged. 'In our profession in York, you have to have a finger in a great many pies.' He paused and then added, 'As for Hardy's ownership of the Dower House, which would have a marketable price of a million pounds at least for its historic connection, that has long been a source of wonder, not to say actual suspicion, especially with his refusal to allow any digging even by the team of local archaeologists he works for. The City Fathers are itching to get their hands on it, add it to the list of buildings of historic interest open to the public, which also adds to their coffers.'

Pausing, he looked at Faro. 'As a policeman yourself, have you not thought it odd that Theo Hardy, a clerk with a limited income and no academic background or qualifications, can afford the upkeep of the Dower House, with servants and a motor car?' He shook his head, 'Where, one might ask, does the money come from?'

Faro shrugged. 'Perhaps an inheritance.'

'We have very carefully examined any such possibilities.' The inspector frowned. 'His parents were working class, father worked on the railway, his mother in a laundry. No siblings, no rich uncles. His wife is an ordinary Yorkshire woman, respectable background, her father also a railwayman, and she worked as a waitress in one of our local restaurants until they married. No money or inheritance there, as far as we can ascertain.'

His frown deepened, and he took a deep breath. 'I'll tell you, Faro, as we see it. We suspect that his income is related to selling artefacts smuggled out of York, that at some stage he has found a treasure trove and is living on the proceeds of that, bit by bit, piece by piece.'

Returning to the Dower House, Faro paused in the garden to consider, in the light of Eastlake's revelations, the faded remains of its mosaic floor as well as the tiny fragments, stones remaining of the walls of earlier buildings.

Recounting details of their meeting to Imogen with the inspector's suspicions, as they prepared to depart for Elrigg, he said: 'It is certainly food for thought.'

She agreed. 'I think it must have occurred to lots of folks, including ourselves. Another mystery, Faro,' she laughed, 'but this is one you are unlikely to solve.'

'I wouldn't even try,' he replied.

CHAPTER EIGHTEEN

Weddings were not regular occurrences or high on the Faros' list of priorities and a society wedding brought trials of what to wear. For their own informal occasion in Kerry with as little publicity as possible, they had worn everyday clothes. Abhorring the S-shaped fashionably corseted figure of the last decade, Imogen's travelling clothes for platform events tended toward a cloth costume with a bell-shaped skirt, the jacket bodice cut away to show a pleated blouse with a lace draped frill from neck to waistband.

In more recent days she had become a convert to the first mass-produced blouses, with high turned-down collars and puffed long bell-shaped sleeves. Ignoring the passion for bonnets of all shapes and sizes heavily endowed with birds and flowers, she wore her abundant auburn curls loose. Besides the dark-green velvet costume suitable for travel and most outdoor occasions, her only concession to evening dress was a turquoise silk gown with a low décolletage, its billowing skirt surrounded by lace and ribbons.

Faro presented something of a problem. He cared little for fashion, his normal attire as long as she had known him being a tweed jacket and trousers. He had an evening suit reluctantly worn, a black dress coat reaching almost to the knees, a white double-breasted waistcoat revealing a stiff shirt front and high collar, with a butterfly bow tie, and close-fitting arrow trousers with braid down the outside of each leg.

Imogen regarded him solemnly. 'You will have to wear a topper.'

Faro groaned. He had an aversion to hats and except on formal occasions went bareheaded; moving from uniform to plain clothes as a detective inspector he had happily abandoned the police helmet. Men in Orkney didn't wear tall hats, he said, and he was glad to find that for most men there was a choice and hats were no longer de rigueur, although he possessed a bowler, which mostly stayed in the wardrobe.

'I will need to buy one, then', he said sadly. 'Hats make me feel uncomfortable and ridiculous.'

With wedding garments carefully packed, they set off early next morning, catching the train to Newcastle and, finding themselves the only passengers in one of the six-seater compartments, were happy to relax. Both had brought books to read, but they were cast aside as they watched the passing countryside in its ever-changing moods. The landscape beyond the carriage window was occasionally filled with the sprawling streets of fast-growing cities, Darlington and Doncaster, none yielding the majestic spectacle of Durham with its castle – 'half church of God, half fortress 'gainst the Scot' – perched high upon the horizon.

'We must visit Durham,' Imogen said, echoing Faro's own thoughts when he had travelled up to York. 'Perhaps on our return journey we could stop off the train and spend a day there.'

Moving swiftly onward into a landscape occupied by the growing mass of industry, the train crossed the bridge over the twisting colourful River Tyne and into Newcastle station. There they changed platforms for the Hexham train and a very distinct outlook from the windows as a very different rural landscape emerged for the remainder of their journey.

On the station platform Mark was waiting, delighted to see them again, and ushered them into the motor car parked outside waiting to take them to Elrigg.

Mark indicated the chauffeur and whispered, 'I like to drive myself, but I thought on this occasion I needed all my concentration.' He grinned. 'There is so much to show you.'

And as Imogen gazed out at the majestic sight of Hexham Abbey, Mark recognised that wistful look and his offer of a pleasant break to park and explore was eagerly accepted.

He explained that the priory had begun rebuilding some fifty years ago in 1850 and was still not quite complete. The Vikings sacked the original abbey and the first rebuilding took place in Norman times, so much of its present appearance was Augustinian. Imogen's particular interest was in the interior with its great nave and the stained-glass window.

'Now essentially a place of worship it serves as the parish church, and if you had been staying at Elrigg for a while longer, I would have brought you back to see the crypt. That's more in Hector's line,' Mark added. 'He and I are on the committee for rebuilding the old priory and maintaining it.'

This was the first mention of Hector and Mark smiled. 'He still lives in the same old rickety estate cottage, can't be persuaded otherwise by Harriet, although there is plenty of room in the castle for him these days.'

And both Faro and Imogen remembered the bitterness of those years ago when Sir Archie, Mark's uncle, had denied his other nephew Hector, an archaeologist, permission to dig on the estate where the medieval foundations of the earlier castle were still visible. This was adding insult to injury as Hector believed that, but for some ancient clause relating to inheritance down the distaff line, both title and estate were rightfully his after his uncle's death.

It appeared that wound had been healed or skilfully bandaged as Mark and Hector were firm friends, the latter having no desire or envy for the title or the estate, his only interest academic in the historic origins of Elrigg.

They travelled towards their destination through the attractive parkland that surrounded Hexham Abbey, passing a fine bandstand and an abundance of trees and bushes, then on past the marketplace, which was a scene of busy activity, with its many stalls of produce. Their journey gave Imogen a chance to study Mark, relatively unchanged by the passing years, apart from thinner hair and a thicker waistline. He was delighted to have their company on this special family celebration, and with a chance to revive old memories, he brought them up to date on activities at Elrigg.

Hector's excavations after twenty years had revealed a few artefacts, now in the Roman wall settlement at Housesteads, a thriving and exciting addition to information on Hadrian's Wall, where excavations begun in earnest in 1825 were now proving to be an interesting tourist attraction.

Imogen seized that information and said she would love to visit the area with its settlements as part of research on the book she was currently writing on women through the ages.

Mark said that could be easily arranged. The Elrigg estate was in easy reach of the wall, so if they could stay a day or two after the wedding, he would take them personally, adding that he was pleased to learn that Imogen shared the castle's interest in the neighbourhood's antiquities and his own particular obsession.

He looked at Faro and chuckled. 'No wild white cattle this time – you will be quite safe, just nice friendly ancient ruins,' he said as they approached the ornate gates and started down the long drive to the castle.

Harriet was waiting to greet them, a stouter more matronly version of the vicar's daughter whose marriage to Mark they had witnessed on that first visit. She hugged Imogen and, shaking hands with Faro, she looked up at him with a radiant smile. 'We were so happy to hear that you were married,' obviously presuming it was long ago, not just recently, when she added: 'especially as everyone thought you were such a handsome couple, quite made for each other.'

The castle was just the same, its atmosphere homely, with furnishings slightly more shabby and faded, indicating a family home with children raised over the years. Imogen was well aware of a contented existence, as she told Faro when they were alone in the guest bedroom.

Touching the century-old tapestry curtain on the four-poster, which was seriously in need of repairs, she whispered: 'All of this is in great contrast to the luxury of the Dower House, but I know which one I prefer.'

Faro smiled sadly. Conditions inside the castle clearly indicated that, along with most of the Northumbrian gentry, times were not easy and money was scarce. 'It must cost a fortune even to keep the roof in good repair.'

They were expected, Imogen realised, to dress for dinner, Mark and Harriet waiting to receive their guests in the drawing room with sherry on offer. As they took their seats before the blaze of a cheerfully crackling log fire, Mark was extremely interested in their visit to York, his eyebrows raised when, in reply to him asking where they were staying, Faro said the Dower House.

He whistled. 'You are lucky. The present building is one the most famous and contains the ruins of the only surviving villa from the Roman occupation. Harriet and I go to York occasionally, we have a lad there – Nick, our eldest, you know.' Imogen calculated that he was the baby Harriet was pregnant with when she and Mark were so hastily and so scandalously married.

'We would love to visit the Dower House sometime,' Mark continued wistfully, to which Faro and Imogen immediately gave assurances that could be arranged, since the Hardys were such pleasant, friendly, informal people.

Harriet sighed. 'Nick is something of a problem these days. Should have done well but he dropped out of public school. Mark was hoping he would help run the estate, but no—'

Mark said quickly: 'He insisted he wasn't an academic, refused to go to university, said he wanted to make his own way, whatever that meant.'

Harriet added: 'A bit of a dropout he has proved to be. Said he would go to York and get a job of some kind on the railway – always loved trains, even as a wee lad.'

'That's all very well, dear,' said Mark, 'but we worry about him. He doesn't seem to want to settle down and I fear he is in undesirable society.'

'A railway clerk.' Harriet gave an exasperated sigh. 'Hardly makes enough to live himself, much less settle down. And he refuses any help from us. We hoped he would come to Mercia's wedding – they were very close as children – but no, he declined, too busy. Maybe he was embarrassed because he could not afford a wedding present. But worst of all,' she paused, lowering her voice dramatically, 'we believe he may be leaning towards turning.' She stopped and gave them a scandalised look. 'You know, becoming a Roman Catholic. The idea has shocked my poor dear father, coming from a line of Anglican ministers.' She looked appealingly at Mark. 'And, after all, Nick is the heir to Elrigg.'

Mark, busy with drinks, hadn't been paying much attention to Harriet's observations. As they looked at him for his reactions, he coughed and said: 'Never been much on religious doctrine myself, don't suppose it would make all that difference – all Christians, after all.' He gave a smile meant to be reassuring and rapidly changed the subject: 'York seems to be the Mecca for everyone these days, since the railway it is regarded as the place of opportunity.'

'But York isn't Catholic,' Harriet said in a shocked whisper. 'The Minster is a stronghold of the Protestant faith, has been for centuries. Father will tell you,' she added with a reproachful look at her husband.

Faro had not anything to add to this conversation, perhaps Harriet had not realised that Imogen was Roman Catholic. There was a sudden feeling of embarrassment before Mark successfully trailed away into the safer regions of taking care of the pheasants and opening the gardens to the public.

Next day, Faro and Imogen were suddenly taken over by the wedding preparations, the infectious excitement and nervous anticipation of the bride-to-be, Mercia, a pretty young eighteen-year-old, who was to marry into the neighbouring family, landowners of the prosperous estate next door. Like her parents, the two young people had been friends since childhood. It was a very reassuring and happy situation, with no economic problems they could foresee clouding the horizon.

The wedding was to take place in the private chapel with a limited number of a hundred guests, the ceremony performed by Mercia's grandfather, the now aged minister who declined to retire. Reverend Cairncross at eighty was still in excellent health, leading an active life at the beck and call of his parishioners and taking an active part in the well-being of the surrounding community. The bride, given away by her father and wearing a wedding dress that had belonged to her great-grandmother, brought a sigh from Imogen and Faro looked quickly at her. Perhaps she was seeing their future and something of her own past. Did she secretly yearn, Faro wondered, for that white wedding he had denied her? Was she thinking of the children she would never give him? An exchanged glance as he took her hand and her wistful look vanished. Few people on earth, she thought, could be as happy in their marriage as Faro and herself.

A touching ceremony for Mercia and her handsome Alex, with a wedding breakfast in the great dining hall of the castle that had survived so many centuries of identical occasions.

Imogen eyed the women guests, aware that those lingering glances of admiration were probably in envy of her slim figure, which the heavily S-shaped corseted ladies with their bewildering assortment of heavily ornamented hats found most interesting.

She had put flowers in her hair as a concession to being bonnetless and realised this was out of her age group, worn only by the very young girls. At least she had remembered her white suede gloves and so had Faro. Although he looked far from happy in that silk top hat, she was immensely proud of the admiring glances this tall, handsome man attracted. One old lady said to her that she and her husband were the best-looking couple there, and added with a shake of her head, even including that pretty young bride and her man.

'Some looks are meant to last and get even better,' the old lady added shrewdly.

They headed towards the village hall with the tenants for a celebratory dance with more food and speeches from the Elrigg family; all were strangers to the Faros from their brief visit twenty years ago. As the champagne flowed the dances grew more hectic, the noise increased, as did the reels. Faro and Imogen slipped out unobserved into the coolness of a perfect evening with the dark shadows of trees against a cloudless moonlit sky, where stars obligingly and romantically shed their own light and they watched a white-feathered barn owl swoop down towards its prey.

At the reception Faro had gratefully taken the alternative offer of excellent whisky instead of the champagne, which Imogen preferred, and having a less hardened head than his, she was almost asleep before her head hit the pillow.

At breakfast next morning there were few diners, and the only member of the family who had survived the wining and dining of the wedding celebration was ready with the carriage, tactfully announcing that he would be taking them to Housesteads. Not Mark, but Hector, whom they had met at the wedding, although with little more than a handshake in greeting there had been little chance to talk. Still something of a recluse, avoiding social occasions, he had declined the reception and retired to his cottage on the estate.

Twenty years had taken less of a toll on Hector than the other Elriggs, he had fared better having aged less than Mark and Harriet, possibly because he continued to lead his solitary bachelor existence and did not share the convivial wining and dining society of the castle.

Faro watched Hector's greeting of Imogen and observing his wistful glances, remembered that he had been in love with her on that first visit to Elrigg.

Although the very thought seemed preposterous now, at that time Faro imagined that Hector and Imogen might marry. He also recalled his own indifference seeing that he had not yet quite realised that he loved Imogen himself. And now observing her laughter with Hector, her charming smiles, he recognised that after twenty years he was suffering from another new emotion – jealousy.

He felt ashamed, since Hector had saved his life that night long ago when he had been shot with a crossbow and was at the mercy of a white bull.

Now Hector was looking across Imogen and saying with a smile, 'Mark said you were keen to see the Roman wall at Housesteads. It would be such a pity to disappoint you on this short visit, so I had just one glass of champagne, then I cleared off home. If you don't mind slumming it, the carriage is better for negotiating the steep tracks, horses are more skilful and kinder to the terrain than Mark's motor car.'

Faro's eyebrows raised at that. It had been Mark's intention to take them both and as if reading his mind, Hector turned to him and said, 'Mark will be very busy today and I fear not very sober. I know it's not like your Scottish weddings with those lethal drams of whisky, but Mark has no great head for liquor, as I know to my cost, having had to carry him home often enough when we were young.' He laughed and, eyeing them narrowly, observed, 'You two are none the worse for wear – the passing years have been amazingly good to you.' His look at Imogen told her more than any words that he had once hoped to have her share them with him. She had been taken aback by his declaration all that while ago, perhaps because she was already in love with Faro.

Whatever the cause for declining him, with those looks unchanged and her life as a writer – clever too – Hector guessed she must still be irresistible to men and that Faro was a lucky devil to have married her.

The weather was not in their favour: although the sun put in a reluctant appearance, there was a brisk wind blowing from the east and the fort looked less than appealing, even menacing with its stones darkened by recent rain.

However, the views as they approached were splendid, across a steep hill, where the path ran past the fort at Carrawburgh – a hard downhill slog on foot, Faro thought, thankful for the carriage with its two sturdy horses, as the road swung abruptly away from beside the wall ditch. Now they were close to a vallum, with the majestic expanse of Sewingshields Crags occupying the horizon before the dramatic run alongside Whin Sill with Housesteads Fort revealed from the fall of the ground and the road below.

Hector, who had taken over driving from the coachman-cum-chauffeur, halted the horses and said: 'We can go no further. We'll leave the carriage with Will here.' And with a grin, 'Are you two game for an uphill walk?'

Faro sighed. There was a chill wind blowing and he had hoped they would be nearer the settlement. 'Housesteads is a good place to begin an exploration of the wall. It is the most visited place of all. For anyone with an urge to walk along a section, that is.'

Imogen found it difficult to carry on a conversation, needing all her breath and energy to climb while holding on to the practical bonnet Harriet had lent her. However, getting closer, the trials of the last few minutes were forgotten as she felt the atmosphere of another world, and as they set foot on the stones, she seemed to hear caught in the wind whispers from the long past, soldiers talking, complaining, stamping their feet in cold weather or looking up the valley in summer sunshine.

Hector was always close by, his warm hands ready and eager to help her over the steeper stones, pausing to point out the remains of buildings. These, he explained, were where that mixed race of legionnaires had settled down in married quarters after Emperor Hadrian had absolved the rule that the men were not to marry, but must make do with the camp-following women or local prostitutes.

'The Romans were also very hygienically inclined,' Hector said. 'Over there' – and he indicated delicately – 'were the communal toilets. Twenty or so seated side by side, as well as the bath house always ready and available with its underfloor heating.'

But Imogen's thoughts were far away, intrigued by the generations who had lived here, legions from distant lands, lost generations, many of whom had been captured as slaves and thrown into a cruel and inhospitable area of Northumberland at the mercy of hostile tribes. In constant danger, yet eventually coming to terms with their destiny.

She stopped and looking round said: 'This was home to so many thousands. Rudyard Kipling wrote a poem about it, called "The Roman Centurion's Song":

'"Legate, I had the news last night – my cohort ordered home! I've served in Britain forty years. What should I do in Rome? Here is my heart, my soul, my mind – the only life I know. I cannot leave it all behind. Command me not to go!"'

Hector laughed and echoed the last words: '"Command me not to go."' His smile at Imogen and her look of gratitude in return signalled a bond between them and that he shared her empathy with those lost thousands of mercenaries.

Faro felt strangely out of it and as Hector's guided tour explored everything, every turret, every fort castle, already feeling footsore, he was quite grateful when at last the rain that had threatened in black clouds finally descended. They hurried back to the carriage, and taking Will with them, found shelter and a warming lunch in a nearby inn.

As they ordered, Hector said: 'Well, Faro, last time I was in Edinburgh with friends they insisted that we climb Arthur's Seat at sunset.' And leaning across the table: 'I was able to throw some light on that legendary king. A monk called Nennius wrote about a post Roman *dux bellorum*, a war leader, and the text recounts campaigns fought between the Christian British and their pagan enemies. There were nine such, at places that lie between the Roman walls – Hadrian's and the Antonine. I wonder did Arthur lead the war bands of the vigorous British kingdoms of southern Scotland?'

And so Faro found himself on common ground with Hector as he recounted the legend that was Scotland's version of Arthur's Seat. The young shepherd who had come across the king and his knights seated asleep at a giant round table, their hounds at their feet, King Arthur with his horn at his side ready to sound the alarm and ride out to save Britain some day when it was in most peril.

Hector smiled. 'He has been somewhat slow about it, has he not?'

Faro agreed. 'There have been many such occasions gone apparently unnoticed by that sleeping king, but it is a curious link that history as well as tradition counts Arthur as a cavalry warrior, and what you have told me is an interesting link with the Roman occupation and the wall.'

Back at the castle all signs of the disruptions caused by the wedding activities were being carefully tidied away by busy servants and grooms. With all back to normal, their visit was over and the wedding had taken its toll.

Harriet put in an appearance, looking pale and saying she was a little tired, while Mark, according to Hector, must be suffering from what Faro judged was a hangover of mighty proportions. And certainly in no fit state to drive a motor car.

Harriet kept her thoughts to herself. Mark had sent apologies about feeling a mite unwell but was seriously pleased when Hector offered to drive the Faros back to Hexham if they promised they would come again to Elrigg, which, although thinking that a remote possibility indeed, they did so as was expected of them, with all thanks and enthusiasm.

A final embrace for Imogen from Harriet: 'It has been so lovely to meet you both again. Do enjoy the rest of your stay in York. I love the place, any excuse to visit,' she laughed. Then a sudden thought turned her smile into a frown. 'I have to see Nick urgently and someone he is anxious for me to meet,' she added. 'A pity that you will be away in the next few days, I expect.'

On the station platform awaiting the train for York, due in five minutes, Faro asked Hector how his digging was going at Elrigg.

Hector smiled and said: 'There are occasional medieval pots and so forth, but as the estate borders the Roman wall, there are interesting possibilities.' He sighed. 'I must drag myself to York one of these days. I've only had one great find in all my years that amounted to more than a few Roman coins, and that was a torque, a neck ring worn by the Roman nobility. How it got all the way to Elrigg I'll never know, someone running from the wall.' He laughed. 'Maybe a jealous husband pursuing his lover's latest conquest. Anyway, I had mentioned it somewhere and I have had persistent enquiries from archaeologists in York, who claim to be authentic buyers of antiquities, wishing to purchase it. They offered a few pounds but not, I suspect, as much as they get selling them on abroad where there are a few millionaires wishing to add such antiquities to their collections and pay dearly for them. A ring worn by a Roman lady would fetch thousands on the market of men whose wives can have diamonds and rubies. These dealers have obviously never heard of treasure trove and, to put it mildly, they are merely smugglers.'

That rang a bell for Faro, taking him back to conversations with Dave Stokes. As the train approached, Hector shook his hand and, turning, looked as if he would like to kiss Imogen goodbye. Instead he said: 'Remarkable that neither of you have changed in all these years.' And then to Imogen he added, 'You look even better, if I may say so. Marriage becomes you.' Faro suspected this was delivered with a shaft of pain from what he imagined he had lost, while Imogen wondered briefly how the years would have treated her had she accepted Hector on that long ago visit.

To Faro, Hector said: 'You never change either, but then you were made out of solid Viking granite.'

The train steamed into the station in clouds of smoke. They boarded, and with thanks exchanged, Hector waved farewell, watching the train slide out of the platform, and with a final sigh for what might have been, he headed back to Elrigg.

CHAPTER NINETEEN

The journey was comfortable, but the sky darkened, and rain-streamed windows obliterated the kind of train journey both enjoyed. Changing trains at Newcastle and having just missed one for York, they took tea in the waiting room. Imogen bought a magazine and a newspaper for Faro, in which there was further information on a Yorkshire murder that had been intriguing him.

Imogen saw the headline 'Tadcaster railwayman released'.

'What's the latest?' she asked. As she wasn't usually interested in crimes, particularly domestic ones, Faro skimmed the details. 'The killer, a popular amateur boxer, has been arrested on suspicion of murdering his wife, accused by the next-door neighbour who heard them fighting and the wife screaming. When the police arrived, there was no body. The husband insisted she had left him, gone away somewhere.'

Faro stopped and smiled. 'Can't have a murder without a body, can they? Not in my experience.'

The York train arrived, so they found seats. Imogen brought out the books they had carried with them for such an eventuality. She settled down to read contentedly and Faro returned to his newspaper, scanning the various articles, apparently, but his thoughts drifted back to Elrigg and to Hector in particular.

This was the first time he had come face-to-face with another man who loved and desired Imogen, although he guessed there must have been many in her travels before and after they met. Never before, however, had he encountered a man who had wanted Imogen as his wife, and meeting Hector again after twenty years had given him food for thought as he kept reliving the moment when it became obvious that they had so much in common, and even in the short time spent wandering around the Roman ruins of Housesteads, it was clear that here were a couple united in their love of history, of antiquity.

Faro was aware of being ignored. No longer travelling abroad together in a scenario of Imogen's engagements in the capitals of Europe, the prospect of domestic life, first in Dublin and now in Edinburgh, with retirement hanging over them, had subtly changed the situation.

He was no longer his own man, free to live his own life, make his own decisions, go here and there as he pleased and as the mood took him. No longer alone, he must consult his wife Imogen on even everyday matters, small items of making trifling decisions that would have been indifferent to him, her choice of a cravat, or approval of a suitable garment to be worn on some occasion, her eager acceptance of an invitation to some meeting or persons she knew but were obscure or of little interest to himself. He now had to consider and – worse – to attend occasions with her that he could not dismiss or refuse because he could not do so without making up an excuse, and being honest was an integral part of his nature.

There was much in marriage, he was learning, of compromise, the desire not to hurt the other's feelings and to be always agreeable. They had only ever almost quarrelled once and that was over the unfortunate business of Imogen's unswerving loyalty to the still missing Kathleen Roxwell, despite Father Seamus's testimony to her character.

It had been a sad lesson and Faro swore that he would never risk again distressing the love of his heart.

He looked out of the window as the train approached York.

The sunshine, so disagreeable and fickle yesterday, had put in a warm and welcome appearance.

Imogen closed her book and smiled. 'Sure now, and it's stopped raining.'

Reaching over, Faro took her hand: 'Hopefully just a few more days, then we will be back in Edinburgh.'

'Home again. And not Dublin this time,' sighed Imogen.

Faro smiled. He was not displeased by this change of plans. It had seemed strange to call Dublin home when most of his life had been spent in Edinburgh. 'We must make the most of our days until the Hardys return. I still have to take you out on the river. You are a good sailor, of course.'

'On a liner, yes. Not so sure about a river, though. Depends on how well you row.' Imogen laughed. 'Anyway, it'll be a novel experience that will be something to look forward to.'

Arriving at the station, they decided it would be a pleasant walk in the sunshine down to the Dower House, as well as some much-needed exercise after sitting in trains.

Reaching the garden, Imogen said: 'I must let Mrs Muir know we're back early. She wasn't expecting us until tomorrow,' she added, hurrying towards the kitchen. That area of the house always seemed isolated, detached from the building entirely along a dark corridor, and it was a miracle, they had decided, that the food always kept hot on its journey to the dining room.

She found the kitchen area gloomy at this hour of the day, very little light penetrating through the one high window. She was glad she didn't have to spend time there, finding it depressing and lacking the cosy warmth that she always associated with kitchens. The rich smell of baking was absent. She felt surprised that Mrs Hardy hadn't made better, more cheerful provision for her servants.

Reaching the door, she heard the murmur of voices and opening the door called 'Hello!' to the three people sitting at the table near the kitchen range.

They literally jumped to their feet, hastily pushing back their chairs, all startled at her sudden appearance, for as she always walked softly, her approach had taken them unawares. In the gloom, there was Mrs Muir, Wilfred and a stranger. At least not quite a stranger. The man whose back was towards Imogen turned round, and to her astonishment she recognised Andres, the customer at the Four Seasons who she had almost forgotten. Andres, the young man she would always associate with the sixteenth-century Dutch portrait seen in the art gallery in Amsterdam long ago.

Mrs Muir stood up and attended to a kettle steaming on the range as Imogen approached. 'Just to let you know we are back, Mrs Muir,' she said, hardly feeling it necessary to qualify that they were a day early.

Busy with the kettle, Mrs Muir nodded, restraining a fit of coughing. 'Very well, madam.'

The two men continued to stare at her, making her feel like an intruder.

She said to Mrs Muir: 'Mr Faro and I intend going on a picnic tomorrow, perhaps we could have some sandwiches.'

Without turning, Mrs Muir nodded. 'Very well, madam.'

There was no more to be said except: 'Good evening, Wilfred.' He smiled an acknowledgement, but although she glanced towards his companion, the introduction to Andres was not forthcoming.

Back in the drawing room. Faro looked up from his newspaper:

'Picnic all arranged?'

'Yes, but something very odd.' Imogen frowned. 'Remember the Dutch fellow I told you about, the one who was at the flower shop on my first visit, then when I saw him again with Sofia he said he had never heard of Kathleen?' She stopped. 'I know he lied. Well, he is there in the kitchen, seems to know Wilfred.'

He was silent, and she said: 'Don't you think that is odd?' He laid down the newspaper. 'Is it, Imo? We don't know much about Wilfred or his friends.'

Faro thought for a moment and sighed. If the man in the kitchen, Wilfred's friend, was the same customer who Imogen had seen talking to Kathleen, and had subsequently denied all knowledge of her, then the last thing he wanted was a renewal of Imogen's concern about Kathleen, especially since the information from Seamus and Inspector Eastlake had made her realise that nothing dire had happened to her cousin, who had good reasons for wishing to disappear.

He said consolingly, 'Wilfred is a man of mystery, it seems, and he wants to stay that way.'

But before they went to sleep that night he said, 'You are quite sure that the man Wilfred was talking to is the same one you saw at the flower shop?'

Imogen didn't want to go into her reasons regarding Andres and the painting as to why she was so sure, but Faro had obviously been giving the matter a little thought.

She said yes, she was quite certain, and Faro didn't question her further.

When they awoke next morning, the sun shone. A brilliant day for a picnic and the basket Mrs Muir had prepared was waiting for them in the hall.

Imogen laughed. 'This is great. Going on the river will be quite an adventure.'

And so it was, but as with most of their plans, this one did not turn out quite as expected.

They set off soon after breakfast under a cloudless sky, and as they crossed the bridge leading to the hiring place for the boats, Faro felt quite jubilant and was looking forward to what promised to be a most enjoyable day if the weather held, for already there was warmth in the sun and the still air. The sea might well be in his Orkney blood, but he had never had the chance to encounter it beyond sailing on the ferry to the mainland and back throughout his life, while for Imogen, the waters around Carasheen were for the fishermen, and the wild Atlantic on their doorstep was not a welcoming prospect for the nervous sailor or swimmer.

Having decided to spend the entire day on the river, they had hired the boat accordingly, much to the boatman's surprise, used as he was to one or two hours away, but Faro had decided they should take it as far as they could upriver and Imogen had left a note for Mrs Muir, who had obligingly packed the picnic basket with adequate provisions.

Handing Imogen into the boat, Faro seized the oars and flexed his shoulders. He grinned; this promised to be the kind of exercise he saw little of these days, a delightful almost unique experience.

'We're off now.' From the other end of the boat, Imogen smiled happily from under a parasol, comfortably relaxed on the picnic rug. 'But don't overdo it, Faro, or you'll suffer for it tomorrow, using muscles not used to such activity. When you get tired I will take over.'

'Thanks, my dear, I think I will manage,' said Faro. Even if he had blisters by the end of the day, his masculinity was a little offended at the idea of being rowed up the river by his wife, who he insisted sometimes in pretending was a delicate female, although all the evidence of her activities over the years pointed to that assumption being far from the truth. In her early days at Carasheen, orphaned in childhood she had been brought up to deal with the tougher aspects of daily life, for there were no modern contraptions in her uncle's cottage and she had all the washing, ironing and cooking to do as well as milking the cow and feeding the hens. She had often compared those times with life in their elegant Dublin flat and the life she had as an acclaimed writer, with fine hotels and servants, and thought how horrified her fans would be if subjected to such a life of toil.

Observing that Faro, after an hour's brisk rowing that had carried them far upstream, must be growing tired and very warm with the exertions, she noticed a small promontory and tactfully suggested they should land there as a suitable spot for their picnic, if he could manage to moor the boat.

'I'm hungry, it's a long time since breakfast.'

'Me too,' said Faro, relieved that she had made the suggestion. 'Nothing like some healthy exercise for giving one an appetite.'

It was a little difficult anchoring the boat on the edge of a grassy slope. Faro leapt out first, gained a foothold, and having borrowed a rope from Molly's drying green for just such a purpose, he managed to moor the boat to a nearby tree. Having tested it first as a reliable post, he handed Imogen ashore on to a grassy stretch, with not too much sunshine and with bushes sheltering it from the wind.

'I wonder where it leads,' said Imogen gazing beyond the bordering trees.

'Probably we're trespassing on to someone's estate,' Faro replied, 'so we should be ready to leap into the boat and be off if they spot us.'

The picnic of salmon and cucumber sandwiches along with salad, followed by cheese and some rich fruit cake was accompanied by a thermos flask of coffee, rather ignored, since Faro had also carried a bottle of wine, which was much more to their taste. The meal over, they lay idly dozing contentedly in the sunshine until distant barking and the intrusive arrival of two Labradors decided them to return, however reluctantly, to the boat without the necessity of an introduction and explanation to the dogs' owner.

They moved quickly, with Faro restored not only by the wine but also by an application to his hip flask, declined by Imogen. Unloosening the boat, they set off, drifting back down the river towards the city. The return journey seemed shorter and, almost in sight of the Minster's towering height, they noticed a small crowd of people lingering by the landing stage.

As they disembarked, one woman rushed forward. 'There's been an accident. A body. What an upheaval. You just missed all the excitement,' she added. 'There was someone drowned. Over there on the other side, below the bridge – a lassie, we think. They wouldn't tell us anything, but it is a place that young people often go to end it all,' she added in a knowing whisper.

'A suicide,' whispered Imogen. Her face paled as she clutched Faro's arm.

Was that the answer? Oh, dear God, Not Kathleen! Please God, no, not that.

CHAPTER TWENTY

Faro could think of nothing to reassure her, for the same thought had somewhat sickeningly occurred to him. So often the case of a missing person turned out to be a suicide and he was taken back to Edinburgh's North Bridge and the immediate remembrance of the number of times in his career he had had the dismal task of recovering the body of a young girl. It was girls mostly, who had jumped to end an unhappy love affair whose outcome had been unwanted pregnancy.

Perhaps despite the theories put forward by Seamus and Eastlake, Kathleen's plans for disappearing had not materialised. Whoever had made them had let her down and, depressed and afraid of being imprisoned, she had decided to end it all.

It seemed such a sad and scaring note to end their own happy day on the river. As they paid extra for the day's hire of the boat and were preparing to find a motor or a carriage to take them to the Dower House, a police carriage drew up and an officer emerged with some constables.

Police, thought Faro, we didn't have a band of police in such cases in Edinburgh. Not for a suicide.

Heading through York, its sunlit day rapidly disappearing into twilight, they reached the house at last. As they were leaving the carriage at the entrance to the cul-de-sac, Dave Stokes was coming towards them.

'Well met!' And spotting the picnic basket: 'Been on the river?'

Trying to push aside the tragic incident they had just missed, Faro said: 'Yes, a great day.'

Dave nodded. 'Perfect weather for it. I've just called at the house, by the way. Babs asked me to invite you both for a meal if you have time before you leave. However, we gathered that you weren't expected back until tomorrow.'

He gave them a coy glance. 'Wilfred was entertaining his young lady in the garden. Weren't exactly pleased to be disturbed, if you know what I mean. On very friendly terms, they were.' He grinned.

Imogen laughed. 'I expect it was the maid, Molly.'

Dave shook his head. 'No, not Molly. I know her.' He shook an admonishing finger. 'I think they were up to something naughty cos they sprang up, looked a bit guilty, caught in the act as it were.'

'Good for Wilfred,' laughed Faro. 'We see little of him, bit of a recluse.'

'Is that so? Well, he said you were away for the day on the river. You missed it all,' he sighed and gave them an uneasy glance. 'Local tragedy.'

'Gather it was a suicide?'

'Might be so.' Dave shrugged and seemed to be choosing his words carefully.

'Young person, was it?'

'Aye, young woman. Perhaps she fell in accidently, we won't know until the doctor takes a look. Been in the water a day or two.' He paused. 'Might not be suicide, either.'

So that was why the police were gathering on the bridge. It might be a murder.

A young woman. The words sprang out at them and Faro felt again Imogen's hand tighten on his arm. Heard her intake of breath as the same thought went through their minds, her unspoken thought. Kathleen, oh dear God, not Kathleen.

Dave cleared his throat. 'We might need someone to identify her.'

A look of horror and a cry from Imogen. 'You think it-it—'

She was shivering uncontrollably, and Faro put his arm around her and led her to the garden seat nearby. 'I'll take care of this, Imo, I'll get all the details. You go inside. Let Mrs Muir know we're back and get her to give you a cup of tea to put those thoughts aside.'

She gave him a tragic look. 'I hope you are right – dear God, I hope so.'

Watching her walk across the garden towards the house, he went back to Dave. 'You can imagine how upsetting this is for Imogen with her young relative missing. As they only met once, I doubt if she has any photograph.'

Dave looked more uncomfortable than ever. 'We only have her description from the police records,' he added awkwardly, and Faro said:

'Yes, your father-in-law informed me that she is not only a missing but a wanted person.'

'Quite so,' Dave replied, obviously relieved that he did not have to explain that Mrs Faro's relative had a criminal record. 'Her description with an indifferent sketch is mid thirties, straight brown hair, mid height, slim.' He looked at Faro. 'Not much to go on, could apply to half the young women in York, but as far as we know they are all accounted for, home and safe.'

Faro guessed there was little point asking what about her last known address, since the police had very real reasons for keeping secret the reasons for their watch over her; doubtless that also applied to her workplace.

He said, 'As I expect you know already, the flower shop denied all knowledge of her on my wife's second visit.' He sighed. 'I realise the difficulty. It seems the only identification will have to rely on your records.' Even as he said the words he knew that would not be enough for Imogen, who would continue to be haunted by the question, was it Kathleen's unidentified body? And if so, then there would be the business of notifying Uncle Seamus in Carasheen.

He said reluctantly, 'I am sure Imogen will want to give you all the assistance possible.' He looked in the direction of the garden seat, but Imogen had gone into the house and he knew what to expect when he followed her.

She would already be preparing to face what she believed was waiting at the police mortuary.

'I believe she will be ready in a few minutes and—'

'No, no,' Dave shook his head. 'There is a problem, Faro.' He drew a deep breath. 'Her head – her face – is almost unrecognisable. We kept the crowd away from the corpse by letting them believe it was suicide. What I am trying to tell you, Faro, is that she had been severely disfigured, perhaps by contact with some floating objects in the water.' He paused. 'Or she was attacked by some person or persons is how we would call it officially. In other words, murdered.'

He put a hand on Faro's arm. 'I think you had better leave it with us, for a few days anyway, until we get the autopsy report.'

Somewhere in the distance in the tranquil sunshine that belied murder, the Minster's clock chimed. Dave said: 'I must go. I will keep you informed as soon as I hear anything.'

Faro went into the house. In the bedroom Imogen was already buttoning her jacket before the mirror. Her reflection told him all he needed to know. This was his Imogen, completely recovered, her tears dried, her mouth set in a line of determination. She gave a sad shake of the head as their eyes met. 'Yes, Faro, you know where I am going.'

He sat on the chair beside her. 'I think you ought to know that there may be a problem. She – whoever – had been in the water for a day or two.' He took her hand, grasped it firmly. 'There was some disfigurement.'

She straightened up and although her glance was tender, there was mockery. 'Faro, darlin', I'm not a baby, I don't need protecting. I've witnessed terrible things in my travels.'

And seizing her cloak she said, 'You must realise I have to do this. I could never rest content – I have to see Kathleen again – whatever . . .' And her voice broke again.

'Then I am coming with you. I'll see if John is around to take us.'

'No need. Let's walk. I know my way round York now, and it is only a short distance.'

A short distance that seemed endless despite their hurrying feet, eager to get there. At last they emerged from the sunlight into the darkened area of the police station, where Dave sat behind his desk.

After their conversation, he looked bewildered to see them. He bowed to Imogen and began stammering out excuses that this was not necessary.

Imogen held up her hand. 'Please, Dave. I only met my cousin once, but I think I will recognise her again. I remember her perfectly.'

'But—' Dave interrupted, his glance at Faro holding a frenzied appeal.

'Whatever she looks like now,' Imogen added firmly. 'If you will show us the way, please.'

They followed him down the narrow white-tiled corridor into the room of the dead, mercifully empty but for one sheeted figure.

Dave said in hushed tones: 'As you will notice, she is quite small. At first we thought she was a child.' He raised the linen cover on the shattered face.

Faro took Imogen's arm as she leant forward, and the attendant partly withdrew the sheet. Imogen gave a shuddering breath, turned to them, and said, 'This is not Kathleen Roxwell, I am absolutely sure.' And looking at Faro, she said in a tone of relief: 'I saw as soon as we came in. Kathleen is quite tall, my height, this poor soul is tiny.' Pausing, she regarded the sheeted length. 'Less than five foot.' And to the attendant. 'May I see her hands, please?'

He drew aside the sheet and Imogen said: 'Calloused, hard-working hands, like a washerwoman. And look, small, thick fingers.' Then indicating the left hand, she pointed out, 'No wedding ring.'

Turning to Faro, she said: 'Kathleen was wearing the claddagh, the traditional Irish ring of two clasped hands that the Crowes at Carasheen always wear. I remember that, because we were both wearing one and she touched hers so sadly, talking about her brief marriage and Henry drowning.'

She stood back from the corpse and clutched Faro's hand. 'Oh, dear God, the poor woman, but she isn't Kathleen.'

Dave thanked the attendant and led them out, glad indeed that Mrs Faro was free of this particular tragedy.

She asked did he need a statement of her affirmation for the missing person file and he shook his head. That would not be necessary.

As they emerged again from the antiseptic atmosphere and filled their lungs with fresh air in the now welcoming sunlight, Dave prepared to leave them. Imogen, remembering his wife was eager to visit the Dower House, suggested that he bring her around that evening.

Dave was delighted, shook hands and turned his steps towards the station.

Imogen took Faro's arm and sighed, saying she would have suggested supper but was not at all sure that Mrs Muir would be able to accommodate the extra guests at short notice. To tell the truth, Faro decided that Imogen was slightly scared of Mrs Muir. When he said so, Imogen laughed. 'Not really, Faro, she just doesn't like me. I can't think why.'

Faro couldn't think why either. That wasn't the usual reaction of servants encountering Imogen, always gracious and thoughtful in her dealings with them. He said: 'Perhaps she resents taking orders from anyone other than Mrs Hardy.'

'At least it doesn't affect her cooking and she is always friendly and polite towards you.' She thought for a moment. 'I presume those lavish quantities of food prepared include Wilfred. Don't you think we should indicate again that we would be pleased to have him join us? I keep sending notes to him.'

Faro shook his head. 'We've made the offer, nothing more we can do.' In truth, he wasn't all that keen on having Wilfred's company. He found the young man's attitude embarrassing, slightly scornful, and superior, as if the Faros were beneath him socially. Which seemed rather odd to Faro considering how the social boundaries never troubled either himself or Imogen, remembering their warm welcome by the Elriggs.

When he said this to Imogen, she reminded him that the Elriggs too had a dropout son who was now living in York. 'I suppose we should try to get in touch with him before we leave, let her know how he is. She was very anxious about him.'

A typical gesture of Imogen's but Faro had to respond. 'I don't see how we can do that without the least knowledge of where he might be living, or whether he would be pleased to see us. It might make him even more resentful of his parents, our stirring of troubled waters. Presumably what he most wants is to forget all about his background.'

Preparing to go down to supper, Imogen was brushing her hair at the bedroom mirror. Her eyes met Faro's in a tender glance and then suddenly tearful, she shook her head: 'Dear God, I wish I could forget it, but I can't get her out of my mind. That poor dead woman.' She clutched his hand. 'Oh Faro, I'm so glad it wasn't Kathleen.'

He kissed the top of her head. 'So am I, my darling. Your Kathleen is still alive. Somewhere. One terror removed.'

But it wasn't really. He knew that Imogen would still fear in secret and that it would haunt their remaining time in York. Suddenly he felt that the days ahead until the Hardys returned were tainted. It would not be a time to enjoy but a time to endure, and he wished with all his heart that they were rushing for a train today and heading homewards.

CHAPTER TWENTY-ONE

Dave and Barbara Stokes arrived while Faro and Imogen were in the garden being serenaded by the evensong of a multitude of birds, enjoying their favourite post-supper activity: sitting on a sheltered seat near the mosaic floor on clear, calm, warm evenings, to enjoy the end of the day and see the first stars appear; listening to that melody, which has been nature's music since the beginning of time, long before man walked the earth with his determination to change and destroy.

Leaning her head on Faro's shoulder, Imogen said: 'Just to think, Emperor Severus and his wife sat here as we do now, all those thousand years ago, and listened to the birds singing. Sure now, doesn't it give you good heart to know of the continuity of life.'

The sound of footsteps denoted the new arrivals. Dave and Barbara – or Babs – his wife, clasping her hands, on tiptoe overcome by the grandeur of the scene before her.

As they were introduced, Imogen had an instant rapport with this comely smiling woman who it emerged sang in the church choir. A pleasing laugh, a sense of humour and the perfect foil for the rather serious and occasionally pompous Dave. As Inspector Eastlake's daughter, Babs established a bond with Faro. Her fair curls reminded him of Rose and, like his daughter, she was also petite. He decided the two would have got along splendidly together.

Very impressed by the mosaic and its history, the Stokes went inside where Babs was silent – overwhelmed, Imogen guessed, by the interior. They sat down in the majestic, seldom-used drawing room while Imogen collected a tray of soft drinks and some biscuits from the kitchen.

Faro had provided Dave and himself with something stronger, and accepting the glass of lemonade from Imogen, Babs smiled and then gave a shiver:

'It's a bit spooky, though. Don't you think so?'

Imogen shook her head and said she thought it was atmospheric, not spooky or ghostly. Babs looked up at the portrait-lined walls. 'It's all those solemn faces looking down at us. Bit disapproving, if you know what I mean,' she added, but that nervous giggle out of politeness did not convey her real feelings of what she felt, which she was to tell Dave later.

Faro had brought in the newspaper to show to Dave, in case he knew anything about the Tadcaster railwayman.

'Oh yes, indeed. Not on our patch, but Babs has been following it from all the newspaper accounts.'

They looked at Babs who had gone suddenly quiet. She

said: 'I should jolly well think so. This husband Reg Bold is an ex-amateur boxer, a great brute of a man, according to the testimony of Mrs Evers – she's the neighbour next door who is great pals with his wife Daisy, who apparently is as small and delicate as her name. By all accounts, the walls in the railway cottages are thin as paper, so you can almost hear folk change their minds. Anyway, the two were always fighting and this particular night it was worse than ever. Mrs Evers heard Daisy screaming for help, so she rushed out and hammered on the door. Couldn't hear anything – silence. Then the great brute opened the door. It was still daylight and she asked to see Daisy. He said she was busy, come back tomorrow. She said, "I want to see her now." As she tried to force her way in, past him, she saw blood on his shirt and on the hall wallpaper.

'Next morning sharp, she was there at the door again. He said what was she going on about. They had made it up as always and Daisy had gone to the shops. But Mrs Evers didn't believe him, she remembered that blood on the wall and went back again later, sure that he was lying and that he had killed her, so she went to the local policeman. He wasn't keen to investigate, said it happened all the time, these domestic fights, and he could go out to one nearly every night. But she insisted, and she was in such a state he got help, but, by the time they arrived, there was no trace of a body but there were still bloodstains.

'Bold said what of it, when they were arguing she'd hit him and made his nose bleed. When the policeman asked where was she now, he lied again and said she'd left him, probably gone to her mother up in Newcastle, but she'd be back again, like always. No, he didn't have the address, he didn't get on with his in-laws. Hadn't spoken for years. Anyway, to cut a long story' – and it had certainly been that , thought Imogen – 'he was arrested on suspicion of violence—'

Dave interrupted, 'But they couldn't keep him indefinitely. However, although the wife hadn't shown up, they were pretty sure he had killed her. But although they made a thorough search, you can't have a murder without a body,' he added, looking at Faro for confirmation.

Babs said: 'Absolute disgrace, that's what it is, letting him go free. All these violent husbands who knock their wives about and get away with it. It's about time someone did something to protect women.' And straightening her shoulders, she gave Dave and Faro a hard look. 'I know you men don't approve, but it's time we women got a say in running the country. Time we had the vote and had some say – I approve of the suffragettes.'

Dave switched the conversation to ask Imogen about their home in Dublin.

Imogen said they had just moved to Edinburgh, it being more convenient with the train line as well as being near Faro's daughter.

Babs said they would love to visit Edinburgh sometime, but they heard Kerry was lovely and were thinking of having a holiday there next summer.

'Go in good weather if you aren't good sailors,' Imogen warned. 'That crossing of the Irish Sea can be terrible.'

The evening took a more convivial turn and the Stokes were delighted to discover that Dower House, among its many marvels, also counted domestic electric light in the main rooms. Babs and Imogen parted with promises to meet again. Babs it seemed was a regular customer at Mary's tea shop in the Stonegate and it was agreed hospitality should be returned by Babs and that the two ladies would meet there for tea and scones.

As she was putting on her bonnet, Babs said to Imogen: 'What is your husband's name?'

Imogen knew what she meant but said: 'It's Faro.'

'I know that's his surname, but what is his first name?'

'Jeremy.'

'Jeremy,' Babs repeated, 'that's a nice name, so why do you call him Faro?'

Imogen laughed. 'Because it suits him better somehow. When we first met, Jeremy sounded all wrong, like a little boy's name. It didn't seem right for a great big man who looked like a Viking, so I called him Faro as everyone else did.'

Babs nodded rather solemnly, regarded Imogen intensely for a moment, opened her mouth and closed it again. She had something to say beyond them being a handsome pair but was keeping it to herself.

Waving farewell, Dave said: 'Nice couple, aren't they? Well, was the house all you expected?'

Babs took his arm. 'The house is rotten at the core, cursed. I can't tell them that, but I just wish they were safely out of it, before it is too late.'

Dave looked at her. 'What on earth do you mean, "too late", love?' He laughed uneasily. 'They can't be in any danger, surely?' He took her hand. 'This is just one of your feelings, isn't it?' he added gently.

She smiled sadly. 'I can't help that. It's what I was born with. I never wanted to be like this, but I just know things.' She grasped his hand. 'Don't tell them, Dave. They'll be leaving shortly, and they are so happy. I wouldn't want to spoil it for them. Or worry them.' Through his arm he felt her shiver. 'But I felt it streaming out of the walls, like an invisible shroud around us.' She shook her head again. 'I don't know what. Not a ghost, but something terribly wrong. I wonder if the Hardys know? If they do they should have an exorcism. It's in sore need of bell, book and candle, if ever a house was.'

Next morning, Imogen decided to spend some time in the library, pursuing her research into the former female prison.

As she and Faro headed in that direction, she said that the library building was her particular favourite, situated in Museum Street beside a multi-angular tower, all that remained of the west corner of the Roman fortress. Outside were the Museum Gardens with pleasant walks and seats for a sunny day, where they might relax with a book or enjoy watching the passers-by. The backdrop was provided by the scant remains of the once-imposing thirteenth-century St Mary's Abbey, the abbot's house a nucleus of another ancient building, the rambling King's Manor.

Faro's usual destination on these excursions together was situated at the top of the gardens with the Hospitium down the slope, the Museum of Natural History with its important relics, including a superior well-preserved statue of a legionnaire and a swatch of auburn hair reputed to be that from a Roman lady.

Today, however, he decided to accompany Imogen into the library and spend a little time reading the newspapers in the Reference Room.

He hadn't discussed this with Imogen, but he had been very interested in Babs's account of the Bold murder. It reawakened those dormant feelings he might have had buried deep in his psyche regarding any unsolved mysteries. Having written Kathleen off after the revelations of her past via Father Seamus and Inspector Eastlake, the fact that she was still alive had been confirmed by the visit to the mortuary yesterday, and thankfully seeing that small body, obviously not hers, should have been the end of it. But for Faro this opened yet another of the kind of puzzles that most intrigued him. A murder without a body.

He read carefully the neighbour's account of what she had heard and seen, and taking out a map, had a careful look at Tadcaster. His mind was made up and when Imogen emerged from the reading room, he asked if she would like another train journey.

'A day in the West Riding of Yorkshire, exploring the countryside,' she repeated. 'Yes, that would be fun.'

'I thought we might have a look at Tadcaster.'

'Tadcaster?' She said. 'Oh, the place where that horrible murder was that Babs was telling us about.'

'The very one.'

Imogen regarded him slyly and shook an admonishing finger at him. 'Faro, you are up to something, I know all your old tricks. What is it this time?'

He shook his head. 'Just interested, you know. Here is a murder without a body but with exceeding possibilities. And,' he added triumphantly, 'I think I might have solved one bit of it anyway.'

Imogen's eyebrows rose at that. 'Tell me!'

'No, I want you to come with me, I might need your help.'

On the branch line train the day promised little to be cheerful about weather-wise, with a dour heavily clouded sky as they travelled across the bleak moors, occasionally dotted with sheep and less frequently by grim dark houses perched up high above rocky formations.

Although questioned frequently by Imogen, who was singularly unimpressed by the landscape, Faro refused to reveal what he had in mind. Instead he took out a guidebook containing details regarding Tadcaster and read them to her. 'Famous as a beer brewing area, the brewery is a fifteenth-century building once used as a meeting place by the Dissenters in the seventeenth century.'

'I've come across them in my research of the period,' said Imogen. 'Protestant Christians who separated from the Church of England.' She paused, regarded him with a sigh. 'I might have guessed what attracted you so much. The brewery?'

'Not at all, I'm a whisky man, as you well know, with an occasional taste for an excellent wine. However, there are some things that will please you. In its earlier days, it was a Roman outpost for York, known as Calcaria. Two miles away is Towton, where a bloody battle of the Wars of the Roses was fought in a snowstorm in March 1461, and a cross near the road to Saxton marks the field where fifty thousand men fought. It's said to be the largest battle recorded on English soil.'

Imogen thought for a moment. 'So if the brewery is not your main interest, what are we here for?'

In answer he tapped the newspaper. 'Murder, my dear.'

As they left the train, the pungent smell indicated that the brewery was very much in evidence, but they walked toward the main street, a terrace of tightly packed, mean-looking houses, which confirmed the neighbour Mrs Evers' words.

'What now?' Imogen whispered somewhat wearily.

'Let's track down Mrs Evers. You might have a word with her.'

'What about?' Imogen protested.

'You're both women. Think of something that might interest her.'

Imogen gasped. 'What on earth? Shall I be a Gypsy woman telling fortunes?'

Faro gave her an endearing smile. 'No, my darling. You are much too refined and well dressed for that.'

Imogen scowled. 'You might have warned me, and I could have brought some cleaning brushes with me. There are plenty back at the Dower House, new ones.'

'No, no, selling things is not you. Stick as near the truth as possible.' He frowned. 'You're a writer – how about the Wars of the Roses, this famous battle just down the road?'

Imogen gave him a hard look. 'I'm a bit young and a bit too Irish to pretend one of my ancestors fought there.'

A pause, then Faro said triumphantly, 'Got it. Say you work for a women's magazine and you're writing an article on keeping hens.'

As Imogen groaned, Faro took her arm and pointed. 'There's a woman brushing her front step. Ask if she knows Mrs Evers. That's a start.'

'Where will you be?'

'Keeping an eye on you, of course. Hurry!'

Imogen was in luck. 'Mrs Evers?'

'Why, that's me, love.' The rather stout woman carefully laid aside her brush, smoothed down her pinafore and adjusted her spectacles. 'And what you be wanting, lass?'

Imogen explained about hens and chickens and eggs, speaking very rapidly and hoping it went over the woman's head.

That had succeeded. Mrs Evers stared at her, astonished. She shook her head. 'I don't keep any hens.'

'Oh.' Imogen put aside the notebook, which she had been flourishing in a purposeful manner. And looking around she said regretfully, 'That's a pity. I don't suppose much happens here.'

It was exactly the lead needed. Mrs Evers eagerly took the bait.

'Oh, yes it does. That's where you're wrong. We had a murder – and what is more I saw it,' she added triumphantly.

Imogen looked suitably startled. 'Really?'

Mrs Evers gathered up the brush. 'If you have a minute to spare, lass, come in and have a cup of tea and I'll tell you about it.'

Imogen looked around. Faro was lurking about the lychgate of the churchyard. 'Oh, I'd love to, Mrs Evers, but you see my editor is with me.' She beamed. 'He is also my husband.'

'That's fine, lass. Bring him in, no point standing about out there in the cold.'

A wave to Faro, whose literary presence as well as his dashing looks clearly impressed Mrs Evers, and half an hour later fortified by tea and fruit cake, they emerged with almost exactly the words that the eager Mrs Evers had reported to the police, along with the parting words that she and Daisy had been lasses together and she still hoped that bugger Bold would swing for her.

Mrs Evers had even produced a photograph at Faro's request of herself and Daisy. Faro had studied it, then passed it on to Imogen without comment after giving it some thought.

Making their way back to the station for the branch

train to York, Faro said, 'That was very well worthwhile. You did very well, Imo, and I saw you having a long look at that photograph.' He paused. 'It confirms my suspicions.'

Imogen nodded and said: 'Daisy, poor soul, such a tiny woman. I think a visit to your Inspector Eastlake is in order.'

'First of all, I need to check my references.'

Imogen looked surprised and he said, 'I believe I have worked it out. We know he killed her but how he got her to York, that needs some clarification.'

Leaving Imogen back at York, Faro spent some time in the railway station, checking timetables and the particularities of goods trains leaving Tadcaster, since there were passenger trains only twice a day – early morning and late evening. If his theory was correct, goods trains would have been chosen by a railwayman carrying a large sack, which could be dismissed as material for work on the railway lines north of York.

The inspector was pleased, although surprised, to have Faro announced and sitting in his waiting room.

CHAPTER TWENTY-TWO

After conventional greetings, Eastlake realised that this was no ordinary visit when Faro stood up and said: 'I believe I am able to tell you the identity of the woman in the river.'

'The suicide we believed might be murder—'

'Is definitely murder,' Faro interrupted. 'In fact, we also have her identity. She is none other than Reg Bold's absent wife, Daisy.'

The inspector sat back in his chair and frowned. 'How do you come by that information, Faro? For a domestic murder, Tadcaster is a fair distance from York.'

Faro outlined his visit with Imogen and their meeting with the neighbour Mrs Evers and how it had ended with the production of a photograph of Daisy Bold.

'When we looked closely at that, the final part of the puzzle fell into place. Standing beside Mrs Evers, Daisy was a very small woman, almost childlike.' He paused. 'And so is the corpse lying in the mortuary.'

'No, we haven't the photograph,' he replied to Eastlake's eager question. 'We had no reason or authority to insist on taking it, however if it will help to "swing" Bold, as Mrs Evers put it, I am sure she will let the police have it as final identification.'

The inspector frowned, he looked doubtful. 'I am sure you are right, Faro, and at last it looks as if we have the murderer and the body. However, what I am finding difficulty with is one seeming impossibility. We know he killed her, but how did her body end up in the river at York, taking in the distances involved?'

'I think I have the answer to that too, Inspector. Bold works on the railway and there is a branch line for goods vans to York several times a day just across the road from where he lives. He would know the timing of these. If you check, you will find there is an early morning one at 5 a.m. that he frequently joined when he was on early duty.' He paused. 'Bold is a big strong man; there'd be few people about at that hour, so all he had to do was to carry her body in a sack and remain in the goods van until the train reached York. He was safe enough. There are no passengers on that train and I doubt whether the early morning railwaymen are much interested in what was being carried by one of their colleagues in a sack.'

'Very well,' said the inspector. 'So when they got to York, how did he put her in the river?'

'The part of the river where she was found is just a short distance from the station, and since there are sheds there for goods to be collected, he deposited her in one of them, locked it, went about his work and then, when darkness fell, probably after midnight, collected the sack, threw it across his shoulder and having carefully bashed in her face to make it unrecognisable, dumped her in the river near the place that suicides often choose.'

The inspector who had been making careful notes sighed. 'Bold must have nerves of steel.'

Faro smiled wanly. 'Nothing like the threat of a hanging to make even the most cowardly take on what normal folk would consider as impossible odds.'

Eastlake stood up. 'Well, Faro, thanks to you, we'll get this under way. Bold thinks he has got off with it, but we will rearrest him and tell him we have the woman's identity – if he knows he is beaten, we may get a confession. He might even think he can change it all and go for manslaughter.' He laughed hollowly. 'Might even think he has a chance, as their bouts of domestic violence were well known. Never meant to kill her, Officer – we've all heard that story. However, that bashed-in face would make it difficult for a jury to agree to a verdict of accidental death.'

As Faro was about to leave, Eastlake thanked him again. 'We would never have solved this one without your help, Faro. Quite amazing how you worked it all out. I understand now how you became a legend in your own police and why we all keep on calling you not Mr but Inspector Faro.'

'Ridiculous,' said Faro. 'I am simply "Mister" these days.'

'Not at all.' said Eastlake. 'We feel it would be disrespectful to drop your title. Retired or no, you have not lost any of your astonishing ability to solve crimes.'

Faro bowed. 'In this case, however, I don't deserve all of it. Some must go to your daughter, Mrs Stokes.'

'Barbara?' His eyebrows rose. 'Incredible – surely not? I know she has been following the case but surely—'

'Oh yes, indeed. Imogen and I had just been in for the melancholy task of identifying the dead woman.' He shook his head. 'We both hoped it would not be her cousin Kathleen, who is on your missing persons list. Your daughter and Dave were visiting us that evening and it was something she said in the course of conversation about Mrs Evers' report and the fact that the victim was a very small woman and the husband a big fellow that touched a chord for me. The woman we had seen in the mortuary was very small and I remembered Dave said that when she was found, at first they thought they were looking at the body of a murdered child.'

There was nothing more to be said.

They learnt later that Reg Bold had given himself up and, as Eastlake suspected, pleaded manslaughter, completely understandable to anyone who had seen this mismatched pair: a mountain of a man who hit his tiny wife regularly, leaving nothing but bruises, until the day he hit her too hard.

Reg wept bitterly in the police station. He hadn't meant to kill her and when he realised what he had done and what lay ahead, he panicked, lost his nerve and decided that he must get rid of her body. Putting on his thinking cap, he was working on the railway with ready access to a goods van, which offered unique opportunities for transporting a body. Perhaps moving it to another place gave him extra time too. If he dumped her in the river in York she might not be discovered for a long time and might even pass as a suicide.

Only the grim task remained to make sure her face wasn't recognisable. In the summing up at the trial, evidence was given by a colleague who Reg had asked for help to put the trunk on the train, saying he was selling some things in York and would need to put it in the luggage van. Reg had then only to wait until the hours of darkness, take her body out of the trunk and carry her down to the river.

In the Dower House, at breakfast that morning, Imogen put an arm around Faro's shoulders and kissed him gently. Beyond the windows, the garden was a scene of busy activity, birds sang and here and there a rabbit flicked a nervous ear.

'Dear little thing. He'll not be popular with the gardener.'

'If you see one, you can be sure there's a whole host of them busily multiplying in the hedgerows,' was Faro's cynical response.

Imogen was silent for a moment, then she took his hand and sighed. 'Faro, darlin', should we be thinking of leaving right now and going home?'

'You are right. Before any other mayhem appears on the horizon.'

Imogen laughed. 'It's all your fault, you know.'

'Are you being too polite to say that I am a jinx?' Faro sighed. All he wanted was to return to Edinburgh, settle down in their new apartment and see Rose again.

Imogen's delicate eyebrows arched. 'You do attract crimes, you know. I have noticed that the great Inspector Faro just has to put in an appearance anywhere. People who invite you should be warned to keep the homicidal department on the alert.'

He said, 'Nonsense.' But he had to admit that this had been a very curious holiday, and their hopes of leisurely exploring a new city from a base in one of the most ancient houses in York had not turned out in the least how they had expected.

'The Hardys should be home this weekend, according to Wilfred. I met him in the garden this morning and mentioned that we were thinking of leaving. He assured me he is quite capable of taking care of things until their return.' Faro shook his head. 'A difficult fellow. He has a way of smiling to himself secretly, as if he is vastly superior to the rest of us, which makes me very uncomfortable.'

'He's always very charming to me. Almost as if he was from another age: bows over my hand, that sort of thing. I feel as if I should curtsey.'

Faro laughed. 'You have that effect on all men, my dear, haven't you noticed? Well, I for one am sure he will be glad to see us go.'

Imogen sighed. 'So will Mrs Muir, although you seem to have found favour in her eyes. She just avoids me.'

'What about Mr Muir? Or is she a widow?'

'I imagine "Mrs" is just a courtesy title, like your Mrs Brook, used by housekeepers in high places to give them extra respect from the lower ranks of servants.'

Imogen opened her mouth and closed it again. She had decided not to bring up the subject of Andres again and dismissed as coincidence the appearance of the Dutchman in the Dower House kitchen, merely accepting Faro's explanation that Wilfred probably had business dealings with the flower shop. Most likely at this time of year the huge garden needed vast numbers of plants and bulbs from Holland.

She stood up and regarded him firmly. 'That's decided, then. We'll go tomorrow. I promised Babs we would have coffee before we leave and I can't let her down. Have a look at the afternoon trains.' She smiled. 'Home again. What bliss. Edinburgh is only a few hours away.' And with a happy sigh, 'Just think. Not much can go wrong between now and tomorrow.'

But Imogen for once was wrong. Much could and did happen.

Meeting Babs at Mary's cafe, which was within sight of the Four Seasons, and walking past the beflowered entrance, Imogen had to restrain an almost overpowering urge to go in and confront Sofia again. She resisted, told herself sternly that all matters concerning Kathleen's disappearance had been resolved and there was no point in muddying the now still waters.

Babs was waiting for her at a window table. Apparently, she was one of the regulars and Mary extended her usual friendly manner to include the elegant Irish lady with the red hair. Her customers were like friends, although she addressed each one formally as 'madam'. However, she seemed a little agitated today.

No, madam, she assured Babs. She was quite well, nothing wrong with her health. And biting her lip, she frowned. 'I am fine but little Amy – that's my young waitress,' she explained for Imogen's benefit, 'it's her I am concerned about.' Before Imogen arrived she had confided to Babs that Amy had not turned up for work this morning once again and that it was becoming a regular habit.

'All to do with this young chap she's keeping company with,' Mary added darkly. 'One of those foreigners, and I'm right worried about the lass. Good-looking fellow, but he's not good for her,' she added with a weary sigh. 'I have this feeling she's mad about him, anyone can see that – hints that he's going to ask her to marry him and take her to meet his family in Amsterdam.' She shook her head. 'I've tried to warn her. I don't believe a word of it – I can see how she's tempted, never knew her parents, poor bairn, came to work for me. I took her in from the orphanage when she was fourteen and' – her eyes filled with tears – 'I'm the nearest to a mother she ever had, so she tells me.' Pausing, she clenched her hands. 'I'm scared stiff something will happen to her, more than having her heart broken by a pack of lies.'

Imogen listened sympathetically. It was a story she had heard often before, unscrupulous men's betrayal of innocence, and it seldom had a happy ending, for all those promises were never meant to be kept, merely the sugar icing, a means to an end. In a short while, having had the thrill of having his way with a pretty young girl, the novelty would wear off or another prettier, more available girl would appear on the horizon and Amy would be discarded and forgotten.

'We women have always been the victims,' Imogen said to Faro, relating the story later. When he looked surprised, she said, 'Not you, Faro darlin', but few men are like you. You're quite exceptional.' She sighed. 'Do you wonder why I am in the fight for women's rights, to have the vote, the right to be educated and be put on an equal level with men?

'Poor Mary, she has a good reason to be concerned for her little protégée – she even asked Babs if her husband or her father, the inspector, could do anything about it.'

Their conversation was interrupted by a newcomer, who introduced himself as one of the archaeologists who had just returned from Egypt. He brought a message to them from Theo Hardy.

CHAPTER TWENTY-THREE

The archaeologist, whose name was Murray, was not bringing good news. Shaking his head sadly he said, 'The Hardys hoped to be returning with the rest of us today but, alas, Theo's leg has an infection and it must be attended to in case it spreads. He is being well looked after by Mrs Hardy, but he will need to remain in hospital over there for at least another week.'

Taking a deep breath, he went on, 'Mrs Hardy has asked me to see you personally. She is very concerned and anxious, as you would imagine, and asked me to tell you that she would be more than grateful if you could possibly extend your stay until she and Theo return.'

Pausing to regard their reaction, he looked around appreciatively. 'Such a delightful house, I am sure you must have enjoyed being here.' Imogen and Faro said they had indeed, and he sighed. 'Such a privilege, living on this spot where it all began, the mosaic tiles in the garden are the very threshold of York's history.'

'We have felt very privileged,' Imogen said.

Murray declined to stay for refreshment. 'I'd love to but must get home,' he said reluctantly. 'I don't live in York, we are way out on the outskirts. My wife and the children will be expecting me, and the stopping trains are infrequent.'

He left them, saying he would be in touch with Egypt and the Hardys would be grateful and relieved to know that they would stay a few days, more or less, and that the Dower House was in safe hands.

Watching him leave, Faro sighed wearily, and Imogen shared his disappointment, realising how much they had been looking forward to leaving for home, returning to Edinburgh on almost the next train.

Shaking his head regretfully, Faro said: 'So we are to keep the Dower House in safe hands, are we?'

Imogen had found that statement extraordinary too. 'What about Wilfred? He's Theo's stepson. Surely, he is capable of being left in charge? Why on earth don't they consider him capable of looking after the Dower House in their absence?'

'Indeed. "Safe hands" seems an odd way of putting it,' was Faro's comment.

It was as well they had decided to stay, as that evening brought unexpected visitors. The doorbell rang while they were having supper and as neither Mrs Muir nor Molly were apparently available, the latter having left for home, it pealed again insistently and Imogen ran to answer it in time to see the new arrivals turning on their heels and about to leave.

'Oh, Imogen, so you are still here. What a relief.'

Harriet Elrigg sprang forward to embrace her. 'Thought we were too late and that you'd already gone.'

At her side, Hector smiled and shook hands with Faro.

'Come in,' said Imogen, and as they followed: 'What brings you to York?'

Removing her bonnet in the hall, Harriet looked round appraisingly. 'What a lovely place, I'm so glad we caught you.' Then she sighed. 'What brings us to York at short notice? You might well ask. Nick, of course. Remember I told you when you visited that we were having problems?' A groan rather than a sigh. 'Well, matters have got worse. He wants to get married to some girl he's taken up with. A shop girl!' she added in a tone of shocked indignation that rang a bell for Faro and Imogen, as almost exactly the same reaction of the elder Elriggs when Mark, the son and heir, married Harriet the local vicar's daughter. Harriet Cairncross, who was not only considered highly unsuitable as the future Lady Elrigg, but was also in an advanced state of pregnancy.

'Nothing much changes does it?' was Faro's observation discussing it with Imogen later. His main concern not the Honourable Nicholas Elrigg's welfare but the presence of Hector Elrigg, already so overwhelmingly delighted to see Imogen again, holding her hand in greeting and gazing into her eyes just a mite too long.

Hector had been ignored thus far. Now Harriet with a fond glance in his direction was saying: 'Hector insisted on coming with me. Mark is much too busy with estate matters. Couldn't possibly tear himself away to come to York and see his son at this time of crisis,' she added bitterly. 'I was so glad when Hector offered, especially as he has always been so good with Nick. Seems to understand him, get through to him much better than his parents.'

Hector's shake of the head and glance in the direction of Faro and Imogen made it quite clear that this was not at all an unusual situation in families.

Harriet went on to say: 'We have long suspected that he is in bad company.' And with a weary sigh, 'As I told you, he is toying with turning Catholic and to that end has struck up a friendship with a priest – he wants us to meet him and we thought we might see him too, though heaven knows precisely what good that will do. His church is just around the corner. Hector looked it up on the map.'

Again, she sighed deeply. 'This foreign girl Nick has taken up with, we think Nick is hoping this priest fellow will marry them. She is Catholic, of course, another reason for him turning.' And suppressing a shudder. 'It is so awful I can hardly bear it, the thought of Elrigg with a Catholic and a foreign wife.'

Faro gave Imogen a quick glance. Harriet had obviously forgotten that his wife was an Irish Catholic. 'Where is Nick staying?'

Again, Harriet shuddered. 'Nowhere permanent – in some cheap men's boarding house, to judge by the fact that he wrote saying letters should be sent to him care of the post office. Not even using his real name – can you credit that? As if he was ashamed of us,' she added in shocked tones.

Imogen and Faro were aware that this was often the usual procedure for poste restante abroad, as Harriet continued: 'I hope he picked up my reply, about where we are to meet tomorrow. An appalling state of affairs, behaving in this furtive manner, like a criminal, as if he had something to hide.' Her eyes widened. 'We can only conclude that he is ashamed of us,' she repeated, her mournful glance begging reassurance and denial.

That came from Imogen, who put her arm around Harriet: 'I'm sure it is all a misunderstanding and that Nick loves you and his father. He would certainly not do anything to discredit Elrigg.' As she said the words, she was conscious of Faro watching her and that he was not at all convinced by her certainty regarding this rebellious lad.

As a distraction, Imogen offered to show them round the house, to have a look at the mosaic floor. Harriet was mildly impressed, her gaze critical.

'Our castle has been there for four hundred years,' she said. 'I don't suppose this house is more than two hundred.'

Faro pointed out gently that it was, as its name suggested, once part of a much older building, to which Hector agreed.

He knew York well and like Faro was a stickler for facts; when, in Elrigg, they had told him about the Dower House, he had decided to look up its history.

'There have been many houses on the site since the Emperor Severus lived here,' he told Harriet as they followed the Faros into the garden to see the mosaic floor, his particular interest.

Kneeling down to subject the faded remains to a careful scrutiny, he stood up again, looked across at the house and said: 'You may be interested to hear that I learnt that this survived and was all that was left standing after the disastrous fire.'

Imogen said: 'Yes, we were told the original house burnt down.'

'It did indeed, a massive conflagration and not just caused by an accident in the kitchen, as was put abroad. This was deliberate, by some right-minded upright members of the York guilds.'

The others gathered round him as they walked back across the garden. 'It had been in the hands of the Straightways family since Tudor times, but the latest incumbents, a couple of Regency lads, had declared themselves outside the law. Amongst other irregularities, it was more than hinted that they went in for black magic, evil worshipping and all that sort of nonsense, sacrificing children and in particular young local girls. It was too much for the guilds and hence the burning, carefully recorded as from an unknown source.'

Harriet asked: 'What happened to the brothers?'

'That is not recorded. They disappeared. Some say they were murdered and died in the fire.'

Imogen looked across at the Dower House, huddled in its ivy-clad walls like one settling down to sleep in the growing dusk.

'How dreadful,' said Harriet, happily conscious of the stainless reputation of God-fearing generations of Elriggs. As far as they knew.

'You didn't tell us any of this before,' Imogen said to Hector walking alongside her.

'You didn't ask me.' He smiled. 'Besides, I wasn't sure of my facts until you left, and when I knew we were coming here, I had a vague recollection of reading something about the Dower House.'

Imogen looked thoughtful and he said gently, 'You were about to leave. Would you have wanted to know all this grisly history?'

'We thought the house was enchanting.'

He shook his head grimly. 'There are two kinds of enchantment, evil as well as good.' He laid a hand on her arm, a gesture noted by Faro, a step behind them and listening to the conversation as Hector turned, saw him and smiled: 'It would have been a shame to spoil it all for you.'

In spite of herself, Imogen shivered. The garden at this hour of the day always looked faintly sinister, like some old landscape painting, its shapes unreal and she almost expected to see the cracks of age on it. She never liked crossing it alone, watchful and uncomfortable with every sound, every rustle, like the ghostly footsteps of all those who had lived and died there through the centuries, and she was always glad of Faro's presence, although pride would not have allowed her to confide her fears in case he mockingly dismissed them as the writer's too-ready imagination.

As they reached the house, no welcoming lights shone, since Wilfred's apartments and Mrs Muir's kitchen were on the north side and the great ivy-covered shape seemed to lurk, waiting to absorb them, while in the garden all was still, no trees moved and no birds sang. Looking back, Imogen saw their ghostly footsteps on the dewy grass, and under the stiffly silent trees the fragmentary stones of ruins, their purpose and origins as human habitations well beyond recorded memory.

Tonight, in the dark of the moon, the silence was oddly oppressive, and Faro was aware of it as Imogen moved away from Hector and took his arm, glad of the comfort and warmth of him.

Walking at their side, Faro asked Harriet: 'Where are you staying?' and Imogen cut in: 'Stay here. We could offer accommodation, I am sure there are plenty of rooms.'

Even as she made the offer, she had an image of the dark twisting corridors evolving into those shadowy, unused, unwelcoming rooms with their creaking seldom-opened panelled doors, up steep, short staircases she had never wanted or – to be honest – summoned up enough nerve to explore on her own.

She had another more urgent thought. The idea of approaching Mrs Muir to prepare rooms and extra meals was by no means encouraging. She was sure the housekeeper did not like her: although she tried to be friendly, Mrs Muir was cold and unfriendly. Wondering what she had done unconsciously to offend the housekeeper, one thing seemed apparent, Mrs Muir was not a naturally unfriendly woman if her behaviour towards Faro was any indication. She sighed. But then she should know, having observed after all their years together, that women of all ages found her husband quite irresistible. She sighed again heavily. Well, Mrs Muir would like her even less if she had to prepare for the Faros' unexpected guests from Elrigg.

However, it was obvious from Harriet's thanks and hasty explanation that she was to be relieved of disturbing the routine of the Dower House.

'We are engaged to visit with the Fowler-Rentons, they have a place just a few miles out of York.' Pausing, she smiled. 'Of course, we had no idea that you would still be here, and it was more convenient for Hector to book us into your station hotel until . . . until we see Nick,' she added wearily. 'Do have lunch with us.'

Through the darkness the Minster boomed out the hour and a mass of more modest clocks throughout the city followed its example in a twitter of response.

As they entered the house, preparing to take their departure, Harriet leant over and kissed Imogen. 'It has been so lovely to see you again, my dear, such an unexpected treat and such a relief. You are always such a comforting friend.'

Waiting while Harriet attended to her toilette, Hector picked up one of the bronze statuettes on a side table and regarded it intently.

Faro glanced at it. 'A reproduction, I expect.'

'I'd like to hope so. But this looks to me like an original piece, in which case it's worth a fortune and should be in a safer place than this, under lock and key in a museum.'

Faro and Imogen looked at each other. There were quite a number of what they had thought of as replicas scattered about the house, and after Hector and Harriet left with last-minute details repeated for the meeting with Nick the following morning, Imogen said:

'If Hector's assumption is right – and we have no reason to doubt it – you wouldn't need a gang to burgle this house. Just one man would be enough.'

'All things considered,' Faro agreed, 'it seems that the Hardys are rather careless, don't you think, if they are leaving priceless artefacts visible to anyone. Is this one?' he added, critically examining a small statuette of the dog god, which might have once graced the tomb of a lost pharaoh before its eventual appearance on Imogen's dressing table in their bedroom.

'It is quite exquisite but so are replicas, only an expert would know the difference.' She shook her head, having decided, based on Hector's discovery, that if there were genuine artefacts lying around, that was the reason the Hardys were so keen on having Inspector

Faro, with his impressive reputation, as guardian in their absence, although she wasn't keen on having him risk facing a possibly violent intruder. When she said this to Faro, he laughed.

'You do me too much credit, Imo. What about Wilfred?'

Imogen shrugged. 'Surely they would feel they could leave everything safe with him.' Pausing she added. 'I wonder if we should tactfully mention Hector's observations. Ask about insurance, for instance.'

Faro shook his head. 'I don't think that would be a good idea. Wilfred is difficult enough dealing with his stepfather's guests. I can only imagine some scornful rejoinder, putting us in our place, that sort of thing.' He thought for a moment. 'One thing we might do is walk round the house and make an inventory of any ornaments that look as if they are original artefacts.'

Imogen sighed. 'That is not going to be easy. I know nothing about antiques, do you, Faro? Or is this one of your hidden talents?'

Faro laughed. 'Alas no, I've always been too busy keeping up with modern discoveries. York, with its addiction to the Roman period, is for scholars and archaeologists.' He frowned. 'Aren't we forgetting Hardy's role? As owner of the house and the estate, surely he must be well aware that he is sitting on a treasure trove?'

Imogen sighed and replaced the tiny statuette, kissing it gently. 'I've grown rather fond of you, my wee doggie. And to think that you may have once graced Emperor Severus's wife Domna's dressing table when they lived here.' She smiled at him. 'Isn't that an exciting thought?'

'Indeed. Except that she was unlikely to have had anything quite as elaborate as one with three mirrors.'

But Imogen had a faraway look, dreaming of that long ago. Such romantic possibilities. Then she sighed and looked around the room, its corners dark in the flickering candlelight, which she preferred as they were more romantic than the modern electric lights. 'That is quite a history Hector told us about the house – black magic and evil brothers. Do you think it was true?'

'The fire certainly.' He shrugged. 'But the rest – who knows? The true story was lost long ago and is probably suffering from exaggeration – the situation embroidered over the passing years.' He looked at her quizzically. 'Would it have worried you, had you known before? Would you still have wanted to come?'

'Of course I would. It would never have worried me in the least.' Imogen smiled. 'We all invent our own ghosts and I'm all for a nice spot of juicy history to enliven the day. And this house is straight from the Gothic romances that are so popular in libraries these days.'

Faro was not quite as adept at stitching on romantic possibilities, and being a practical man was always concerned with more realistic prospects and darker suspicions. Imogen broke into his thoughts:

'There is one person who could help. If Hector is to be here for a day or two, seeing he is so knowledgeable,

I'm sure he would gladly make an inventory.'

Faro's nod and murmured reply concealed the certainty that Hector would be delighted with any excuse to spend some time going round the house with Imogen.

CHAPTER TWENTY-FOUR

Meanwhile, Nick Elrigg was dreading the meeting with his mother tomorrow, grateful only that his father would not also be present. Communication between them had grown increasingly tortuous as he grew older and came into contact with what he was pleased to call real life and people who did not live in castles and have titles and property to inherit. People whose interests lay in wider issues like making the world a better place for everyone, rather than in attending hunts and society balls to further business issues, or to make excellent marriages for sons and sell daughters to the highest bidder – particularly when property was involved. Whether that daughter was in love with the man chosen for them was scornfully swept aside. In Elrigg, as in most other upper-class homes, property and extending one's small empire was all.

These were the constant topics he brought under review with the new friend he had found in York. Some twelve years older than Nick, he shared his principles but from a different angle, not political but religious.

His new friend, Father Joe Ingles listened patiently, agreeing that more attention be given by people like the Elriggs to the condition of their tenants, to the homeless and hungry outcasts of society who, as a parish priest, were his main concern. He did not care for riches, although Nick found it astonishing that a fellow who had started off in Edinburgh as a policeman with a promising career should have made this alternative and quite astonishing choice from down-to-earth tough law-keeper to this, as he imagined, head-in-the-clouds clergyman.

Nick did not yet know the circumstances of what had brought about Joe's change of heart – that information was something he kept to himself. Nick knew only that Joe had decided that mending broken lives and saving souls was more desirable than walking the streets of Edinburgh on the lookout for sordid and unwholesome crimes, with a regular income for doing so provided by the City Police.

In one of Nick's long monologues, Joe realised that this new-found friend had not received a spiritual reawakening to the true religion but that the real intention of the Honourable Nicholas Frederick George Elrigg choosing to convert to Roman Catholicism was defiance of his father and the desire to throw a stone in the still but often muddy waters of the aristocracy.

Joe also realised that Nick was afraid of his mother

who was the real power behind whatever went on under Elrigg Castle's ancient battlements, where they still hunted with crossbow and arrows, a medieval ritual carrying on an ancient tradition before rifles and bullets made killing animals a little less arduous.

Nick implored Joe to meet his mother who, he inferred, was coming specially to York to convince him to put aside his present rebellion and slum living. She wanted him to return with her, turn over a new leaf and re-enter the portals of respectability by considering his father's latest suggestion of a suitable bride – a girl from the 'right' family who would no doubt go on to produce a son and heir and so secure future generations.

'Mother has conveniently forgotten and does not care to discuss the circumstances of her own very unsuitable marriage to my father. She was the local vicar's daughter, she and Father were childhood sweethearts. They had a shotgun wedding,' he grinned sheepishly. 'She was expecting me any day at the time. It did not go down well with Elrigg society.'

He laughed bitterly. 'She doesn't like it now when I have to remind her that history repeats itself. This time an Elrigg heir and an ordinary shop girl, a foreigner – and as if that wasn't the worst thing that could happen, a Catholic too.'

Joe watched his expressionless face and asked slowly. 'You are in love with her?'

Nick bit his lip, frowned, and with a shrug of resignation said: 'I think so.'

Joe gave him a hard look and he went on almost apologetically. 'You see, I don't really know what being in love is. But I expect I am, because she is really nice, quite pretty and we laugh a lot.'

That answered Joe's question. He knew all about what being in love was. He had suffered the agonies it can cause and would never forget the girl he had loved and lost so tragically. He wanted to say: being nice, pretty and laughing a lot are not quite the same as taking a partner for the rest of one's life, living with them every day for better or for worse. He kept back those warning words.

Suspecting that this foreign girl symbolised Nick's act of defiance, it had all the right ingredients to throw another spanner into the workings of Elrigg society.

'Is that your intention then, to marry this girl?'

Nick frowned again, a doubtful shrug. 'Well, I do like her, and I know it is reciprocated,' he added eagerly and smiled. 'I rather think she is in love with me and we would be happy together.'

Joe looked at him. Good-looking, yes, in a first-glance superficial way, but there was a weakness in those classical features too, hinting at caution and trouble ahead. Joe refrained from asking the obvious *Living on what?*, aware that Nick had little to offer in the important matter of earning his daily bread. He had confessed to Joe that he had not done well at school and had dropped out of university, neither regarded by his family as of any great importance since his future was secure and had been from the moment of his birth. However, to their alarm, Nick had set on a course determined to change all of that by becoming a rebel, and perhaps on what they regarded as bad advice, thinking he might seek his fortune independently. With no particular talent to offer in up-and-coming York, its growing affluence provided by the railway and a flourishing chocolate factory suggested endless possibilities.

Joe had met Nick in one of the dreary lodging houses for down-and-outs on his visiting list, and after their first few words realised that this lad was out of his depth, eager to tell his story to anyone with time and patience to listen. He needed help, and after a couple of meetings Joe had offered him lodging in the long disused church premises next door to St Columba's until he found suitable employment and a better place to stay. Joe had occasionally thought of making the lodging into a presentable flat but never had either the time or inclination. A couple of rooms adjacent to the church hall were adequate for his needs, and living on the premises preferable for the offices of conducting daily services.

Nick was touchingly thankful and, moving in with his few possessions, looked around and at the dictate of a hopeful imagination saw the dusty shabby rooms converted into a suitable first home for himself and the girl he now intended to marry. He had also almost immediately confessed, perhaps more from gratitude than conviction, thought Joe, that he had always been attracted to the doctrines of Roman Catholicism. Joe listened thoughtfully, but more cynically considered this to be yet another spanner to hurl into the sedate and conventional C of E at Elrigg, where his grandfather Rev. Cairncross's family had for generations past been the local vicars.

Joe sighed resignedly. Nick's was yet another confession to his ever-growing list. He dismissed a fleeting thought of the Dower House and sighed again. What was said in the confessional was sacred, the priest acting as mediator between the suppliant and God, with divine right to grant forgiveness. This he explained to Nick, ready to mutter away at weekly wrongdoings, such as laziness and telling white lies to this young foreign girl, pretending not to know that she was declining his advances and saying 'no'.

Confessions. What a burden the good Lord had placed upon priests. Having to bear so many secrets that could never be revealed.

He sighed more deeply this time. Secrets not revealed to the police not even to bring a criminal to justice and enlighten the suffering of those penitents anxious for reassurance, especially when one word from him could end it by revealing what he knew. But bound by the holy rules he had to remain silent and watch both parties suffer their own particular agonies.

In the meeting at the hotel the next day, coming in suddenly from brilliant sunshine and blinking against the dim interior, Joe was surprised by an additional two faces he had least expected in conversation with the rather stout and imposing lady he took to be Nick's mother, Lady Elrigg. At her side, hovering protectively, a good-looking middle-aged fellow, Nick's archaeologist second cousin Hector Elrigg, who he addressed by the courtesy title of 'uncle'.

But most surprising of all for Joe was to meet again, to his delight, Inspector Faro and his lovely wife, Imogen, who seemed to know Nick's family well. Introduced by Nick to his mother and then to his uncle Hector, Joe turned to Faro and Imogen.

'What a pleasant coincidence,' he said, greeting them warmly. 'I had no idea you all knew each other.'

'They are our old and dearest friends,' said Lady Elrigg sternly as he shook hands with them and Imogen smiled at Joe: 'So you are Nick's friend. What a small world.'

And after an exchange of the usual platitudes among friends who had met after a long period as well as ones who had never met before, they sat down to lunch.

Where newcomers regarded those who knew each other well with interest, some were like Faro, who felt the invitation had come by politeness only because Imogen had the Elrigg connection as Mercia's godmother.

He looked at Nick, the reason for Harriet's visit, beloved son and a constant matter of anxiety, and without any intuition a glance in Joe's direction suggested that they were sharing the same conclusions. Both had vast experience of human nature and a growing realisation, built on appearance, that this good-looking young man would never be able to make up his mind about anything for long.

Faro's main concern and disquiet, however, rested on Hector, seated by Imogen: heads together, they were laughing. Like old friends. He wished with all his heart that Hector was not here in York with Harriet Elrigg. His mission, Faro felt sure, had less to do with taking care of her than seizing the unique possibility, if the Faros were still in York, of seeing Imogen.

He looked across at them again. They were talking seriously now, Hector recommending something from the menu, and others in the restaurant must have noticed that they made a strikingly good-looking couple.

Observing them as old friends and remembering that Hector had once asked Imogen to marry him, in Faro's eyes – and perhaps those of everyone who knew him – Hector was still in love with her.

Faro suppressed a sigh and wondered why it should bother him; it was just that they were of a similar age to have much in common, and looked well together, while Faro was beginning to be made more aware that he was twenty years older than his still beautiful and youthful wife, increasingly conscious that because of his dangerous life with the police, and scars left from brutal encounters with killers, he was already beginning to find other disquieting symptoms. The injured ankle that kept him in Edinburgh after Imogen's departure for York still troubled him and he blamed it for not being able to run so fast, as it was becoming alarmingly difficult to keep up with Imogen's tireless energy.

She was seated opposite him across the table near

Nick and Joe and suddenly he was aware of her eyes on him, a look of yearning; a small and tender twitch of her lips said it all and told him that today, even though she enjoyed the attentions of Hector and had been sincerely glad to see him again, Faro was and always would be the love of her life.

As for Hector, Imogen had known from the moment they had first met, even though they were soon to part, perhaps never to meet again, that holding her hand in a gesture of farewell he was in love with her. She was sorry about that; love unrequited seemed such a waste of life and she must be cautious. She didn't want to hurt him or any man who loved her. Through her years of travelling alone she despised members of her sex who led men on with false hopes of promises, just for the satisfaction and pride that a man's admiration brought to their vanity, the pleasure of attention given to them regardless of the heartbreak and misery of rejection.

Aware that seated between two handsome young men made quite a picture on a dull day in a York hotel, Imogen had never considered her looks important. To those who knew her she said that beauty was merely an accident of birth that one did nothing to deserve. It could also be a curse in attracting attention from men for the wrong reasons, and she would always prefer to be admired and acknowledged for what she had worked hard to achieve in establishing a successful career as a writer.

Even as she thought of that she looked across at her beloved Faro, still unable to fully appreciate that this great man was hers until death did them part. Watching him talking to Harriet, she thought that in all the years they had been together, he had never seemed to grow older. The years seemed to pass him by, an excellent frame untouched by the years, the once fair hair still profuse, now silvered, the well-shaped nose slightly crooked, broken long ago in a struggle with a criminal, a mouth with full lips straight from the statue of a Greek god. Made for kissing, she had decided long ago, and the slightly narrow deep-blue eyes still seemed to dig deep into one's soul – one could never lie to those eyes, she had told someone, trying to describe him.

Such a dear lovely man, there wasn't much evidence of that selkie Orkney grandmother, except hopefully longevity linked to the remarkable fact that Sibella Scarth, lifted from the sea as an infant, had been a beauty who had survived well beyond a hundred years.

CHAPTER TWENTY-FIVE

Over lunch at the hotel, Faro and Imogen had been delighted to see Joe again and learn he was a friend of Nick. Both men were young, of a similar age, and with looks that would turn a few female heads, particularly the young priest, thought Harriet, and decided that his church's vow of celibacy was such a waste. He should have stayed a policeman and made something of his life. She could hardly credit it when Nick told her a few minutes ago that Joe had thrown away a promising career to take on a life of poverty in holy orders.

She considered him carefully. Well educated, most of it self-taught had she known, very nicely spoken, a soft gentle voice, she thought, and a direct gaze that would encourage one to confide, or did they call it confessing in that religion, she wasn't sure.

Nick had been telling them how grateful he was to Joe, although he was careful not to mention the shabby rooms next to the church he was occupying, sure that his mother would demand to see them.

Once Harriet got over the shock of wondering what her reverend father would say if he saw her sitting down to lunch with a Catholic priest, she gave vent to a sigh of relief. If one ignored the dog collar, he seemed just a nice, ordinary and attractive young man and not at all as formidable or unapproachable as she had imagined. Hopefully, was she seeing a gleam of light at the end of her particular dark tunnel? Perhaps she could get this young friend of Nick's alone and persuade him to use his influence to send her son back to Elrigg and to his rightful hereditary birthright in society, the life to which he and his future generations belonged.

The lunch ended and the group prepared to leave. This hotel was where the Elriggs were staying before moving on to the stately mansion a few miles distant, home of the Fowler-Rentons. Nick remembered a daughter met on one occasion when they visited Elrigg. A plain, dowdy girl with nothing to say for herself except that she would inherit the family fortune as an only child, she therefore figured high on his parents' list of suitable brides for him.

His mother had already urged him to come with them, assuring him that of course he had been included in the invitation, and he now wondered in fact if accessibility to the Fowler-Rentons' place was the sole reason for their visit to York. The sudden thought shocked him, it seemed so cunning and underhand, a betrayal that increased his determination not to comply with their wishes. Although he loved his mother he was appalled at her suspected treachery, and feeling mutinous he followed her upstairs to their suite.

Saying goodbye, Harriet had already taken leave of Faro and Imogen. It was unlikely they would meet again this visit, she said sadly. In fact, it had been such a bonus, such a stroke of luck that they hadn't left York, and she added a final word, renewing the invitation that they were always welcome at Elrigg at any time. Hector, meanwhile, bowed solemnly over Imogen's hand, murmuring that it had been such an unexpected pleasure.

It was a pleasure and even a relief for Faro to see him go, although he felt a pang of sympathy observing Hector's unconcealed adoration for Imogen, his heart reflected in his eyes, and realised that Hector Elrigg was by no means the first man to have loved and lost Imogen Crowe in her long career and in the many countries she had visited.

As the Elriggs disappeared upstairs, watching them go Imogen took his arm and whispered she would have greatly enjoyed being a fly on that wall, listening to the arguments that would inevitably follow, with Hector in vain trying to maintain peace and logic.

Meanwhile Joe was waiting for the Faros in reception and as he had church offices to attend, asked might he accompany them back on the short walk to the Dower House? Walking down the hotel steps, he asked whether they had they met Nick before.

Imogen said this was the first time as he had not appeared at his sister's wedding.

Joe shook his head and sighed. 'He was determined to avoid that important family occasion, although I did my best to try and persuade him to go.' He paused and thought for a moment. 'He means well, as young rebels so often do. They are so earnest in their beliefs that they have discovered a unique plan to set the world at rights and can't understand why no one discovered it before.'

Faro smiled. 'Are we not all brought up to believe that Jesus Christ got there before us?'

Joe laughed. 'As always, Inspector, you are right.'

Imogen said sadly, 'He has so much going for him, good looks and charm, but he seems very young. He's only just a couple of years older than his sister Mercia, and I can't help thinking that had he not been male and the rules of inheritance not specifically proclaimed him as the heir to Elrigg, Mercia might have it in her to make a better laird. I gather from Mark, her father, that she has a terrific interest in the estate and on occasions has already been known to challenge the factor's opinions.'

Joe was silent. Realising there wasn't much he could do to sort out the domestic problems of the aristocracy, he said: 'All I can do is provide him with a prop to lean on, someone to listen to his woes.'

Imogen asked delicately: 'What about this business of wanting to convert to Catholicism?'

Joe shook his head. 'Time for that later. He has a lot to learn and understand what he is taking on, first of all.'

There was a slight pause before Imogen said: 'And what of his intention to get married?'

'That I don't believe in at all. I am certainly not intending to encourage him to do either at the moment. Marriage for him would be a disaster.' He looked at her. 'I am not in the least convinced that he is a young man deeply in love and ready to commit himself to all that marriage implies.' He sighed deeply. 'I fear poor young Nick's idea of the shop girl and his conversion are just thorns to thrust into his parents' sides.'

Joe parted company with them at the entrance to the Ironside, heading to his church. They crossed the road into the vast garden of the Dower House where Wilfred was walking his dog, a small mongrel with a vast assortment of ancestors, including a whippet. Small, sharp-eyed, and always on a lead, on one occasion Imogen had stopped and, eager to be friendly, bent down and stroked his head, but the creature had cringed away.

'What is his name?'

Wilfred, regarding her overtures with distaste, had said: 'Ratboy – catching rats is his main purpose.'

'Really, are there rats in the house?' she asked in alarm.

He had looked at her scornfully. 'There are rats everywhere. You cannot go more than ten yards in any direction here without encountering them.'

She had always been scared of rats and Wilfred's reply, although possibly exaggerated, was no consolation.

'Do they do a lot of damage?'

'We manage to keep it to a minimum,' he said coldly,

as if the subject bored him and giving the lead a sharp tug, he had moved off. She watched them go and thought there was none of the loving companionship between a man and his dog that she had been brought up with at Carasheen and had witnessed in Edinburgh with Rose and Thane in Solomon's Tower, or of Thane's utter devotion to Jack and their little girl Meg. Thane was one of the family, as Imogen believed a dog should be, not like this poor wee mite, thin-looking and afraid, as if he was more used to kicks than cuddles.

'When I met them walking in the garden for the first time,' she told Faro, 'I realised the true meaning of the word "hangdog".'

At least he was quiet or had been trained not to bark. Not a guard dog, they would never have known there was a dog in the house, and watching them from a window or meeting them occasionally in the garden, she felt that neither dog nor master were out for pleasure or exercise, judging from Wilfred's reaction. True, he often carried a rifle, so perhaps he was on the lookout for something for the kitchen pot, although it had never yet appeared on the menu.

Ratboy's treatment bothered her. 'Surely a dog should be allowed to roam free, instead of pulling along on a lead,' she said to Faro. 'It's a shame to keep him restrained with all those trees and things dogs like to sniff, especially in such a lovely garden.'

As far as Mrs Muir could see there was nothing Ratboy could destroy as the formal borders protected the plants and her vegetable garden was safe from all but wild birds. There were daffodils everywhere now; soon they would die off and bluebells would take their place.

On the day after Harriet and Hector visited, Imogen met Wilfred in the garden alone, carrying a rope lead and rifle, but there was no sign of Ratboy for whom he was whistling shrilly.

'You can't have lost him, he must be somewhere,' she said.

Wilfred merely scowled and ignored her. At last Ratboy appeared, ran to his feet and crouched low. Imogen felt shocked, the cringing dog obviously expected a blow, which she imagined would have been gladly forthcoming by the angry look on Wilfred's face had she not been present. Bending down, muttering angrily, Wilfred fixed the lead and hurried back to the house, ignoring her remark: 'I think he must have found a rabbit hole.'

Both soil-begrimed muzzle and front paws indicated that he had been digging and as she continued her walk to collect flowers to take to Mary for her tables when she met Babs in the cafe tomorrow, she came across upturned earth, a newly dug hole quite near the mosaic floor. Curious, she laid down her flowers on the seat and kneeling down, she saw a bone.

Had Ratboy been burying a bone? Taking a nearby stick, she poked – and sat back in horror.

A bone, no! Dear God, the lower jaw of a skull with gleaming teeth grinned back at her. She ran into the house to get Faro and found a visitor waiting for him. Inspector Eastlake stood up. 'Your husband asked me to look in but I'm a little early. I have tickets for a concert.'

'He should be here any moment,' Imogen said. 'He was going to look something up in the reference library. But thank heaven you are here, Inspector.' She shivered suddenly. 'I would have been coming for you. I've just found the remains of a skull. I think Wilfred's dog dug it up in the garden. Please come.'

The inspector needed no second invitation.

As he bent over the displaced earth, Imogen watched horrified.

Is it – was it – murder?

He straightened up, laughed and patted her arm. 'Mrs Faro, if you will get me something to wrap it in, I'll have it looked into at the station. But nothing for you to worry about, I assure you. Even at first glance, I think that this fellow is probably hundreds of years old. Young when he died, such splendid teeth. They looked after them then; not so much sugar around in those days – healthy diets.' And carrying it carefully as they walked back towards the house, he said: 'Anyone digging in this garden, or on the estate surrounding here would most likely unearth human remains from time to time.'

Pausing, he pointed towards the gate. 'All this land around the Irongate here was once a kirkyard attached to the Catholic church down the lane there, in medieval times.'

In the hall she found a discarded paper bag. 'Will this do?'

'Excellent,' he said, and tipping the skull in carefully he regarded her solemnly. 'Happens quite frequently, the archaeologists are always finding human bones and think nothing of it, in fact any digs below the surface in York are liable to hit ancient burials and whole skeletons. Not only from Roman times, there were the plague pits outside the walls. Like the one under the station hotel that they discreetly don't mention to customers.'

In the middle of this conversation, Faro arrived and was told about his wife's dramatic discovery. After giving Faro a look at this lower jaw of an ancient skull, it appeared that the reason for the inspector's visit was to invite them to a police concert.

After he left, Imogen said: 'After Ratboy's discovery I was so glad to have Inspector Eastlake on hand. I panicked, I can tell you.' She shuddered. 'Thought we might now have a murder on our hands.'

He smiled. 'You always have a mind to murder, Imo.'

'I got it from you. It must be catching.'

Faro rubbed his chin thoughtfully. They were both thinking the same thing about that invitation. Was this the inspector's sole reason for coming in person or was he seizing an opportunity to look over the premises?

Faro's frequent visits to the reference library were adding to the picture he was compiling, the still almost negligible suspicions carefully sifted through as Imogen asked whether it had occurred to him that the gruesome discovery might be the reason Theo never allowed the archaeologists access to the gardens.

'They are all very keen to get in here because of the historic association with Emperor Severus,' she said, but Faro merely frowned. He was almost certain of the existence of a deeper reason, remembering Hector and the artefacts.

And again, a thought shared as Imogen said, 'Do you think this is the reason the Hardys can afford to live here? Has Hardy come upon a treasure hoard and is keeping it secret? Has he been selling pieces and smuggling them abroad over the years?'

CHAPTER TWENTY-SIX

There was no reason now to cancel appointments, their reluctant obligation to the Hardys had made that clear, so meeting Babs next day morning at Mary's cafe, Imogen was surprised to see at her side a dashing young man in the gold-braided uniform of a ship's captain.

Babs smiled at Imogen and said proudly, 'This is my brother-in-law, Captain Brian Stokes.'

Watching him bow gallantly over Imogen's hand, introduced by Babs as her new best friend, she added: 'Brian comes to York quite frequently while his cruise ship is in Hull and we're delighted to have something entertaining to offer him this time. As well as the pleasure of meeting you and Inspector Faro, he will be coming to the concert with us.'

As they sipped coffee and ate Mary's delicious scones, Babs teased him about whether he had found a wife yet on all his exotic cruises.

He gave an amused but weary sigh. 'Don't listen to her. She has been trying to marry me off to any of her friends who would have me. Regardless of the fact that I am a bachelor born and bred, and have every intention of remaining so.' Although used to Babs's comments, Imogen recognised that this particular bachelor had an eye for the ladies, judging by his appraising and lingering glances in her direction, and Babs too noted that, as she told Dave later, his younger brother was quite swept away by her lovely new friend.

He insisted on paying the bill and as Mary thanked Imogen for the pretty posies of flowers for the tables, Imogen was aware that she was not her usual cheerful self. Amy the young waitress was not in evidence, and when Babs tactfully commented on the fact that Mary was attending to the tables herself this morning, Mary sighed.

'Amy didn't come in this morning, third time this week. I'm really worried about her, not angry – she would never lose her job with me,' she added loyally. 'Know that, for like I told you, she's as close as any daughter could ever be.' And in a whisper she added: 'It's that foreign fellow she's obsessed with. Daft about him,' she groaned. 'I wouldn't care, I'd make allowances for young love, but I'm not happy about him. I'm sure my poor Amy is in for a broken heart.' She paused and shook her head. 'I just hope he doesn't get her in the family way and leave her.'

She would have said more about what was really worrying her, but the young sea captain was waiting for the ladies at the door. Some of her money and valuable jewellery had gone missing from the house and she suspected Amy's sweetheart had pinched those antique earrings and bracelet when he was visiting her while Mary was at the cafe. She was in a cleft stick, all right: she couldn't mention it, Babs being married to a policeman, and Amy would be implicated. But one thing she was now certain about. This wasn't a romantic elopement, as Mrs Stokes had hinted. Amy was in some sort of danger and if she didn't appear by tomorrow, Mary was going straight to the police station to notify her as a missing person.

Seeing them to the door, Imogen was not taking Babs's romantic suggestion lightly. With all that Mary knew about that girl, she must have had an instinct that something was amiss.

The Stokes were delighted that Faro and Imogen had accepted Eastlake's invitation to the annual police concert in the aid of charity for bereaved gentlewomen, particularly those whose husbands had died in heroic activities, such as firefighting, accidents on the railway and other dangerous occupations. It was a big occasion and Dave said this would present the Faros with the lighter side of police life in York while Babs told her eagerly not to expect any long speeches or anything of that nature.

Dave laughed. 'It is very low-brow entertainment, a bit lower than I imagine you are used to in the higher echelons of Edinburgh, Inspector Faro. You know the sort of thing, though, comic acts and dancers.'

'Yes,' said Babs, 'but there is one serious turn, a ventriloquist whose dummy tells fortunes.'

Dave laughed. 'If anyone believes them. It's all a bit of a joke.'

'Not always,' said Babs quietly.

'Oh, do be quiet,' he said with a tender glance. 'You have to forgive Babs, she's inclined to be psychic. It's a condition no one seems to have found a cure for.'

Babs giggled and gave him a playful smack.

They were to meet first of all at the Stokes's house near the Bootham gate. Once the family home of Inspector Eastlake, after his wife died some years earlier the Stokes were persuaded to sell their own modest terrace house and move in with him. The arrangement worked exceedingly well, a simple happy home life very different to the ostentatious Dower House and the kind Faro and Imogen would have chosen had they decided to live in York.

When they arrived, Brian was already well established, drink in hand, and after an introduction to Faro, in the course of conversation it emerged that Brian had his own ship now and ran a passenger craft taking people on short cruises from Hull across to the Continent: Amsterdam and back again was high on his itinerary.

In the crowded concert hall, they found their reserved seats. Brian had managed to have a seat next to Imogen and was resplendent in the gold braid of his captain's uniform in the front of the stalls, alongside the Eastlakes as honoured guests preparing to enjoy the usual variety theatre programme. A slightly subdued, more modest imitation by local ladies of the daring high-kicking chorus line of Le Moulin Rouge was followed by excerpts of *La Bohème* by two performers from the opera society.

Their act was a great hit, encores were demanded and when the applause settled down, two comics in drag took the stage telling slightly off-colour jokes that received roars of laughter.

In the interval, Imogen and Faro saw the two comics at the bar and said to Brian that they made very convincing females.

Brian laughed raising his glass to them. 'Very convincing ladies, except for the hands, legs and feet.' He shook his head. 'Definitely men's and no amount of disguise could conceal that ultimate giveaway. Mind you, I approve of this new fashion that with shorter tighter skirts, ladies now display ankles, which could have been considered indecent in the old queen's day, when it was rumoured she even put covers on the legs of the grand pianos.'

Faro laughed when Imogen looked at him and asked if that was true. 'He has been to Balmoral,' she said to Brian.

Faro shook his head. 'I'm afraid I was too busy chasing criminals on that occasion to notice the grand pianos.'

'But then you never notice nice legs,' she said reproachfully, a little hurt, proud of her small feet and dainty ankles that were no longer to be hidden under vast skirts.

In the men's room, Brian, who had already had one drink too many, confided in Faro that women's legs were his main attraction. 'I notice them quite casually, even walking in the street, and more often than not I'm surprised when the face I expect to be young and a stunner, is that of an older woman, like Babs's housekeeper.'

Faro was silent and regarding him curiously. Brian asked, 'With some men it's bosoms, of course. What's your preference?'

Faro found this conversation mildly embarrassing, shy at discussing sexual matters with other men, even in his young police days.

He shrugged and smiled. 'A little higher, attractive hair and eyes.'

Brian looked at him and nodded. 'Well, you certainly got both in your lovely wife.'

The bell rang announcing the interval was over and next, topping the bill, the ventriloquist who, contrary to the usual, was a female, the dummy a wicked-looking male doll with a painted smile, in evening clothes on her knee.

Babs whispered to Imogen: 'She is good, definitely a true medium, often seems to hit things bang on the truth and that's why Pa and his colleagues invite her. Once she even helped them track down a criminal. That is why the police associate with her. Madame Felicitas is a true Romany who would never have been invited or accepted to such a gathering normally.'

As the polite applause welcomed the medium, Babs said, 'She is amazing, she can even find lost people sometimes.' At which point Imogen made a resolve to be introduced to her afterwards and ask about Kathleen.

There was a now hush in the hall, everyone preparing to listen carefully and take the newcomer seriously, some shouting questions to which the dummy gave sharp and witty answers. The theatre lights had been dimmed with only the spotlight on the Romany ventriloquist and the dummy she called her son. Ignoring calls about did he have the crystal balls, she merely smiled and said that wasn't needed, her son had all the answers. Shouts varied from the serious to the ridiculous, such as where did someone leave his lost spectacles and who stole my party shoes. One policeman asked daringly where they might find the latest bank thieves.

The dummy's name was Archie, and watching him turning his head here and there to answer questions from the audience, he seemed incredibly lifelike and Imogen was suddenly afraid. She felt her flesh creeping, certain that this woman was no music hall joke and this act was to be taken seriously.

Finally, there was a call for silence and some eerie music on the violins in the orchestra. Archie looked back and forth as if searching the hall. Silence for a moment, then he croaked: 'I have a message from the beyond, I think it is from Egypt, because there is mention of the ancient rulers, the pharaohs.'

This was greeted by stifled laughter as he continued. 'The message is from a woman who has passed over, a royal personage who says her name is Amy . . .' He paused as though listening and whispered: 'Say that again. Oh, Amelie. She says their son is ruling now but no one knows, it is still their secret. This pharaoh is in danger.'

Archie's head sank to his chest in apparent exhaustion. He seemed to be asleep and then jerked awake, head up grinning at everyone and throwing out a succession of spirit visitors for the audience's attention.

Imogen realised that most were lucky shots in the dark, deceased mothers and lost babies, husbands and dead wives. Everyone applauded as Archie and Madame Felicitas left the stage, but at her side Imogen was aware that Faro was not responding.

Together they left the auditorium and went into the reception area where drinks were being served to guests. She looked around for the medium, but Babs said she had left, she never stayed afterwards.

Imogen sighed and whispered to Faro, 'A pity, I was hoping to have a word.'

He gave her a sharp glance. She shrugged. 'There was someone who might have known about Kathleen.' Standing by his side and looking at his face intently, she was certain that, although he smiled and applauded the superintendent's welcome speech with its witty comments, he was not quite himself. He turned down the offer of a drink when they were passed round, and later declined the invitation back to the Eastlake house for a nightcap, saying he had already had a nightcap too many. He was tired. She saw him exchange a look with Eastlake, and there was a whispered aside.

On the journey home in the cab provided, he was strangely quiet. Imogen took his hand as they walked across the garden where the dark house waited. He put down his cloak and sighed. Yes, he said, he had enjoyed the concert.

Imogen looked at him. 'But what did you think of the Romany lady and her remarkable assistant?'

Faro shivered. 'Never cared for ventriloquist's dummies, bit weird. Fortune-telling is daft enough.'

'Not always. My grandmother was a Gypsy born and they have strange gifts.'

He regarded her sternly. 'As do you, my dear.'

She smiled. 'And you don't have to be a Gypsy to know one truth that never occurred to anyone else.' Pausing, she put a hand on his shoulder. 'I am sure that the significance of reading "pharaoh" as a ruler of ancient Egypt and not as Faro, your name as pronounced in Orkney, would not have been understood by anyone in the audience.' She waited for comment but there was none, he seemed far away, and she asked gently, 'That gibberish about Amy—'

'Amelie,' he interrupted sadly. 'Amelie was her name. Haven't thought of her for years.'

'And a son? What was that about?'

George, Grand Duke of Luxoria, was one secret he had told no one, not even Imogen. Now he said wearily:

'Sit down, Imo darling.' This was one promise he could keep no longer, Amelie long dead would have to forgive him. And he told Imogen how it was. Amelie Grand Duchess of Luxoria was goddaughter to King Edward's mother, the old queen. She had escaped to Scotland from the husband who meant to get rid of her to seek sanctuary with the queen at Balmoral and everything went wrong. It ended up with Faro, who had been commanded to look after her, listening to her tragic story of a cruel tyrant and a bitter marriage to a serial womaniser. All her husband had ever wanted of her was an heir and when she failed to produce one, with his current mistress pregnant, Amelie narrowly escaped with her life. Once she was dead he could marry this other woman, who he was confident would bring him an heir.

Listening to the bare bones of it, Imogen was thinking doubtless Amelie fell in love with Faro. What woman wouldn't, she thought, based on her own feelings that he was irresistible. Or perhaps the Grand Duchess had regarded him only as her means to keep her kingdom and stay alive.

Faro was saying he was never quite sure how it happened. They spent one night together. It had a strange magic, something he had never known before or since, as if they were trapped in a web of enchantment, and Amelie wanted to stay with him, but she had to leave. Nine months later he received a cryptic telegram: WE have a son.

Imogen had listened silently. 'Did you love her?' she asked slowly.

He shook his head. 'Not as I love you, infatuation perhaps. The madness of a moment.' He regarded her sadly. 'Would it matter to you after all these years?'

She sighed. 'Not the infatuation bit. You were never my only lover, I never pretended that.' She thought. 'Only the son you were telling me about. The child I could never give you.'

'We never wanted children, Imo. I had Rose and Emily and it was too late by the time we got together. You were travelling and we always seemed – to me, anyway, but perhaps as a man, I was presuming wrongly – that we were enough for each other. Were we not?' he added gently.

She didn't respond to that question, aware in the depths of her secret heart that a child would have been the fulfilment of her love for Faro. 'This son, have you ever met him?'

He nodded. 'Once, once in a lifetime. He was at boarding school in Scotland, and as the man he acknowledged as his father had died, the Queen commanded that I was to take him back to Luxoria so that he could take his rightful place by his mother, her beloved goddaughter's side.'

'Did she know you were his real father?'

He laughed. 'Probably – I wouldn't be surprised. The Queen knew everything.'

'Even down to her personal detective being father to a member of European royalty? Well, well.' She frowned.

'Did you never want to meet him – secretly, I mean? Did he know who you were?'

'I think he guessed the moment when we were travelling across Europe and we happened to see our reflections in a mirror.' He smiled wryly. 'He was my image and I knew then how impossible, even dangerous, it would be if I ever showed my face in Luxoria.'

'What happened to Amelie when you met again?'

He sighed. 'I saw him reunited with her, safe. And I knew the reason for the urgency of my mission when she told me that she was dying.'

He was silent and passed a hand over his eyes. 'Dear God, I haven't thought of her for years. A deadly secret, Imo. And so it must remain. You are the only living person who knows the truth.'

She laughed gently. 'And I am not likely to go around boasting that my husband fathered one of the heads of European royalty.'

CHAPTER TWENTY-SEVEN

At an interval during the concert, Brian bowed low over Imogen's hand and including Faro asked if they would like to come on one of his cruises for invited York passengers to Amsterdam.

Faro was delighted at the prospect: living in the Dower House despite the surrounding attractions of York was beginning to feel somewhat claustrophobic.

Overheard or perhaps even suggested by Babs, she whispered later to Imogen that his was a business that seemed to thrive, and although he evaded saying how much these short cruises took, she guessed they were very costly, as on the occasions when she and Dave went along she noticed that the passengers, none of them known to either of them, were wealthy folk who wished to stay incognito. She also suspected that not travelling under their real names included not associating with the other passengers.

Imogen was surprised at that, but Babs said the cruise offered quite a daring experience, especially for young men. Brian had told her that all cities, like London, Paris, Edinburgh – and even Brighton since the notorious Prince Regent's days – under the respectable front they exhibited to the world had their secret hidden places, where high-class brothels and opium dens could be frequented, and those in Amsterdam were not regarded illegal as in Britain.

She smiled at Imogen. 'It has been known for even local worthies to slip away for the weekend, especially as Brian is so well organised – he even hires a special compartment on the Hull train. As for what is on offer in Amsterdam, Dave and I are quite immune, I mean to the sex and opium, but we like the museums and the pretty houses and the food is quite different from ours. Such a novelty. I remember meeting the Hardys on one of our jaunts. They were also pretending it was the Rijksmuseum that was their reason for being there.'

Babs regarded their acceptance of Brian's offer delightedly. She was obviously very fond and proud of her brother-in-law and enjoyed his impromptu visits.

'I believe he has an apartment in London too. We are always being urged to visit him there.' Looking fondly at Imogen, she clapped her hands. 'This is such an opportunity for you and Inspector Faro, if there is a cabin available. They are usually booked months ahead.'

'The ship is quite tiny as cruisers go,' Brian

said, 'built especially for negotiating up rivers and canals, but strong enough for the sea crossings to the Continent.' He frowned at Imogen. 'Perhaps Mrs Faro and her husband would prefer one of the hotels in Amsterdam.'

Babs giggled. 'Not those you recommend to your wealthy passengers, Brian, they nearly always provide extra facilities, at a cost.'

Brian choked uncomfortably and had the grace to blush.

Imogen said hastily, 'Oh, Faro and I always prefer being on the sea. My husband is an islander from Orkney and will enjoy your cruise, but please, please don't call him "Inspector". He has been retired for a while now—'

At her side Babs said in shocked tones: 'But everyone calls him "Inspector". It's a mark of respect.' And to Brian: 'No one can forget or want to forget that he is a legend in his own time—'

'I think he would be very happy for everyone to forget it,' Imogen interrupted hastily.

Faro was very enthusiastic at the prospect of visiting a new place and even the anticipation of a new train journey down to Hull. And Amsterdam would be an interesting new experience; he had never been there and the idea of a sea voyage, even a short one, was most appealing.

Because of his Orkney background, the sea drew him like a magnet and this totally unexpected cruise with the Stokes and a change of scene away from their enforced stay at the Dower House was just what he needed. Feeling it necessary to oblige the Hardys and stay on when he had actually been on the verge of a welcome return to their new home in Edinburgh, had led to the Dower House becoming quite oppressive.

Imogen was quite excited about it: 'I'm so glad you approve, I want you to see Amsterdam. I haven't been there for – oh, twenty years.' She remembered it was in the Rijksmuseum that she fell in love with the sixteenth-century portrait of Andres. How delightful it would be to stand before it again, although she had only the vaguest memory of the man who had been at her side on that occasion. One of many she had met and been attracted to briefly before Faro entered her world, claimed her life and swept away all memories of previous loves.

And so the plans were made. Brian had all the necessary arrangements in hand. Fortunately there had been a late cancellation due to illness, or so it was reported, so with a cabin vacant they would leave by early train to join the cruise at Hull. Brian promised to accompany them ashore at Amsterdam, show them the sights, as he called them, and how to enjoy the night life since York, he said, was so innocent compared to the wicked goings-on over on the Continent.

Dave and Babs were pleased that the Faros would share this new experience with them, with Babs already making lists of what were bargains for Imogen to buy in Amsterdam, and bubbling over with enthusiasm. Her inspector father, when told of their plans, added his comments that it would be a unique opportunity for the Faros to see the lighter side of life on the Continent. He always appeared slightly ashamed, even apologetic, for his son-in-law's brother, who he considered a bit of a rascal, suspecting that some of his activities with that ship trembled on the edge of the law.

Dave, however, was devoted to his brother and as a retired policeman turned a blind eye to his activities even if, as Eastlake insisted, he would not be averse to smuggling if the price was right.

Dave said sternly it was none of their business, something he preferred not to think about.

Inspector Eastlake had to wearily agree. He liked his happy family and, near to retirement, wanted nothing to disrupt it. He was deeply devoted to Dave and only sorry that Brian, whose parents had wanted him to follow in his elder brother's footsteps, had refused to become a policeman and joined the mercantile marine at seventeen. He went on to make excellent progress as well as his fortune, eventually leaving with enough to own his own small ship.

Boarding the train next morning, Faro was surprised to see Inspector Eastlake in the station, hovering near the platform.

'Are you coming with us?'

'No, not my scene at all.' At that Eastlake drew Faro aside and looked around to see that they were alone before continuing, 'It is you I wanted to see.'

He coughed nervously. 'I wonder if I might ask you a great favour. I am expecting a small package from Amsterdam and it occurred to me that you might be of assistance, especially as it is essential that it is in my hands as soon as possible.' He paused. 'You see, it contains material that is vital as evidence for one of the cases we have under investigation, and I decided not to have it sent by mail.'

As Faro was wondering why he had not asked his son-in-law this great favour, Eastlake said, 'In matters of such importance to national security, I don't wish to burden Dave, and of course not Brian – or anyone else for that matter.' And regarding Faro intently, he went on, 'I made this decision to ask you because of your connection with the police and your reputation. I know you can be trusted implicitly with a highly secret mission.'

This put Faro in something of a quandary: although he felt he could hardly refuse a request from a police officer in high authority to help an investigation, he had a certain reluctance about the responsibility of accepting such a mission.

'It will be handed to you during the cruise as inconspicuously as possible from a contact who is helping us, and I will be waiting to meet you here on your return.'

Eastlake made it sound very simple but nevertheless it was still the sort of thing linked to secret agents and spies, which Faro was very glad never to have seriously been a part of, although he had shared many secrets relating to the royal family as personal detective to the late queen.

The train was gathering steam, doors were being closed, the guard's whistle in evidence and Eastlake, after exchanging hugs with his daughter, left them.

Babs had been surprised to see her father there. Observing him talking so earnestly aside to Faro, she said to Imogen, 'You must be very important people for Pa to spare time in the early morning,' while Dave added with an admiring glance in Faro's direction, 'Only time he has come to see Babs and me off at the station was on our honeymoon, long ago.'

The journey was not as impressive as Faro and Imogen had hoped. The heavy clouds in York had followed them and now deposited streams of rain down the windows, obscuring what landscape managed to emerge, a hardly admirable sight mostly obscured by passing through areas that had long ago fallen victim to the rapid advance of the Industrial Revolution.

When they reached Hull, all that Faro remembered of the city was that it was the birthplace of a national hero, William Wilberforce, who in 1833 had succeeded in getting the act for the abolition of slavery passed through Parliament.

At the railway station they picked up a carriage to transport them with their luggage to the dock where the cruise ship awaited. Surrounded by noise and bustle everywhere, with rain thankfully ceased and a thin sun putting in an appearance, they went up the gangway. Imogen, now very clothes conscious about what one wore on a cruise, was subjecting the other female passengers to a careful scrutiny, sure too late that she had packed all the wrong clothes. The few other passengers, however, had one thing in common: expensive-looking leather luggage. The ladies were wearing expensive-looking furs, suggesting that they were not trusting the unreliable spring weather. The men were elegantly attired too, wearing headgear more in keeping with an evening out than a brisk sightseeing tour of the city.

Imogen glanced at Faro. Hatless as always, he had as little taste for toppers and bowlers as he had for the well-trimmed moustaches and beards, the fashion set by King Bertie. However, his decision met with Imogen's approval. She was glad that he had always been clean-shaven and intended to remain so.

The cruise had eight other passengers: two tall ladies in their late thirties, unescorted, who remained on their own, talked to no one and kept their own company, and were sometimes to be seen holding each other's hands on deck; two couples, one a man and his wife – were they married to each other? Imogen wondered, considering their self-conscious wariness; then another youngish couple who were definitely not married to each other, this given away by the nervous, slightly excited but apprehensive look about them that suggested they were slipping away to Amsterdam on an illicit and very expensive weekend.

Her friendly smiles ignored, Imogen turned away, hoping silently that they would find it worth all the trouble.

As the ship slipped down the river, leaning on the rail, enjoying the slight breeze, were three of the quartet of tough-looking men she had encountered at the Four Seasons and Mary's cafe. She had not expected to see them in this least likely place, Brian's cruise ship, their city suits exchanged for working men's overalls. That was indeed strange, and she felt a need to point it out to Faro who had not seen them before. But Faro, whose mind was now fully engaged on the rather tricky business Eastlake had thrust upon him, was not inclined to regard Imogen's remark about their appearance with any significance.

'What are they doing on a cruise ship?'

'Working, by the looks of them,' was the reply.

'I last saw them making a delivery of flowers from Amsterdam to the Four Seasons flower shop.'

Faro did not consider this remarkable and said: 'Possibly they need the money, and I dare say our Captain Stokes pays well for experienced engineers, especially those well acquainted with Amsterdam.'

Imogen had to accept the logicality of that response, although she felt uneasy, apprehensive even, as she remembered in particular the incident when she had forgotten her umbrella in Mary's cafe, and now the presence of the three brought back full force her anxiety – her concerns regarding the missing Kathleen that she had been persuaded to put aside.

Seeing her doleful expression, Faro said: 'They are Dutch, they could be just getting a passage home, you know.'

Not in workers' overalls, she decided, already pondering how she could talk to Brian and share her uneasy feelings.

CHAPTER TWENTY-EIGHT

Babs was waving. 'Come along you two. I'll show you your cabin. Next to ours. And very nice too.'

It was indeed. Babs opened the door into a small but elegantly furnished sitting room where a large porthole offered starboard views and privacy on the portside. Delighted by Imogen's enthusiastic response, she walked across to a handsome bedroom which had, rather than the two sleeping bunks Imogen had expected, a large double bed, fitted mirrored wardrobe and a separate cupboard containing a washbasin and WC.

The interior of the ship was much larger than the exterior suggested. Cleverly designed so that nothing was wasted, every available space was put to good use. Having their meals at the captain's table was optional, some passengers for obvious reasons desired service from stewards in the privacy of their cabins. Brian told them that Babs and Dave always sat with him and the

Faros were happy to join them, while a few of the other passengers were seated in what looked at first glance like a small, elegant cafe with subdued lighting. The kind one would expect to find in expensive restaurants ashore, if it wasn't for the portholes overlooking the sea.

Brian said the weather forecast was good, it promised fine weather and a smooth crossing. After the meal with its excellent four courses and appropriate wines, finishing off with brandy and liqueurs, Brian grinned.

'This is normally where the gentlemen retire with brandy and cigars, however on my ship they have to smoke on deck – that's the rule. There is no facility for a game of billiards, although there are card tables and you are welcome to a game of poker.' And to the ladies, he stood up and announced:

'The lounge is yours, to play cards or whatever your inclination.'

Neither Imogen nor Faro had any desire to be separated. They had spent little time together and decided to wrap up well and sit on deck to watch what promised to be a splendid sunset over the sea.

There were few couples who shared their enthusiasm and the only crew Imogen observed were two of the overalled ones dismissed by Faro when they boarded as workers. Imogen, however, had an uneasy feeling that there was more to their presence than merited casual employment.

Faro was answering her questions almost by yes or no and had also seemed quiet, almost watchful, throughout the meal.

'I'm cold,' she said. 'Let's go inside.'

As soon as they closed the door she turned and said: 'Well, Faro and what is wrong with you?'

'Nothing, my dear,' he said brightly, removing his jacket. 'Now what should be wrong after that excellent meal?'

Regarding him candidly, she replied: 'Nothing, as you say, darlin', but you're not yourself.' He was frowning and she asked: 'What was all that business with Inspector Eastlake as we were leaving?'

He shook his head. 'What business?' but his pretended innocence was wasted on her.

'Come now, you know me better than that. After all these years, you can't keep secrets from me. I can read you like a book.' She pointed a finger at him. 'You and Eastlake, you are up to something. He certainly was not behaving like a man who had just come to see his daughter off on a cruise.'

Faro sighed and put down the guidebook he had hoped would distract her attention. 'You win, as always. Very well, I have to presume that Eastlake will approve of this secret being shared with my wife, who would have made my life and this cruise a misery otherwise.'

She sat down, smiling. 'Come along, let's hear it. Cross my heart and hope to die.'

'Hope not,' he murmured, and pouring her a brandy and himself a preferred and quite substantial dram of whisky, Faro told her in as few words as possible of the arrangement with Eastlake.

She listened silently. At the end, she sighed. 'Is that

all? No identification who this fellow is to be, what he looks like?' She shook her head. 'I don't like it, Faro, I don't like it one bit. You don't know what you have let yourself in for. This might not be just an innocent handover. It might be dangerous.'

'Dangers are something I can deal with. I've spent a lifetime with them, so I'm used to it.'

She regarded him, her gaze solemn and somehow sad. 'Not any more, Faro. You gave that up when you retired.' And she didn't add what that short silence was indicating, that she was afraid for him.

He stretched over and took her hand. 'Sorry, you made me tell you, but let's not start building mountains out of molehills. Let us just enjoy Amsterdam and take what comes. Perhaps Eastlake's confidant never got the message we presume was sent to him. These things happen.'

They slept well that night, the gentle motion of the ship on a smooth crossing in a cloudless starlight sky a bonus to the warm comfort of their bed. Next morning, the sounds outside indicated that they had reached Amsterdam. Although it was early, Faro was awake, washed, shaved and walking the deck while Imogen still slept. Watching the busy dockside's activities, bigger ships that overshadowed Brian's cruiser and reduced it to the proportions of a rowing boat were busy loading and unloading bigger cargoes than his select passengers.

Now, leaning casually on the rail, Faro decided this would be the perfect opportunity to be approached by

Eastlake's mysterious messenger. But apart from some of the passengers, including the two silent ladies who had decided to walk a few steps on land, he had the area around the ship to himself.

Before going ashore, while the ship's arrival and papers were formalised by the captain with the customs, the passengers were left to enjoy a substantial breakfast. At last it was time to find their way into Amsterdam, where Brian had a guide awaiting to show them the city. 'A time-saving measure,' he said, and with a wink, 'he knows all the places that will interest you most, gentlemen, as well as the best goods to buy.'

After following the guide – who spoke excellent English – for a while, Faro and Imogen realised they would be happier armed with Faro's excellent guidebook read avidly since the cruise was planned. Now, stepping discreetly aside from the guide's orbit, in the shadow of a shop door, he unfurled and consulted a map.

Whilst he did so, Imogen gazed along the canal road. What they hadn't expected were bicycles; although now no longer novelties in Britain, where the motor car and cabs had taken over from carriages, here they seemed to be popular and in everyday use.

Faro put aside the map, as Imogen pointed towards them with a meaningful glance. They had both tried out Rose's bicycle as her recommended means of transport in Edinburgh. They could ride without falling off and the roads with their linking bridges by the canals would be safe enough.

Walking swiftly, a little distance away they discovered that bicycles could also be hired, and the man seemed used to English tourists. He offered them a tandem, indicating with a smile that the gentleman could do all the hard work pedalling on the front seat.

And soon they were breezing along enjoying the scenery, stopping at a cafe at the base of one of the tall, elegant houses on the canal, and as it was some special anniversary with flags flying and bunting across the houses, they were soon stopping to admire local residents who wore the traditional Dutch costumes, complete with clogs.

After some bicycling along the sides of the canal, they decided to exchange the tandem for a horse-drawn carriage, their final destination the Rijksmuseum. Imogen had long awaited this moment and as they climbed the steps and entered one of the galleries with their exhibitions of Rembrandts and Vermeers where Faro was inclined to linger, Imogen was now eager to return to the gallery she remembered and the painting of Andres she had fallen in love with and been haunted by ever since that day in Amsterdam long ago.

She remembered the exact space where it hung and almost ran towards it.

But the space was empty. Empty.

She stopped, clutched Faro's arm. 'It's gone, I can't believe it. It's gone.'

He stared at her in amazement as breathlessly she explained to him about her earlier visits.

'Darling, Imo,' he said consolingly, 'don't take on so. You were just a girl. That was twenty years ago. Galleries do change their exhibits from time to time, you know. Wait a moment,' and he went over to a gallery attendant seated at the door of the room where he tried unsuccessfully in English to ask about this missing painting.

Imogen stepped forward. Her French was excellent and fortunately understood by the attendant, who merely shook his head sadly. He had never seen the portrait the lady was interested in; it was before his time as he had been here for only the past ten years. He confirmed her worst fears. He had no idea where it might have gone, maybe to another gallery. He had never heard of this particular portrait by Vermeer. Too bad.

Such a disappointment, Imogen thought, walking away sadly, even knowing that Faro and the attendant's conclusion was quite right. Twenty years was a long time for pictures to remain static in a popular gallery that needed to keep up with changing times and fashions in artistic taste.

She sighed, realising that the moment she had been looking forward to as soon as the cruise to Amsterdam was mentioned had gone for ever and taken with it the dream portrait of a young man she would now never see again.

They returned to the ship and were greeted by Brian, eager to know if they had enjoyed Amsterdam, what they thought about it all. Had they been impressed by the different kinds of food and what had they bought as souvenirs?

'None? Not even a pair of clogs each?' He was surprised and felt they had wasted golden opportunities spending so much time in an art gallery among paintings from the past, when the present had so much on offer outside at the various places the guide had so enthusiastically indicated.

We are such a disappointment to him, thought Imogen. She felt as if they'd let him down and wasted such a great and generous chance he had given them.

'You see, we found bicycles for hire and couldn't resist them as a means of getting round the city,' she said to Brian, who shook his head. Bicycles had never figured in his life's adventures.

Faro made no comment throughout their conversation, his thoughts were elsewhere, alert now for the messenger. Half expecting that he would try to deliver the package while they were walking round the city, he soon gave that up as very unlikely, unless he had a list of everyone going ashore, so he must be on the cruise ship.

The following day's programme of seeing the additional sights Amsterdam had on offer was cut short by heavy rain, and for Faro there was still no sign of Eastlake's expected messenger. However, to compensate for a disappointing day, passengers were treated to an excellent supper with free champagne and entertainers – clog dancers as well as a baritone.

From the amount of applause the latter's appearance brought forth he was apparently a local hero, an opera singer who rendered a mournful ballad, the words in Dutch beyond the Faros, only his facial expressions, his tearful eyes telling them that this was a tragic tale of lost love.

Again, a cloudless night, so they decided to spend some time on deck. Returning first to their cabin for something to wear more appropriate for the night air, Faro went to the table at the porthole, turned and said: 'Imo, this cabin has been searched, presumably while we were at dinner.'

'How do you know, it all looks the same to me.'

'Observation and deduction,' Faro sighed slowly. 'Small things have been shifted. These flowers, for instance, were facing a different way. A book I left on the table has been opened and the bookmark replaced on the wrong page.'

'That's the observation, what is the deduction?'

'We still have to work that out. The beds were made this morning, the room dusted earlier and nothing's been disturbed.'

'One of the stewards, perhaps?'

'Unlikely,' said Faro, opening the wardrobe and as a matter of precaution going through the pockets of his outdoor jacket. To his surprise he encountered a sealed envelope. He withdrew it.

'Our messenger has delivered,' he said triumphantly. 'This was not in my pocket when we were out today. It has simply been put here while we were at the captain's table.'

'Before or after the room was searched?'

'Presumably no one thought of searching in an obvious place. It's like disguises. They don't expect the everyday, the ordinary, and were wasting time in search of a secret hiding place, often a weak link with even hardened criminals.'

'So the messenger must be one of the crew.' Or one of the faintly sinister trio of Dutchmen in their working overalls, thought Imogen, but said nothing as Faro felt the envelope and said, 'Hardly a package, it feels just like a letter.'

'What are you going to do with it?'

'I'm going to wear my jacket and lock the envelope in my case – seeing as I am carrying the keys for our luggage, it should be safe enough.'

As they prepared to leave the cabin, Faro said, 'I'll send a wire to Eastlake, as we arranged – message received – not to the police station, but to his private address at Bootham Road.'

On deck a chilly wind was ruffling the sea; it would no longer be warm, with clouds gathering on the horizon and bringing rain in their trail.

The passengers were gathered in the lounge. There was a small orchestra and couples were dancing, even the two ladies, holding each other stiffly and solemnly.

'Shall we?' whispered Imogen.

Faro sighed. 'If you wish, Imo, but it is not one of my few talents, take my warning.' And as they walked towards the floor, he listened to the band. 'And I haven't had much chance to learn to waltz.'

After a round of the floor, Faro began to feel dizzy and worse, nauseated. He drew Imogen to the side seats, sat down, then stood up hastily. 'Darling, I think I'm going to be sick.'

'You're never sick,' she said.

'Mussels!' he replied and fled across to the exit.

He was just in time to reach the rail and part with the excellent dinner the cruise had provided.

He stood leaning there, hoping that was the last of it and he would feel normal again. He leant over, looked down at the sea and suddenly the deck was empty no longer.

Rough hands seized him.

As he tried to whirl round and face his attacker, he saw the flash of a knife blade and a voice said:

'Hand it over or you will be very sick when we throw you into the sea with your throat cut.'

CHAPTER TWENTY-NINE

His reaction was instant, born out of a lifetime of such dangers. Still feeling weak, he was aware that he had come face-to-face with his adversary, and that whatever the package contained was valuable enough now to cost him his life.

Whoever his attackers might be must have been watching him. It was even possible that his plate of food had been poisoned.

His thoughts of necessity were rapid but disordered in the face of death. He was a big strong man still, however, and not the poor, sick older passenger they expected to deal with. An easy number. As he turned and bent down as if helpless, suddenly he leapt up and butted the man who stood over him in the ribs. He heard the knife clatter to the deck and as the winded man tried to regain his balance, the other one who had been on the lookout rushed forward.

Could he deal with them both?

Faro was himself again. Faro who knew how to fight, who had used his wits over and over to save his life all these past years. Fight or flight, he felt the surge of adrenalin.

Was the second man armed? He was, he saw a gun raised. The ship at that moment also felt the swerve of the sea, which doubtless saved him from death.

He had nothing. Nothing but his fists and his feet.

All sickness had left him, all he had to do now was survive.

He caught sight of a shadow, a drift of satin and suddenly he was no longer on his own.

A gunshot and then Imogen's calm voice. 'Drop that gun, or I will not hesitate to shoot your partner.'

The gunshot had raised the alarm. Suddenly there were footsteps, people rushing on to the deck, and the two men and their pursuers melted into the darkness. The ship swayed, dealing with the first lash of what promised to be a storm at sea of unquestionable ferocity.

Imogen put her arm round Faro. 'Are you all right?'

Passengers had reached them, frightened figures, their faces tense with anxiety, leaning over demanding, 'Did they hurt you, sir?'

Faro straightened up. 'No, missed by miles, thanks to the kindness of the ship lurching at that moment.'

They went down the steps followed by two of the couples already muttering, loudly demanding answers for this disgraceful scene.

Brian appeared flustered and anxious, trying in vain to give angry passengers soothing answers and reassurances, protesting: 'Nothing like this has ever happened on my ship before. This is the first time any passenger has ever been attacked.'

'And almost killed,' said someone.

'An assassin with a gun, too. Meant business, that one did,' said another.

Escaping to their cabin, Imogen shut the door and Faro sat down on the bed. suddenly utterly exhausted, and without a word Imogen handed him a large whisky and said wryly:

'I suppose it should be brandy to settle your stomach.'

He smiled: 'I prefer this. Thank you. Now, may I ask where you got the gun from?'

She sat beside him. 'A relic from my travels when I went to some places in Europe that I was warned could be dangerous, especially for a young woman alone. In Morocco on one of my tours, talks in the area, I met a man I think was a former gangster from New York.' She grinned. 'He rather fancied me and without demanding any favours in return, decided to instruct me in the arts of using what he called the "lady's weapon".' She held it up. 'Small but deadly, I was advised to always carry it. Oddly enough, your daughter still has a Derringer from her days in America.'

'Surely you didn't consider it necessary on a pleasure cruise?' Faro said. 'Brian will be most offended.'

Imogen sighed: 'I was uneasy, somehow, always a bit suspicious about Eastlake's plan. It made me suspect danger and I didn't care for you being involved, especially when we've heard rumours of smuggling artefacts and doubtless worse between York and Amsterdam.' Pausing she looked thoughtful. 'We don't know much about Brian, being a retired policeman's brother doesn't guarantee respectability.'

Faro nodded. 'Same thought did cross my mind, that Brian's luxury cruises may have another role to play.'

She shook her head. 'Mm . . . could be right but it's none of our business – or Inspector Faro's now,' she reminded him. 'But somehow, Eastlake's mission for you – that set all the warning bells ringing.' She laughed. 'My Romany blood, you know.'

She looked at him as he stood up and refilled the whisky glass. 'Feeling better? Not like you to be sick, especially on this ship's menus.'

Faro sighed. 'My selkie blood, I suspect. Grandmother Sibella could never abide fish, and we all inherited that with seafood, to a degree. Might be hearsay, but I can't touch shellfish – I'm afraid greed got the better of me at that seafood place in Amsterdam.'

A tap on the door announced Brian demanding anxiously, 'Are you two all right? Sorry about that.'

'Did you catch them?' Faro asked.

He shook his head. 'Two of them got away. Jumped overboard. It was pretty dark, but I think they were picked up by a ship following us. I got its name, we'll have them picked up in Hamburg. You maybe haven't noticed but the ship has slowed down – just recovered a man out of the water. The third of that trio I took aboard.' He groaned. 'More fool me.'

'Will you hand him over?'

'Only to the mortuary, I'm afraid. He was quite dead. Had his throat cut.'

'Robbery, was it?' he asked Faro, then gave Imogen a curious look. 'Good thing you were on hand. Don't meet many lady gunslingers on my travels or in this part of the world.'

Imogen refused to rise to the bait and said: 'The two of them were part of the trio I noticed you had hired when we set off. I had seen them before, in suits, and I was a bit suspicious about the workers' overalls.'

Brian gave a weary sigh. 'The three so-called engineers I hired. I guess I should have been a bit suspicious too. Wish you had mentioned this earlier, Mrs Faro,' he added. 'The warning would have come in handy. Villains!' And to Faro. 'They must have marked you down as a rich chap with a weak stomach and taken a chance on that.'

'Possibly,' was all Faro would say, to which Imogen added for his ears only:

'I think we have the identity of our mystery messenger.'

'The one with his throat cut,' was Faro's response, 'so he won't be telling Eastlake any useful information.'

Brian was frowning, preoccupied with the disaster that had hit him, already viewing the inevitable consequences. He said stiffly: 'I owe you all an apology. If this news gets abroad, then my cruises will take a beating, especially among those who conveniently like to travel incognito for personal reasons.'

He sighed. 'My own fault, being a bit careless

about hiring crew on the spur of the moment without references. If I'm a bit short-staffed, I tend to take likely-looking lads at the quayside who volunteer. Sorry about that. Attempted robberies give cruises a bad name. And this one will have to be cut short. We'll return this time with a dead man and a bevy of scared passengers, I can tell you, all demanding compensation and terrified of being called as witnesses to a robbery as well as a murder.'

Brian was called away by one of the stewards. A lady passenger reported some of her jewellery stolen. He groaned. 'This has never happened before, either,' he added bitterly, to which Faro and Imogen had unworthy thoughts that maybe she was taking full advantage of the incident with hopes of extra compensation.

As their door closed on Brian, Babs and Dave arrived, full of alarm.

Imogen repeated the story of how Faro was on deck, being sick, and how there was then an attempted robbery. Babs was very upset.

'It could have happened to any of us, so awful for you on your very first cruise with Brian.' Imogen and Faro insisted that the cruise had been memorable, which it certainly had been, and Babs and Dave stayed and had a drink while the storm died down and the ship rolled into smoother waters, heading back on the return journey to Hull.

'Thank goodness, none of us would have slept tonight if that storm had kept up. Little ships like this one weren't meant for stormy seas,' said Babs, wishing them goodnight. 'Poor Brian, what a disastrous cruise – and they are always so marvellous.'

Babs's words left Faro feeling guilty, as if his involvement via her policeman father was the reason for this catastrophic ending. And there was still the question of the identity of the murdered man.

'If he was, as seems likely, a spy among the Dutch smugglers, how could he also be Eastlake's mysterious contact in Amsterdam, and where did he fit in handing over the incriminating document that Eastlake was awaiting and almost cost you your life?' Imogen wanted to know. The only answer seemed to be that the murdered man's contact with the police spy in Amsterdam had been revealed or observed by the two cut-throats.

When they arrived at Hull next morning, Eastlake was waiting. Faro spotted him and said in tones of relief: 'There he is.' She regarded the inspector resentfully, wondering how he had had the effrontery to put her husband Faro in such dire peril. Faro hadn't expected to see him on the quayside in Hull, presuming the document would be handed over when they reached York.

Imogen remarked on his appearance. She was still angry at the danger his mission had put Faro in, watching him edge forward anxiously.

And there were more problems waiting for the end of this particular luxurious cruise. They had missed the York train, the next at midday. This aroused more mutinous murmurs from the stranded and already depressed passengers, and Brian realised that he must provide alternative transport to York for them.

He hired a trio of motor cars to take them and their luggage. Seeing them safely seated, he said to Babs and Dave who were also being accommodated:

'No, I must remain with my ship. The police have arrived, including your illustrious father-in-law,' he added to Dave, watching Eastlake in deep conversation with Faro. Imogen had noticed the uniforms swarming over the decks. She was undecided whether to wait for Faro or whether he would be returning to York in the police car with Eastlake.

If Brian had any notion of what was taking place between the two men, except that it probably concerned the murderous attack on Faro, then he was concealing it tactfully and said to Imogen: 'You go with Dave and Babs, it will be quicker for you. There will be endless forms to complete, numerous interviews.' He sighed deeply 'The next few hours will be hell.' And to his brother, 'Expect me back when you see me,' he added, giving last-minute instructions to his crew, while murmuring in conciliatory tones to those of the passengers who saw in the uniformed policemen another chance to air their grievances regarding the disastrous shortened cruise, their wearisome travel and expected compensation.

Imogen watched Faro, who waved to her from Eastlake's motor. She would have given much to be with him, feeling very uneasy at being parted from him at this time. There was not a lot of conversation either on the drive back to York, seated behind Babs and Dave among passengers now angry and tired, many of them thoughtful, no doubt busy inventing believable excuses that would be valid for their incognitos and the lies they had told to enjoy that illicit visit to Amsterdam.

The sight of the Minster occupying the horizon brought sighs of relief from weary souls. Imogen shuddered as she envisaged the very different arrival Faro would have received if she hadn't had the intuition to be armed.

Imogen was more interested in the young man who was also waiting as the motor cars gave up their passengers. He looked up and saw her watching him. She took Dave's arm. 'It's him.' She looked around, wishing she could see Faro.

'I've seen him before.' Dave was regarding her with a puzzled expression. She could hardly tell him that the young Dutchman was the image of Andres, whose portrait she had been telling Faro about in the Rijksmuseum.

Who was he looking for? Imogen remembered the first time she had seen him was with the three men in Mary's cafe who had boarded the cruise ship in workers overalls, two trying to kill Faro on the deck.

So, on whose side was this image from the portrait of Andres?

Part of the answer came from Eastlake. On the drive to York, well ahead of the disgruntled passengers' motorcade, he said that the package from Amsterdam, which almost cost Faro his life, was from one of the police informers who had been shot, severely wounded and was likely to die. He wanted them to know that the document enclosed contained evidence that artefacts and drugs goods were being smuggled from headquarters at the Dower House to Amsterdam, and that the man in charge of operations, they knew, but could not prove, was a well-known Dutch gangster named Lucas Jannsen.

Eastlake shook his head sadly. 'One of the four Dutchmen, the alleged florist delivery man, was working for us.' They had accepted him since his mother was from Yorkshire and he had established contact with the British spy in Amsterdam, who had gathered evidence about the smuggling of artefacts.

'Poor Carl, I'm afraid it was him under the blanket on Brian's ship, and he's now headed for the mortuary. Somehow, they had found out the evidence had been given to him to pass on to a passenger on the cruise ship, unaware of your real identity as Inspector Faro. But that evidence, once the cryptic messages are sorted out, will reveal who is the leader behind the smuggling and the artefacts from York via the Four Seasons flower shop.'

Faro would have hazarded a shrewd guess that Wilfred was involved in his stepfather's absence, and that Jannsen was the man, wanted by the York police, seen by Imogen with Wilfred and the housekeeper at the kitchen table in the Dower House.

Faro had been dropped off at the Dower House by Eastlake. Imogen was in the garden with Dave and Babs who had returned with her to collect a recipe for parsnip soup Mrs Muir had promised Babs.

Imogen ran to Faro and hugged him.

'I'm so glad to see you, darlin',' she whispered.

'Me too.' He kissed her. 'I have a lot to tell you.'

Walking at their side, Babs said: 'Our arrival took Wilfred by surprise. He was in the garden with the lady friend Dave saw on a previous occasion. The same one he noticed had such elegant ankles,' she added with a giggle. 'But this time we certainly weren't going to be introduced, much to his disappointment.'

As before, she had been hustled quickly out of sight, presumably going through the house and out by the front door.

'Strange,' had been Dave's comment as Babs picked up Mrs Muir's recipe.

'I'm glad you have got on her good side,' sighed Imogen. 'She doesn't seem to like me at all.'

Babs's eyebrows raised when Faro shook his head. 'We get along fine too, but poor Imogen.'

'I don't know why. Can't think what I've done to offend her.'

She was conscious of a stillness in Faro at her side. She had recognised this before as a sign that he was not inclined to share something with her.

She would ask him later. 'What was all that about – in the garden?'

He smiled. 'Just a thought.'

'I think I know what you mean, Faro. I should have

guessed. Our Mrs Muir has taken a notion to you – not the first lady by any measure – and she is madly jealous of your wife.'

Even as she said the words, she had a feeling that was not quite true or quite logical. There was something much more important, but looking at Faro, she decided that had he been a cat he would have purred.

He laughed. 'Maybe you are right, but I'm trying not to be vain.'

'Or encouraging, I hope,' she added sharply.

There was indeed something she was missing. Remembering Dave's tale of his first encounter with the retreating figure of Wilfred's girlfriend, Faro was superimposing another incident when he had observed Mrs Muir gathering vegetables for the supper. As with a feeling of triumph, he guessed he had the answer, at that moment, Imogen was also recalling that the Crowes had small feet and was not far behind him.

Waving goodbye to the Stokes, they went indoors to make a cup of tea, when suddenly the doorbell rang.

Imogen opened the door to a distraught Father Joe.

Almost inarticulate, he gasped out what they wanted least to hear.

There had been another attempted murder.

CHAPTER THIRTY

Joe slumped into the nearest chair.

'Dave told me you were back, I wasn't expecting you until tomorrow. He said there had been trouble on the cruise, a man murdered.' Trying to take control, he sat up, taking a deep breath: 'There has been an attack on a young girl, in the precinct of my church, the rooms occupied by Nick.' He shook his head and regarded them intently. 'I am afraid he is involved.'

'His shop girl, you mean?'

Joe nodded miserably. Yes, she was the girl Sofia from the flower shop who Nick was considering marrying. He was in tears, said she had promised to meet him in his lodging but when he came in, saw her lying there, he was sure she was dead.

Joe went on: 'He was in a terrible state. He had never even told me her name, until then. What was he going to do? I asked was he sure she was dead, and he said of course. So I went back with him with only minutes to prepare before a family arrived for a baptism.'

He paused, frowned. 'She certainly looked dead, I did a quick check. It was rather dark. I couldn't detect any pulse but there were no visible marks of violence.' He sighed deeply before continuing: 'Poor Nick, he seemed on the verge of collapse. He asked me what should he do. I said he must inform the police. He said no, they would think he did it. It was always the way, the person who found the body was the main suspect, he gabbled.

'I said nevertheless he must do so. I couldn't go with him as I had people already waiting in the church.' He shook his head. 'I'll never know how I got through that baptism, it seemed endless, but when they left I rushed next door.' A despairing gesture. 'No sign of Nick or the body. So I went to the police. They asked a lot of questions. Who normally occupied these rooms? Where was he? There was no sign of the girl. Nick was nowhere to be found so they went in search of him.

'Then Inspector Eastlake came in, invited me to a seat and said, "You will be glad to know there was only attempted murder, Father. The young woman recovered consciousness sufficiently to stagger over and gasp out that her young man, who happened to be the same Lucas Jannsen we had just arrested, had tried to kill her."

'And the whole story came rolling out. Seems that the two had been together a couple of years and she had been helping him with the smuggling activities via the flower deliveries, he promising her marriage, until suddenly he was no longer interested. He'd found someone else, a waitress from the cafe across the road—'

Could that be Amy? Imogen wondered. Eastlake went on:

'In retaliation, Sofia used Nick – or thought she was using him – to make Jannsen jealous. Here was a lord's son who loved her and could give her a good life, but none of this was having the required effect. In a battle of words with Jannsen, who had followed her to Nick's lodging, she hit out at him. He retaliated, she fell, hit her head and was knocked out.'

He sighed. 'That was how Nick found her when he returned.' Clasping his hands in despair, he added: 'I had no idea what to do. Before the inspector's revelations, prayer had failed me as it would fail Nick, once he was arrested,' he added gloomily.

'It was a terrible day, and that evening he came to the church in tears. Relieved to know that Sofia was still alive, his main concern for the scandal back at Elrigg. Poor Mummy was heartbroken that her precious boy was associated with an attempted murder at his lodging in York.'

Not as heartbroken as seeing him, her only well-beloved son, sentenced and hanged, had been Joe's immediate thought as he continued:

'He decided that Inspector Faro might know what to do, but I hope I discouraged him.'

Faro said nothing, about to go to the railway station to

collect tickets for their imminent departure to Edinburgh.

As the young priest left, Imogen thought about him compassionately. If Nick could no longer stay at the church lodging, he could have taken refuge in the many rooms of the Dower House, but that was impossible as they were leaving. It couldn't come soon enough for either of them, and Imogen knew Faro would warrant no delays.

CHAPTER THIRTY-ONE

Retracing his steps to the Dower House, tickets in hand, seats booked on the next Edinburgh train, Faro felt rather jubilant. He wasn't leaving with an unsolved mystery after all, he had the answer to Imogen's problem with Mrs Muir. But on second thoughts, he decided to keep this to himself and dig a little deeper; even with Imogen's high intelligence it seemed unlikely that she might have worked this one out.

He had another reason for withholding information: if he told Imogen the whole issue regarding Kathleen, he might rekindle the fire adding additional fuel to the hope that she may be able to renew her relationship with this new-found cousin.

He sighed. For the moment he would continue down that line on his own, going over again meticulously the scene when their unexpected arrival had upset Wilfred walking in the garden. Surprised at being caught with his girlfriend, it had been Dave, then Babs, who had reported that they both looked startled and guilty.

Now, even as he watched their retreating backs, anxious not to be confronted and hurrying in the direction of the kitchen, the scene was superimposed by a discussion with Dave Stokes that rippled a chord of memory from Faro's early days with the Edinburgh Police. How, in early training, young policemen learnt that there were things very difficult to disguise, that they must recognise and accept that most criminals, including murderers, had no distinguishing features. In fact, the best disguise and chance of escaping the law was being someone you passed by in a crowd and never gave a second glance.

There were other issues that were giveaways, however, such as Captain Brian Stokes had also suggested, most particularly: walks. Walks were very individual, and it was hard to disguise them, a fact most criminals never considered.

He recalled one afternoon recently when he was alone in the garden and Mrs Muir had appeared, busy collecting vegetables for their evening meal. They exchanged a cordial greeting as she walked past, about the weather and what they would like to eat for dessert. She did not linger, casting off her gardening gloves as she spoke. She had smooth white hands, with little evidence of rough work, and he had wondered how she had achieved the rank of housekeeper through the lower ranks.

As she had walked away, he chided himself on noticing for the first time remarkably small feet and trim ankles, despite the rest of the rather shapeless bulk of her figure. He shook his head: what would Imogen think of him taking note of such things?

But there was more to it than a typical male observation. Faro shook his head; indeed, he must be getting old for where were his usual powers of observation and deduction? They had certainly failed him.

He straightened his shoulders resolutely. This time he knew he had the answer. It was there before him, just waiting to be put into words.

He had reached the kitchen door when he was hailed by Inspector Eastlake, crossing the garden.

'I thought you would like to know that you are no longer required as guardians of the Dower House. The Hardys will not be returning.' He flourished a piece of paper. 'This is from the ship. They are on their way to America, apparently for Hardy's health but, in actual fact, because if they came home they would be immediately arrested, as we now have all the evidence needed to close the case on their smuggling activities.' Pausing, he sighed. 'Thanks to our man in Amsterdam who gave his life to provide it. And a special thanks to you, Faro, for your help in obtaining this. It would seem that Wilfred and Mrs Muir have left us and are on their way to join the Hardys, unless they can be intercepted before they reach Portsmouth.'

Faro looked at him. This was his chance to reveal all, but before he could do so, the inspector continued with a happy sigh. 'The City Fathers will be delighted that they will now be able to acquire the Dower House to add to their list of their historic sites. They have had their eyes on it for years but could never persuade Hardy to sell. Now, that will be cancelled out by the criminal costs involved.'

As he hurried away, Faro realised that Wilfred and Mrs Muir had indeed left. He joined Imogen at the kitchen table, while around them the house had already begun to shroud itself in the deep silence of emptiness.

Imogen looked at him. 'Must have had everything packed and ready, well ahead of the inspector's visit and just such an emergency.'

She stood up. 'I've made some tea.' He sighed. The confrontation he had feared, a resurgence of her anxieties regarding Kathleen, was inevitable. It could no longer be delayed.

The answer that had come to him in the garden before the inspector's arrival was like some thunderbolt, from watching Mrs Muir gathering vegetables that touched on a previous encounter he had dismissed as of little importance, seeing Wilfred and his girlfriend also vanishing in the direction of the kitchen.

That had been Faro's moment of revelation. Whilst he posed no threat to Kathleen, having met only Mrs Muir, he now knew why the housekeeper avoided Imogen so carefully on all occasions. Imogen, who would not be fooled long by a wig and specs and some unbecoming clothes used to turn a slim figure into a middle-aged woman. But although slim legs and neat ankles had not registered with Imogen, they were a giveaway to men like Brian.

Now there were other strands to consider: Wilfred and the young woman they presumed was the girlfriend, and Faro guessed now why they had very good reason to be anxious not to be recognised. They had taken a chance to spend some time together in the open, believing that they were free for the day, and had it not been for the disaster of Brian's cruise because of the attack on Faro and his return to the Dower House with Imogen, they would have got away with it.

With the arrest of the Dutchmen who were Faro's attackers, Wilfred would have recognised the danger of whirlpool-like panic spreading – particularly among Captain Brian's wealthy passengers, for their own darkly private reasons. Once the police were informed, there would be interviews and investigations since the two murderously minded Dutchmen were connected with the smuggling activities. As for Wilfred, he was not going to linger but had been poised for immediate flight.

When Faro reported the inspector's revelations to Imogen, as a prelude to what else he had in store, she smiled.

'Did you not tell him what you – or rather we – had guessed?'

While he was still thinking up an answer, she stretched out her hand and lifted from the opposite kitchen chair a grey wig and thick spectacles. 'I am perfectly aware now why she had good reason for avoiding any conversation or contact.'

She smiled sadly. 'I should have realised that I had the logical answer for Kathleen's disappearance, her transformation into Mrs Muir, but it was her shoes that actually gave the game away.' She thrust out her own small feet and wriggled them. 'All the Crowes have tiny feet, you see. Remember we talked about Mrs Muir not being a widow but that "Mrs" is a courtesy title by which housekeepers kept male servants and other undesirables at a respectful distance?'

'I gave that further thought,' said Faro. 'In this case I was right about her being a widow. Once, when she removed her gardening gloves, I noticed the third finger of her left hand was pale and worn below the joint, like the hand of someone used to wearing a thick ring of some kind.'

'Ah yes, the claddagh leaves quite an indelible white mark.'

Faro nodded: 'It is now all abundantly clear. Mrs Muir didn't dislike you or resent you being in charge of the Dower House in the Hardys' absence, because she never existed.' He frowned. 'At some time, it had fitted the smuggling plans for Kathleen to take over the role of housekeeper, as well as providing a safe haven.'

He paused. 'I was safe enough as we had never met, but you were going to be a problem searching for this missing cousin.'

Imogen frowned. 'Dave happened to mention that Wilfred's young woman had long brown hair. That stuck in my mind somehow, and now I realise she was afraid of me with good reason; even our eyes meeting might have aroused vague memories of that first brief meeting before she disappeared and led me to realise that I was talking to Kathleen Crowe, who for some obscure reason was pretending to be Mrs Muir.'

'She must have been terrified every day at the thought of you now staying indefinitely in the Dower House.'

'Do you think the Hardys knew her identity?'

'It certainly looks like it, given the inspector's evidence that the Dower House has long been suspected as the headquarters of the smuggling activities.'

Now that the reason for Kathleen's disappearance had been solved, Imogen still found it hard to reconcile her role in a gang of smugglers, except for her possible connection with the Clan na Gael, a group of Irish Americans who funded the movement to free Ireland from British rule, who had presumably recruited her. Her first action leaving the flower shop had been to steal money from the bank and thus regrettably get her name on to police records.

Faro said: 'There was another piece of evidence regarding the identity of Mrs Muir, which had seemed odd at the time. Do you remember Father Joe's reactions to her presence here?'

'Yes, he seemed uncomfortable by her appearance. I remember him going into the kitchen to thank her for the meal, and when I remarked upon this, you laughed and said she's probably a Catholic, one of his parishioners.'

Faro said triumphantly, 'And there was the answer, of course. As Kathleen Crowe, she was probably one of his congregation at the Mass, and the young priest had recognised that she was also Mrs Muir.'

'He must have been very anxious, wanting to know, needing to confide in someone to learn the truth – a heavy burden, since the sacred nature of the confessional bound him to silence,' said Imogen.

It also explained his odd behaviour afterwards. Here was a young man with a heavy conscience, with a secret, perhaps even a confession that he could not share.

CHAPTER THIRTY-TWO

As if aware that he was the subject of their conversation, Joe appeared at the door, shocked by the revelations about the Dower House, always ready to believe the best of everyone. But the topic of his concern was not Kathleen, aka Mrs Muir, but Nick Elrigg who, hardly surprisingly, had been terribly shaken over recent events concerning his shop girl.

'Poor Sofia. But in a way it jolted him back to reality and the realisation that the world he was trying to find didn't exist. Its doors would for ever be closed to him.'

Joe sighed. 'We will always be friends, although as I told you, I have discouraged his ideas about conversion until he has time to learn what it entails. At the moment, it's little more than a means of upsetting his parents and their centuries-old traditions.

'He never had any intention of marrying Sofia. She merely fitted in with his family-wrecking scheme.'

He shook his head. 'Certainly, he is free to stay with me in York as long as he wishes, but his uncle Hector, to whom he seems thankfully close and who I gather understands him, has suggested he return to Elrigg, share his cottage on the estate and renew his one-time interest in archaeology.'

He smiled. 'Dig out some sort of career for himself. Hector will be arriving for him within the next two days and will know how to resist all attempts to marry him off. After all, he has succeeded very well on his own account. They can remain two bachelors together, if that is what Nick wants.'

Eastlake came to the Dower House with two policemen. 'The Dutchman Jannsen had been very anxious to include Wilfred Hardy as well in this smuggling business, but as you know, he and the Roxwell woman have vanished into thin air, or as we believe, en route for Portsmouth to join the Hardys' ship to New York. They were obviously well prepared for such an emergency.'

He paused and looked at Faro. 'Thanks again for your help in Amsterdam,' he added casually, to Imogen's indignation, apparently forgetting that dangerous interlude had almost cost Faro his life. 'You helped cut short the investigation involving the English branch of the smugglers' flower shop delivery men, all of whom have been rounded up and, eager to escape long sentences, one has offered to turn King's evidence, as has the girl Sofia.'

He stood up to leave and bowed to Imogen. 'I expect you are both anxious to get back to Edinburgh, and don't forget, we owe you a debt of gratitude.' He sighed. 'The vicinity around the flower shop is still one of intense police activity. Although it looks as if this case is closed, there will always be smuggling, I'm afraid. Others will take their place.'

Faro could have added a few helpful footnotes but had his own reasons for not wishing to open what might be another can of worms and delay their now imminent return home to Edinburgh.

Meanwhile Imogen's thoughts were with Mary at her tea shop across the way, her customers enjoying, along with her delicious scones, the spicy gossip regarding the Dutch smugglers. Mary would do her best for Amy's broken heart, as she dried her tears, both of them fully aware that Amy had had a very lucky escape, and with time's healing, would live to love many other days.

For Faro and Imogen, the holiday was over and they were really leaving this time, their luggage packed, waiting for Dave's motor car to take them to the station and the Edinburgh train.

'No, I'm not really sorry to leave. It's been an adventure and certainly an experience,' said Imogen, still feeling bruised that she had allowed her feelings for Kathleen to cast a blight on what had started off with the intention of a carefree holiday. As for the Dutch sixteenth-century Andres also being the wanted criminal, Lucas Jannsen, she could only shake her head and reflect that life did throw up some very strange coincidences indeed.

Babs was in the car with Dave, ready to wave au revoir and already planning to visit Edinburgh next year.

She wasn't alone. Snuggled close in her arms, a little black dog, with a darting red tongue, happy and as smiling as any dog could possibly be.

'Isn't he darling?' she asked as Imogen stroked him, unrecognisable as Wilfred's ill-treated Ratboy.

As the train for Edinburgh steamed into the station, its arrival was accompanied by the sound of church bells across the city as well as the mighty Minster's chimes, appropriate to a Sunday morning blessing.

The doors closed. The guard's warning whistle sounded.

'We will miss them. They've been lovely,' sighed Babs wistfully, while the joyful bark of the tiny dog proclaimed that he had found his happy ever after.

Settling down side by side in the comfort of the six-seater compartment, Faro took Imogen's hand:

'Happy now, Imo?'

Her kiss was enough. 'Good to be going home.'

Then with a stroke of devilment, remembering Joe's last remark, Faro said: 'Are you sure you didn't want another day in York, just to say hello to Hector?'

She gave him a sharp look, and said crossly, 'Sure now, and why would I be wanting to waste a day on Hector Elrigg? He's nothing to me. There's only one man in the world, is the answer to that one.'

Seeing his expression, she took his arm snugly, smiled impishly into his face.

'And in case you don't know or can't remember his name. It's Faro.'

AUTHOR'S NOTE

I have taken some geographical liberties with the fair city of York: the Irongate and the Dower House are fictional.

Faro and Imogen first met in *The Bull Slayers*.

ALANNA KNIGHT has had more than seventy books published in an impressive writing career spanning over fifty years. She is a founding member and Honorary Vice President of the Scottish Association of Writers, Honorary President of the Edinburgh Writers' Club and member of the Scottish Chapter of the Crime Writers' Association. Born and educated in Tyneside, she now lives in Edinburgh. Alanna was awarded an MBE in 2014 for services to literature.

alannaknight.com